Michael
and the
Ice Princess

A Mystical Romance

Michael and the Ice Princess

A Mystical Romance

Mary Mendenhall

SECOND EDITION

Michael and the Ice Princess is a work of fiction.
Any resemblance in the narrative to specific historical dates
or characters living or dead is purely coincidental.

Originally published in hardcover
by Avon Books, London, 1997
ISBN 1860339379

Copyright © 2011 Mary Mendenhall
All rights reserved.

ISBN: 1463581866
ISBN-13: 9781463581862
Library of Congress Control Number: 2011910092
CreateSpace, North Charleston, South Carolina

For Richard, once upon a time.

The Lady Poverty

I met her on the Umbrian hills:
Her hair unbound, her feet unshod.
As one whom secret glory fills
She walked, alone with God.

I met her in the city street:
Oh, changèd was her aspect then!
With heavy eyes and weary feet
She walked alone, with men.

– Evelyn Underhill

Arrogance is a downward ascent.

– Saint Gregory of Nyssa

I

Hard Bargaining

The life-pulse drummed in his temples, blending with the rhythmic pounding of his stallion's great hoofs against the footpath. He abruptly reined in his mount and turned toward his companion, throwing his head back in exultation and drinking in a deep draught of mountain air.

"Pieter! You dawdle! Is it not a most excellent day?" The sky lay heavy and warm above him, yet there was a crisp freshness in it—a sky between seasons. The other rider soon caught up with him. They cantered alongside the meandering river, its bank speckled with the glowing coals of autumn leaves; their brilliance flowed through his senses like liquid gold from a furnace.

He was going to be a father. His wife could give him no greater gift: a child, made in his image and likeness. His to mold, to influence, to guide through the twisty maze of life in a sometimes hostile world. How good of her, to give him an heir to carry on his name! He must buy her a present...

Nicolai had told him of some wondrous handicraft down in the bazaar, and it was toward the town he urged his horse, cutting across his subjects' harvested land, churning up the harvested clods of emptied fields. Peasant heads turned in curiosity and admiration at the horsemanship of the two men, who soon regained the footpath and dismounted in the square, at the entry to the shadowed stalls of the bazaar. He left his attendant to tie the horses and glanced about him with sweltering pride. All was as it should be: peaceful, quiet, orderly.

"I'll buy her the most expensive thing of beauty in the market," he confided, striding handsomely in, his spurs a-jingle. A scarlet cloak billowed behind him, fastened to the shoulder of his tunic by means of a silver brooch depicting a dragon encircling a ruby bright as blood.

Crude tables lined smooth stone walls, their cracks moss-filled, their dressed faces slowly crumbling away in the ever-present drip and dank. Shadows stretched deep here; occasional shafts of dust-laden sunlight pierced through cracks between broken roof tiles, barely allowing a buyer to examine the wares. Bemusedly he took in the piles of leather boots and jerkins, the gaudy scarves, cookery, baskets, tools, and hand-wrought trinkets. His armed companion, obviously a knight of some rank, followed him closely. He was soon surrounded by gasps and stares. Men removed their caps; women drew their shawls closer about their faces. Ducking beneath a low archway, he stopped in a narrow passage.

There, on a rickety table surrounded by a display of an odd and varied collection of amulets, small fabric bags probably containing herbs, hand-crafted jewelry, and dusty vials holding liquids of several hues, Something had caught his eye.

The vendor, a pale young woman with uncovered head, smiled but did not look up from her beadwork. She waited, her hands busy, until he touched a small pewter figurine on the table. He lifted it carefully into the light of a muted sunbeam, scrutinizing the craftsmanship. The dull metal swirled with iridescent color, a liquid rainbow playing over its surface. It was finely detailed and skillfully made, not a seam or mark of a rasp noticeable. The delicate shape of a leaf-clad child looked up pleadingly, its tiny hand raised as if to reason with its examiner. It flooded his memory with the warmth of age-old faery stories—and the voice of his grandmother who told them.

The perfect gift.

"How much for this?" he asked in his most lordly tone. His voice satisfied him with its intended effect: the air sparked with anticipation.

But the voice that answered was calm. "That's quality, that one, Your Majesty," said the woman, engaging his eyes. "It'll cost you dear."

"How much, then?"

"I won't take less than twenty gold pieces for it." Something about the way she spoke reminded him of grease, but he didn't flinch. He had bartered before, in battle.

"You must be joking. For a plaything made of pewter? It's not worth even one."

"But it is, Your Majesty, for I've paid dearly for it myself. There's not one like it in the world." A smile twitched at her mouth. Why he should believe her, he didn't know; she was toying with him. He wanted to put it down decisively and walk away laughing, but the craving grew stronger; the thing burned in his hand. He would not part with it. To gain bargaining leverage he gently replaced it, and settled back on his heels to consider. His attendant approached, sullen.

"Leave it, Sire," he counseled softly. "There are more fitting pieces for the queen."

"Ten silver pieces is more than enough, my good woman," the king offered in patient condescension.

"No, my lord, it's not."

"Then it will be, and you can oblige your sovereign in a generous showing of your allegiance to him."

"You'll do well enough to take it, Mistress Barbara," the vendor in the next stall advised harmlessly. But the woman stood her ground.

"Allegiance is earned, not bought—or even suggested." Her voice was low but growing cuttingly sharp. "You would not bring your loyal subject to further poverty, would you, Sire?"

"It's obvious you didn't make it," he answered obliquely, his gaze wandering among her other merchandise to find relief from the eyes which bore into his. The figurine was the only sculpted work on the table. "Perhaps it came to you through unjust means."

"Your Majesty is unkind as well as unfair to accuse me in my place of business. I know its worth better than you do"— her volume rose alarmingly, like the tide in a storm—"and I've asked a reasonable price. You've no right to impoverish me!"

Her passion was wasted on his stony face. He reached into his purse. Seizing the little statue in one angry hand, he turned to go, pushing a gold coin into the woman's outstretched palm. But with the other, she grabbed his forearm before he could withdraw it, her fingers a vise, her face a brittle mask.

"You shall have to pay for it, though. The coldness of your heart will bear its fruit. There is a power greater than yours." Her voice had sunk low again, but it now came through clenched teeth. "The debt will remain. You'll look for me, then, but I'll not be here for you to repay. No. I shall seek you out, instead." She smiled, satisfied. Her grip fell as he retreated, the pewter figure in his hand and a burning rage on his face.

He thought to have Pieter arrest her for treason or at least insult, but the words themselves struck him as flimsy evidence. She was mad, that was all. Besides, what could a little beggar woman who sold charms and powders in the depths of the bazaar do to the king? The shadows dispersed as he re-entered the sunlit square, but he shook his head against a growing doubt that he had done well in the bargain. He mounted his stallion elegantly, but on the way back, he did not gallop.

The blight of a cloud was passing over the castle, its stalwart towers marred by shadow. No matter. He would give the present to his queen in the morning, when she could better admire its delicate shape. It was beautiful, yes—but hardly worth twenty gold pieces. He marveled that a subject of his could be brazen enough to try to take advantage of him. She was mad to ask for so much.

People can certainly be selfish, he mused as he rode through the gate.

There is the person who buys much for little,
yet pays for it seven times over.

– Ecclesiasticus

II

Reaping the North Wind

Three soft knocks shattered the silence of the king's chambers.

"Is that you, Nicolai?"

"Yes, my lord."

"Come in." The steward entered with a stately bow. "Look over there," ordered the sovereign, throwing his bejeweled hand in the direction of the mantel. A cheery fire blazed on the hearth. Nicolai's searching eye caught the new addition.

"Why, it's exquisite." He picked up the figurine and turned it over in his slender hands.

"She doesn't like it."

"Amazing. Why not?"

"She says it looks sad; she asked me to put it somewhere out of her sight."

"It must have cost you a fortune," reflected the steward, returning it to the mantel. The king only grunted at this. "Entirely worth it, my lord. As to the queen, perhaps it's a shifting whim of pregnancy. She'll come to like it, I'm sure. In the meantime, you've chosen a fitting spot for it."

He became aware of Nicolai watching his hand open and close in undecided emotion, and stopped his fidgeting. They gazed on the statuette together, and the monarch thought for a fleeting instant that it gazed back. But it was beautiful, he reasoned inwardly, and if his wife wouldn't look at it, he would enjoy it: a lingering portrait of childhood innocence—his childhood, filled with stories and dreams and freedom to run barefoot along the banks of the wandering river. Free from the worries of being a king. His was only a little country, after all, hardly more than a city-state fragment of an ancient empire. Drained by the blood-letting of the Crusades, it nonetheless depended on whatever skilled governance he could give it. So he set his life upon ruling it in justice and keeping a precarious peace with his neighbors.

And now he would be a father. Let the winter come, and the famines, and the armed conflicts... All would be well. He laughed, clapped Nicolai on the shoulder, and jauntily left the room.

His hopes fell before the last of the dying leaves had left the trees. Winter struck early, hail soaking hay still out in the fields; the north wind blew harsh and chill. Snow whirled and mounted in stormy drifts. Villagers huddled in freezing misery while wolves howled in hungry anguish outside. Every hearth in the castle was alight, but no amount of fire seemed able to warm the place.

The queen was brought to her bed on the Eve of Holy Innocents, her labor long and arduous in the cedar-paneled chamber. The cold fingers of dawn reached through the frost on the colored glass when Brigid, her maid, brought him news.

"Sire."

He had dozed off; the word and a light touch on his shoulder gently jostled him awake.

"Well?"

"You have a daughter," she said, softly.

His thoughts blurred and hardened. It would have to be a girl, on such a night. He sat upright, now seriously awake.

"And the queen?"

"She is ailing, my lord. It was a difficult birth. She asks for you." With a heavy step, he followed Brigid into the hushed room. His wife lay pale and quiet. No lusty baby's cry could be heard, only the crackle of fir cones on the hearth. His eyes surveyed the chamber: the midwife held a thickly-swathed bundle near the fire. He went straightaway to the bedside to take the queen's hand. She opened her eyes to smile weakly at him before a cloud fell across her face.

"My lord king," she murmured, her dark eyes tired. Then, "I'm so cold. They wonder if she will live… I've asked for the priest to come with his chrism."

God, he thought, swallowing. *A sickly child. A girl.*

He beckoned the midwife bedside, so he could look at his daughter in the dim light of the lamp. The little face was serene, and ashen-still.

"She needs to be close to her mother," he found himself saying distantly, with some tenderness. "Perhaps they can warm each other." Once the babe had suckled herself and her royal mother to sleep, he left, knowing he would have to be summoned back for the hastily arranged christening. Passing the stone archway of the chapel, he prayed that his wife would be alive to name the child. He hadn't a notion of what she should be called.

Two hours later, he stood near the mantel, staring at the faery figurine swirling there in pewter. The door timidly opened, and a page announced the Mistress Brigid. The king turned to welcome her.

"Sire," she greeted with a deep curtsey, awaiting permission to speak. He nodded coldly. "My lady regains her strength."

"The child?"

"She lives, by God's mercy. We had a time getting her warm, though." He was far away. "The priest is here; will you come?" He sighed and followed, but Brigid hadn't done with her talk. Her words drifted backward, over her head in the echoing corridor. "She's beautiful, your daughter. Like her mother."

But the child was very quiet; well, so was the queen. For all he knew, the nursery might have been the chapel or the crypt.

Winter flowed by, storm drifting over snow, life in the castle a sleepy retreat from the cold world beyond its thick walls. Physician and priest alike could find nothing wrong with the newborn—except that she needed more cover than other infants.

"You don't hold her much," his wife remarked one evening.

"She is... so small. And she cries when I take her."

"Not always: she's smiling now. I wish you would look. And she's strong."

Strong maybe, but always and forever cold. Especially her little feet.

"She might be, but you're not. How many months does it take a woman to get over childbirth, anyway?" His impatience silenced her. Maybe spring would bring a change, she found herself hoping. For all of them.

Their private council continued long after moonrise.

"She's dying, Nicolai. And there is something wrong with the princess, I know it." He shook himself from personal concerns to address the business at hand. "Pieter tells me there are eastern spies asking questions in town. I need to strengthen my borders, before something happens." He was particularly concerned about his covetous eastern neighbor. Monarchs seemed more power-hungry since the Crusades; little kingdoms were being devoured by bigger ones all the time.

"With what, my lord?" the steward asked. The king trusted him with all his major decisions. Only Nicolai was shrewd enough to suggest, rather than direct, the king's thoughts. Only the two of them knew that a rebellious stronghold taken two years ago had fallen not because the king was a brave commander or a strategic leader, but by the negligence of a little doddering man who had failed to lock the postern gate. The victory had won the monarch much acclaim; he owed much to Nicolai for keeping the secret.

"With what, indeed. A show of force. A tournament, come spring, or..." His voice wandered. Nicolai waited before offering his own suggestion.

"Or an alliance. He hates the infidels as much as you do. Bide your time, Majesty. If there were a tragedy—the queen's death, God forbid—such a distraction could open the way for negotiations."

"What sort of negotiations do you mean, Nicolai?"

"Perhaps an arranged marriage would strengthen your fellowship..."

"He has no son."

"No, my lord, but he has a daughter, only about ten years younger than yourself."

The king colored with anger and then suddenly flashed, "I'm not a widower yet, damn you. You would rid me of my own queen for expedience?"

"Of course not, Sire. But there is the reality of your kingdom to be considered."

"My kingdom. My wife. My daughter... Did I tell you, Nicolai, that someone cursed me in the market when I bought that?" He was looking toward the mantel.

"No. What kind of curse, my lord?" The steward had a miniscule knowledge of sorcery, and this intrigued him.

"A curse of coldness."

"I'm sure it's reversible. One has only to find the right practitioner."

"Look into it for me, then, Nicolai. And arrange a meeting with the physician in the morning. The weakness of these my women-folk—natural or not—has gone on long; it has fatigued me."

"A good reason to be rid of it, Sire. Shall I bid you good night?" The king raised his hand in assent and parting. The oaken door closed fast and quietly, and he was left alone in a twisting labyrinth of thought. So: evil had found him after so many years of righteous and uneventful rule. There was no lock strong enough to keep it out—from the kingdom, the castle, or himself.

How the mighty have fallen!

– King David's lament

III

Maelstrom

Nicolai waited until the last strains of the funeral procession had wafted down the river valley. It was a beautiful day; the sun at its warmest since the king had gone to the bazaar eight months before. The spring thaw would have reached even the high mountain pass, so his way would be clear.

Strange that the queen had asked to be buried in the town churchyard, away from the castle grounds, but it gave him more time. And his alibi was secure: he had left earlier that day to visit his ailing sister in the west—the king had even provided the coach and a disguised double.

No one would intercept him.

The kitchen was empty. Nicolai stole into the scullery, overturned a jar of drippings, and shoved a dry log onto the fire. An untrained kitchen wench could easily put in too big a piece of wood... In a matter of moments, the sparks flew out as he worked the bellows; a few conveniently landed on the spreading drippings. Tiny tongues of flame lapping at the oil crept toward the door, the dry straw, the waiting piles of thatch.

Before the drifting smoke signaled an alarm, the king's confidant slipped up the stairs and into a small room adjoining the royal nursery, where the princess slept beneath an eiderdown coverlet atop a thick fleece. He had planned it well; her lone attendant hurried out to help quench the fire. He had chosen the plainest, warmest wrap: a cast-off hunting cloak of her father's fell over the sleeping bundle, and Nicolai made his escape out of the castle while the cottony clouds of summer floated leisurely in a powder-blue sky.

He'd contrived to go by foot, up and over the steep and rugged track behind the stronghold rather than through the town. A coachman had instructions to meet him on the southern slope, where the path joined the road, six days later. By then he would have crossed another small kingdom and a wide river to his destination: a low cottage in the hill country where a second cousin of his tended sheep with her unsociable husband.

It was the perfect place for his secret—far away from any town, secluded, private. And safe: his dear relative had fallen out of grace with the family and was seldom visited. He himself knew her just well enough to be recognized. She would not even know he was working in a king's household, and he wouldn't tell her.

Being a blood relative, she would be obligated to keep the child for a year or two—long enough for him to discover the means to undo this little curse that bothered the king so much. It wouldn't take long. He would visit; not so often, though, as it might arouse suspicion.

Dressed as a peasant farmer, Nicolai made out that he was recently widowed and taking his baby girl to a better life. She helped him the first few days by being fussy. "She misses her mother," he would tell any who took notice. People pitied him, offering rides in their carts and free hospitality. It was going so well. Milk and bread appeared as if by magic to feed her, and the small vial he carried to dose her at night kept his sleep undisturbed.

The ferryman at the wide river shook his head at the poor farmer's plight and declined Nicolai's offer to pay for passage. It was during the trip across the languid water that he found the brooch tucked into a fold in the fleece, its clasp gripping the wool—a metal stowaway.

"Ah, so that's what's been pricking you," he said to the bright-eyed infant, who had just noticed the sun playing on the ripples of the water. "A parting gift from your papa, eh?" He unfastened the silver dragon; he should leave no trail. It would sink quickly, even if someone did hear the small splash...

"No," he said, reconsidering. "It's only fair that you should have it. It'll just be a pretty plaything where you're going, anyway." She heard his almost-caring tone and cooed at him while he replaced the brooch in a deep pocket of the hunting cloak.

The king's trust in this matter warmed him. The monarch would, of course, be doubly, even triply indebted to this faithful servant when the princess returned unharmed and un-cursed to her father's castle. Smiling with satisfaction at the future display of gratitude, Nicolai gathered up his little ward and stepped off the gangplank onto the southern shore.

The late afternoon sun threw a long shadow behind him as he trudged up the last long hill, panting and blowing. His cousin the shepherdess was sweeping the cottage and had just appeared outside the door, besom in hand. Nicolai waved, but paused to catch his breath while she awaited the as-yet-unknown visitor.

"Is the man at home?" he asked her finally.

"Aye," answered she, shielding her eyes from the sun. "Have we met?"

"Surely you know your own cousin, Joan!" He tossed back his hood and grinned at her.

"Nicolai! What mischief are you up to now? You're no farmer, that's sure... and heavier than last I saw you."

"Can we step inside?" he said quickly, aiming her in the direction of the door. Before she entered, she called her husband to come.

As if he were one of the sheep, thought Nicolai, as shepherd Jacob emerged from a copse of dogwood trees.

Nicolai unwrapped the baby near the thick glass of the one tiny window, where it was warm. The shepherd's skeptical look vanished when he saw her dimpled legs kicking the air.

"...So I thought you might like a little girl's company, Cousin, for a while, seeing as you don't have any children of your own yet—or I would have heard, wouldn't I?"

"I want to know why you picked us, of all people," interposed the shepherd in a gruff voice. A courtier he was not.

"Of course you do. Well, her papa's going away, for a time, and he doesn't want any sneaky invader or traitor carrying off his child in his absence, only to demand a fat ransom upon his return. And this is the safest place I know of, and the two of you the safest people." Jacob crossed his arms and rolled his eyes, and this did not go unnoticed by the speaker. "And you'll be well compensated for your generous care," Nicolai went on. He flamboyantly produced a heavy leather pouch, and dropped it noisily on the rough table before falling silent.

Jacob reached to pick it up as if it were a snake poised to strike. He opened it gingerly and peered inside. "Silver, Joan. Not a single copper among them."

"I shall be back next year to look in on her, maybe even take her home." Nicolai looked pleadingly at Joan. "Her mother's dead, Cousin, and her father wanted her to have parents, not just guardians, to begin her life well."

The shepherdess had already taken her from Nicolai's arms.

"What's her name?" Nicolai merely frowned at this. Joan looked to Jacob. "What shall we call her, then?" she asked, stroking the red-gold curls.

"Miriam will do," Nicolai stated. He had thought about it on his way: something common-sounding but unusual in the region. It would make finding her that much easier. Or, as a backup, provide an excellent reason why she could not be found at all, later.

"Miriam. It sounds, uh, Hebrew."

"Yes, yes it does. Exotic, don't you think? And I'm glad that you see the importance of keeping this confidential. Is there a boatman on duty in the evening?"

"You aren't staying with us?" Joan protested.

"There's one evening boat, but I'd wait until morning if I were you," offered her husband.

Well, you're not me, thought Nicolai, *thankfully.* "I have to be getting back, Jacob. But I'll stay longer on my next visit, I promise."

The shepherd grunted.

"I'll walk you down the hill then," Jacob stated. "You'll just make it before sunset."

"Good-bye, Joan."

"Oh, Nicolai, I wish you'd stay. The baby will miss you."

"She seems to have gotten used to you already," he concluded.

Joan didn't press him anymore. She turned back into the cottage, a child in her arms and a wondering smile on her face.

Jacob stood at the landing. His wife's cousin—he could call him a guest—had donned his hood and hastily boarded the last boat north. Silver coins glinted gold in the fading light as they fell from Nicolai's hand into the ferryman's. There was a breeze blowing through the river basin that the shepherd didn't like, but he lifted his hand in parting as the boat cast off. The two men had talked little during their descent; they didn't have much in common. Nicolai was obviously important, to somebody, somewhere. Jacob found himself wondering what his guest's hurry to leave was all about. He watched the craft glide away with the twilight before he scrambled nimbly up the hill, toward home and his new family.

A spring squall blew up quickly; the pelting rain had drenched him by the time he reached the doorstep. Inside, the baby was nestled in the just-emptied wood box, sleeping soundly. Joan told him that the child had taken the goat milk and mash easier than any orphaned kid. He smiled, stamping water off his boots.

"Didn't seem to want to catch up with you that much, that cousin of yours."

"No, he never did."

"He did have one piece of advice, though—I mean for her."

"What was that?"

"He said we should be extra careful to keep her warm."

Nicolai had pulled it off. The plan was flawless, brilliantly executed. He was another Merlin, rescuing a royal heir from certain danger, holding the key to his country's secret. And it was safe with him; he could return now to the king in full confidence, his own power not only intact, but manifestly increased...

They were midway across the river when the storm struck. It lashed mercilessly at the boat, tearing him out of his reverie, and hurled him over the side into the dark water. Panic seized him as the small craft floundered, snatched away by the elements. A fleeting thought of the infant princess flashed in his mind as a cold wave covered him. There was not even time to pray.

He had taken everything into consideration but his own mortality.

Were a man in a mountain of ice, yet if the Sun of Righteousness will arise upon him, his frozen heart shall feel a thaw.

– John Bunyan

IV

Twilight Dawning

His pacing footsteps reverberated like incessant clockwork from the flagged stone floor of the great hall. It had been more than a month now, and still there was no sign of Nicolai. He could have sent a messenger; he could have been far less secretive about it all. He could have… The king's thoughts spun in endless arcs, winding shapelessly through a maze of suspicion, tragedy, and anger. He trusted no one now and kept his musings inside, heavily bolted and barred within the castle of his mind.

The princess' disappearance consumed the tiny kingdom. A country-wide search was ordered of course, and for a time the dungeon (a former storeroom) rang out with the tortured cries of brigands arrested for their shady looks and averted eyes. The king restlessly immersed himself in the affairs of governance, mechanically moving from one decision to the next, but without queen or daughter, he hardly felt at home anymore. And while he grieved in distancing silence, the kingdom hibernated.

Only a few whispered voices spoke within its murky sleep.

"Mistress Brigid, you're out late," the sentry commented.

"Can't sleep, not when the stars are so bright, Sir Pieter."

"You miss your mistress, I think."

"Don't we all?" She looked up with pert, hazel eyes, though he could not see their fire under the cloak of night. "Especially his Majesty."

"He doesn't show it."

"No, but he aches inside," she stated. "Misses both of them, he does. Keeps so busy because he's miserable. Well, it won't last forever."

"I'm glad to see you're so sure about that."

"God's at work."

"In the king?" the knight answered, taken aback. "I only wish he was."

"He is," she answered definitely. "Keeps it secret, though; doesn't want anyone to get in his way. Least of all his Majesty." She bid him a cheery good-night and sauntered back to the dead queen's chambers, looking up at the night sky.

Pieter was relieved that Brigid didn't say much during the day; her confidence in an unseen world embarrassed him.

As the trees in the castle gardens once again exchanged their gay summer gowns for the fiery garments of autumn, the king awoke from his lethargy. He threw himself into the great chair upon the dais, drummed his fingers on the ornate armrest, and thought. He was wasting time, bemoaning his losses and inventing excuses, and he knew it. Something had to change. He called for pen and ink, and as soon as they were brought he began to doodle upon a scrap of vellum.

"Ha!" he cried, stabbing the parchment with a black blob. The new chief steward emerged from behind the pillar where he always seemed to hover in attendance, like a shadow one didn't notice until it moved.

"My lord?"

"Ah, there you are. It's been a dogged summer, eh?"

"That it has, Sire."

"Winter is coming apace, and we all need a change."

"Indeed, Your Majesty."

Could no one hold a decent conversation anymore? All anybody ever did these days was agree with him. Well, he wouldn't let it bother him; that was how subjects treated their king. Nicolai, however... no. That was once, and this was Now—a different era altogether. He must step up to it. He cleared his throat to make his pronouncement.

"There's to be a new emblem. Brand new. The former is to be done away with." He dramatically removed the silver brooch from his shoulder and casually tossed it to the steward, who was unprepared for the gesture and juggled it, befuddled. "Here, look at this." The king poked the scrawled drawing at him next and dictated a fervid description: "A seven-rayed golden sunburst on a field of royal blue. The central stone is to be topaz for our royal apartments and either gold or amber for the furnishings. Yes—and have the stones polished and set against a light metal so they can catch the light—that will be better and less costly than gold for the larger ones. Gold thread on blue silk for the standard. For the jewelry, the sunburst in yellow gold on an enameled background, if it can be done. When a sample of the devices are set and ready, have them brought to me for approval."

"Yes, Sire. And the current ones?"

"Well, what about it?"

"What's to be done with them, my lord?"

"Leave them for now, until everything has met with my satisfaction. Then replace every seal, banner, shield, medallion—everything on which that infernal dragon lies—in the kingdom." He added, *sotto voce,* "We must look to better times, forward. We can't have all these ancient dragons skulking about."

"Yes, Sire," came the submissive answer. It was a good change, not least in the effect it was having on the king. The steward turned to go, then looked back in hesitation.

"Excuse me, Sire, but what exactly will you want done with the old ones?"

"Burn them, melt them down, sell the stones. We could do with the revenue. There must be nothing left."

"Yes, Your Majesty." The steward bowed and left to call a meeting of all the masters of the guilds: stonecutters, wood carvers, jewelers, weavers, blacksmiths, armorers. In these uncertain times, the new order would be more than welcome. The craftsmen would be happy for the work – and delivered from dangerous boredom.

Simplify, clean up the image, decided the king, rising from his chair. The color change would certainly make the castle warmer, more welcome. He would replace the draperies, the bedclothes, the tablecloths; everything would match. The rest of the day he spent in a thorough tour of the great house, taking note of every place the dragon curled around its red treasure. And he would have less filigree, more Spartan line in the metalwork. *Clean. Clean and warm.*

He passed the chapel and halted, retracing a few steps to peer inside. It could use more light. And the carved wooden corpus on the crucifix—it would have to go. Too depressing.

"But Robert, it means new work, the king's work. You've got a son now, a family to support." The master carpenter would not listen. Chopping up the carved seals for firewood was cruel thanks for hours of backbreaking labor—his best, most heartfelt work. They would be gouging them out of chairs and chests, chiseling them out of the handcrafted oaken tables, pounding them off the marble faces of the pillars... it made him sick to think about it. He would have nothing to do with any of it. To ask a man to stand by and watch his work being destroyed was too much.
"I'm sorry, sir. Ye'll have to find yerself a new master. There's plenty carpenters here can wield an adze and chisel as well as I."
"No one does the fine work so well, though, Master Crafter."
Robert pursed his lips and scratched his bristly chin. "The new emblem won't be needing so much in the way of fine work, sir. Not in the wood, anyway." Returning his leather cap to his head and bowing stiffly, he resolved to leave the purged castle as soon as possible. He would go south, where the weather was warm, he muttered as he left the hall, to be a simple working man, making really useful, beautiful things. He would leave off carving altogether, and he would stay far away from images and symbols, of kings or nobles or anybody else.

The Father is with him all the time, but it may be long ere the child knows himself in His arms.

– George MacDonald

V

Castaway

"Miriam!" The peasant woman's herding voice rang among the hills, searching for the girl she called daughter. A summer breeze caught a strand of dark hair and threw it against the cotton of the matron's cap. She hadn't long to wait; the child soon sprang up over a rock-dusted knoll, back-lit by the early morning sun, her curly hair an aura of burnished gold. *How she loves to run,* thought the mother as the agile feet bounded through mossy turf, springing the girl forward into the wind.

"Hurry, child, it's shearing day." The little shepherdess pivoted in mid-stride, turning into the timbered barn where ricks stood as barricades and strong hands waited to channel the sheep toward the rhythmic clipping of the shears. She'd learned her part in tiny bits: two years ago she was stuffing fistfuls of new-shorn wool into baskets for sorting and washing. That year, too, she'd learned to card the wool and watch it untangle into soft, spin-able fibers. She had no interest in working the spinning wheel then, being too small to reach the treadle, but she liked very much to gaze at its turning—it sang whirring lullabies to her as she lay in the little corner straw pile near the stone hearth.

She couldn't manage a grown sheep on her own, but she was welcome; she was too conscientious to get in anyone's way. Today she would help hold the ewes while the crossing blades snipped off their thick coats. Many summer days' walking had strengthened her limbs, and night watches against wolves had toughened her will and courage. Miriam took a quick draught from a skin bottle hanging nearby, giggling as a trickle of white milk ran down her chin. She loved burying her hands in the wool, feeling the warmth of the soft creatures beneath their matted fleeces. And she was conveniently small enough to restrain them without crowding the shearers.

She watched in admiring wonder as a struggling ewe relaxed, limp in her hold, suddenly passive and seemingly waiting to be undressed. The shears deftly made their way up its belly, the fleece peeling off in a thick, seamless blanket. Over and over it happened, the smell of lanolin and sweat thickening the air around her. Pools of sunlight swirled through holes in the roof, filling the barn with a dusty cloud edged with tarnished gold. Her concentration ebbed. Then, suddenly, there came a feeble bleat and the ewe she was holding gave a start; the dulling blade had nicked its skin.

Blood flowed softly, crimson and warm.

She coughed and tried to catch her breath: something was choking her. She gritted her teeth hard, trying to regain her hold on the creature which now lay tense and still while the shearer bared its flanks, but the room was spinning. She was caught in its whirl, being twisted into its woolen thread. Her eyes widened and her jaw dropped in terror as the blades opened and shut—she didn't notice when they stopped—and now she was the passive victim, looking up with liquid, stupid eyes at those who wanted her wool, stripping her of her only protection against the harsh elements...

Being thus harvested was too horrible to bear, and little Miriam fell back, senseless, onto the wool-strewn floor. The shearer hastily dropped his tool while the half-shorn sheep rose confusedly to hobble away, besmeared with a spot of red dribble. Much fuss was made over the girl who had so gaily entered the barn an hour before. Strong arms bore her off to her alarmed mother, who gave a sharp, questioning look to her husband as if to say, "Now will you believe me about the child?"

Sometime later, Miriam woke. She immediately begged Joan to let her rejoin the sheep. She wanted to hold the naked ones, she said, to keep them from getting too cold, although she knew well enough that they were herded into a crowded pen for just such a purpose and that the afternoon was warm. Joan cautioned her to wait, but the girl fidgeted and fussed so that the woman relented, insisting nonetheless on walking with her down to the sheepfold.

Miriam was quiet the rest of the day, and grew strangely tired as the sun journeyed toward its setting. The shepherdess had watched the girl's meandering among the shorn sheep, speaking softly to herself, touching them with significance, peering into their faces. After dinner, she disappeared again, this time to the corner where she slept. Ever vigilant, the tiniest sound would wake her, so Jacob motioned his wife to step outside, where they could breathe easier and talk freely in the stretching twilight.

"Were you there when the fit came upon her?"

"I was; but it were no fit, Joan. There weren't so much as a cry. No jerking, no foaming at the mouth…" He paused as the background sounds—flies buzzing, sheep bleating, the glimmering murmur of the tiny brook—filled the wordless gap. "She were overcome by something."

"When she awoke, she told me she wanted to go warm the sheep. She seemed so sure of how they felt."

"Aye, it were feeling that done it; too much feeling. You taught her faith, I taught her letters, but who taught her to read the sheep, the sky? Ach, but she reads everythin'—stars, wind, sky together. She wants an answer, but to what? I cannot help her if she canna put into words what it is she wants to know."

"There are many things about her we don't know."

"Ye needn't tell me, wife," he answered, eyeing the edge of his boot. "The village priest was here, a few days back. Did he talk with her any?"

"Yes, earnestly. They two seemed to understand each other. But when she'd gone back, to help you…" Joan sighed, pursing her lips slightly.

"What'd he say then?"

Her eyes were away, out on the fields. "He said that she had a pretty imagination and could tell the sweetest stories. He commended me on her manners, but he didn't seem to think she was odd."

"I wonder the talk hasn't reached his ears." Jacob was thinking of the village children and their whispers of "changeling" and "star-child". Joan had heard, too. What parent could miss overhearing such things?

"People know by now that she's fostered. Children always find names for things they don't understand."

"Even the other day," he recollected, "when we were up in the high meadow, she seemed so at home. She threw pebbles in the brook and climbed a tree. She raced the dog and picked berries. But when we come back…"

"She was so quiet. I remember."

"Aye. It were as if she met someone, or found out a secret—an' not a secret fit for little girls—or, or suddenly she come of age. She's too young to do so much in the way of wonderin'."

"Is she? Babies wonder about everything, seems to me."

"Do they, now? An' how would you be knowin' that?"

The woman held her peace; they'd never had one of their own.

No, thought Jacob, with a mild bitterness. After meeting her, he had fled the austerity of the cloister for the solitude of the hills. Here he found space to think, to break at heart, to melt in his spirit like the winding glacier above into the watercourse below. But she was barren. He carried a curse of his own making. If only he'd taken his final vows… He changed the subject.

"I hope that uppity cousin o' yers comes soon, because, if the truth be told, I'm gettin' too fond o' that girl, Joan. We got to try an' keep her mind on her work, treat her as any child. We can't go about making her feel more different—than she already do, I mean—just because we don't rightly know who she is." The awkward speech hit its mark.

"I can't help but fear for her a little," Joan admitted. "He may never come back."

"Then she's ours, woman, for good or ill, until God lets us know what's to be done about her. He does seem to be takin' his time though, don't he?"

"Oh, Jacob, you of all people, wantin' God to hurry! There's nothing the matter with him, or his ways—you know that as well as I. So why should we two mind bein' kept for a moment in the dark, standing outside his window?" Her voice fell from scolding to pondering. "Sometimes even the waiting can be sweet."

They grasped callused hands for a minute or more before Jacob turned toward the barn and his wife back into the cottage, where the little shepherd girl smiled in her sleep, chasing lambs in a dreamland meadow.

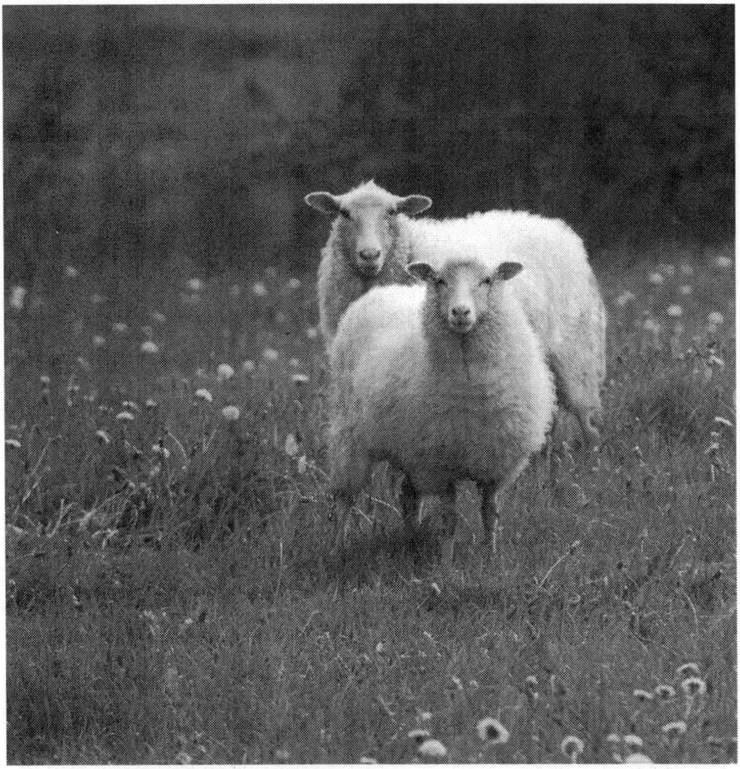

He who lives alone is eaten by the lion.

– East African proverb

VI

Tête-à-tête

The yellow light, reflected from the emblem highest in the hall, played upon the smooth floor like the sun's rays on the surface of a golden pool. An ambassador stood, his smooth hands crossed in front of his elegant robe, waiting for the king to finish reading the document. The monarch's eyes darted down the page and across again before looking up; when he did, it was with head tilted sideways to examine his solicitor in earnest intensity. Despite the scowl he wore, he had hoped for—even anticipated—this meeting. It came as no surprise to him. His response was both confident and practiced.

"He knows we cannot withstand him by force."

"Yes, my lord."

"And these... terms and conditions, Lord Basil—they seem to be of mutual benefit." It felt good to come to the point; he never did like subtle negotiations. So he leaned forward, bold and direct. "What is his true motive in all of this?" The ambassador smiled calmly, hardly taken aback.

"I believe it is one of compassion, primarily. He, like yourself, wants to preserve the peace between us. He also has the means to extend his borders, but he is not willing to do so at the expense of your friendship. He knows that you, like himself, have no male heir, and he pities you for it. His daughter is of marriageable age and would grace any court, and he would like her to be near him as his years increase. You, being an orderly, capable ruler and his nearest neighbor, he deems the most prudent choice."

It was all in the document, but coming from the lips of this skilled orator, it sounded irresistibly logical and absolutely safe. In fact, he could think of no clever alternative. His eastern neighbor was civil, shrewd, and educated—no barbarian tyrant. The pause lengthened, awaiting the speech's concluding remarks as the window behind the dais let the midday brilliance into the council chamber.

"Should there ever come an heir by this union," the ambassador went on, "the kingdom would still pass through you by inheritance... And a formal liaison—ties by marriage—with a stronger realm would mean increased security for your own." The king scarcely heard this last remark, distracted as he was by a warm stirring at the thought of siring a child.

"Yes." He cleared his throat and sat up straighter in the heavy chair. "It is not an unattractive arrangement. However, the benefits you propose could still be a long way off. How will your sovereign guarantee this, ah, security, until this future heir—if ever there is one—comes of age?" The answer was, as he expected, sensible and ready.

"He will gladly lend you several of his knights and their retainers to fortify your borders, as well as supply you with a counselor of his choosing..."

"Such as yourself, perhaps, to supervise my governance."

"No, Sire," Basil answered with a patient smile. "To better forge a unified kingdom, if in the course of events an annexation came to be. Your authority would remain intact. You have already earned his trust and admiration. Why else would he propose such favorable terms?" Right; it was damn good of him, that sneaky neighbor, and clever. Clever, and pleasant.

It could work.

"Oh." He scrutinized the face of his opponent or soon-to-be colleague, unable to decide which. "It is agreeable. I should like two days to compose a fitting response."

"No less time would be expected," came the gracious reply.

Later, he stood alone on the rampart, sorting out his tangled thoughts. So. He would be a little vassal-king of the beautiful mountain-clad valley. It was a friendly solution, so much better than another bloody siege. He was tired; tired of fretting over his defenses, mostly over how to fill the vacuum left by the vanished crusaders of his father's reign without burdening his people with the cost of building a bigger arsenal for their protection.

And he was tired of being alone.

He gazed steadily into the new emblem, all awash with the golden rays of a dying sunset, imploring it for wisdom. He could still be king, without any obligation to a lost princess who might turn up unexpectedly to demand an inheritance. He smiled, wanly, at such a notion. If all went well, he would have none left to give her.

The servants noticed the change instantly. Never had their sovereign welcomed a visitor in such fashion; never had such a refined ambassador as the sagacious Lord Basil appeared at this court, so pleasantly mingling with the few nobles amid the most lavish entertainments their king could afford. The banners hung from the roof of the great hall, shimmering in their silken blues and reds and ablaze with appliquéd cloth-of-gold.

But no one knew what the celebrated occasion was until midway through the feast, when the king stood up to make the announcement: he was getting married again.

If my hand slacked, I should rob God, leaving a blank instead of violins... he could not make Antonio Stradivari's violins without Antonio.

- The violin maker

VII

Project

Robert Crafter stood on the threshold, leaning against the door frame with his arms crossed, watching his nephew at work. He used to work like that too, once, when he was young; reveling amidst a growing pile of wood shavings as they fell from his plane, counterbalancing his weight on each smooth stroke.

In the work shed, his apprentice paused just long enough to brush back the sweat from his eyes with a coarse, upturned sleeve. He was planing a cedar board and had come up against a knot. He stopped to run his fingers along the grain and frown, then reached for his sharpening stone. A few minutes more and the blade was singing again. The pungent-sweet shavings curled away in spiral ribbons; their fragrance wound around him like smoke.

There was no knot too tough for Michael, the graying carpenter thought. Give him enough time, and he would overcome them all. Built to wrestle with manual work, his nephew was a keen learner, taking in Robert's few spoken lessons seriously and applying them in earnest. "If you have a beautiful piece of wood," he'd said once, "you do everything you can to turn it into a beautiful piece of furniture. There'll be knots and nicks to smooth out, and cuts and calluses on your hands, but the work's always worth it in the end." And Michael took him at his word.

"Well, Father," said a tawny fellow appearing just behind him. "Come see the table." Robert turned with a short sigh to follow the young man into the house.

"It's fair enough to look at, Jon, but the joints could be tighter." Robert squatted beneath the tabletop, inspecting and poking his stubby work-worn fingers into the corners. "You might use a peg or two to firm it up."

"I had to leave some space for the pine pitch, Father," answered the other, rationally. "But it's good work, and I started on it only two days ago." Masters were always pickier with their own children. "Michael's been at his four days already and hasn't even started on his mortises yet."

"Michael's tables will outlast yours by twenty years at least," Robert said, standing.

"I know that, but he spends so much time on them, he'll never make a decent living. And in twenty years' time, I shall have made many tables." Here he was, measuring himself again. Robert had warned Jon against it, said it was better to stick to the board in front of you than the future beyond. "We don't make tables for kings, you know, Father," came his son's chiding. Master Crafter retired at the remark, reminiscing. If he only knew...

Jon loved the fruits of his labor, but his cousin loved the work itself. Robert remembered speaking with his nephew about his choice of trade.

"You ought to be a stone carver, the way you fuss over the wood."

Project

Michael had been busy sanding and answered with a hearty laugh. "I haven't the patience for it, Uncle. You could spend your whole life on a work site and never see the cathedral or whatever-it-was finished." It was true; woodwork meant visible, tangible results. "Well," he mused, "columns and lintels I might manage, but there isn't much room for variation on those. You can't invent as you go, not with stone."

Robert knew exactly what he meant; nothing compared to the live grains and textures of once-growing timber. Stone made beautiful outsides, for castles and abbeys and manors. But wood changed a structure into a home—an everyday chapel even, where a well-built table could be an altar. Robert's homespun fear of God had gotten into every room in the house, in the shape of furniture.

"Could you see me hammering away at a gargoyle for five years?" his nephew had asked then, tilting his dark-haired head. No, thought the older man; Michael was much too practical for gargoyles. Still, his work was art, and whether he knew it or not, he would be a master carver.

The pounding of a mallet brought Robert's mind back to the present. Jon was tightening the table joints. He measured a triangle between the legs at the corner, and called to his father who had wandered into the adjoining room to get a drink.

"I think I'll use corbels instead of pegs. They would serve the same function, and give it some decorative value. What do you think?"

Robert set his cup of ale down.

"Sounds a good idea. Make them smooth, though. Legs don't like splinters." Jon didn't smile, but neither did he understand that his master-father was talking about the legs of people and not furniture.

45

Begin to be now what you will be hereafter.

– Saint Jerome

VIII

Besieged

If there was one thing that Michael liked better than the smell of fresh wood, it was the smell of warm bread. He often made extra trips behind his master's simple house to fetch the odd tool, so as to catch Mistress Crafter in the act of baking. Even with the scraggly beginnings of a fairly thick beard on his face, his bouncy step and happy whistle betrayed a boy-child on the inside—a simple, hearty fellow whom nothing bothered very much. The townspeople liked him, though the brilliance in his dark eyes escaped the notice of everyone but Robert and his wife. He could talk with anybody, it seemed, and feel perfectly at home wherever he was: in the street, in the square, in the greenwood, or in the work shed.

Master Crafter and his nephew sat in the little shop, washing down their midday black bread, warm from the oven, with almost-as-warm ale from the jug, when a commotion outside caught their attention. At about the same moment, Jon burst breathless through the open back doorway.

"The burgomaster's getting ready to assault that castle on the hill—the one he says is his. A call has gone out for men-at-arms, including all the guilds..."

"Doesn't he have enough to worry about?" asked Michael, exchanging glances with his uncle. He was sitting on the workbench swinging his legs, a habit Jon found coarse and irritating.

"Maybe he wants to fill his coffer and slow down the taxes," suggested Robert calmly.

"Yeah, maybe. Maybe he's just hungry for power."

"He's supplying all foot soldiers with leather armor and weapons," added the son, feeling ignored.

"I guess you're going, Jon."

"I think I'll stay home," mumbled Michael, his mouth full of bread.

"It's not an option, Father. Those who don't come are to be fined fifty silver pieces."

"That's ridiculous. Who's got that kind of money?"

But Jon had turned to his cousin.

"It would mean a chance to distinguish yourself, Michael."

He was dowsed with uproarious laughter.

"What happens if you don't fight and can't pay?" his cousin asked.

"You go to prison. Simple."

"Well then, Jon, I guess we'd better visit the armorer's," Michael acquiesced, sighing dramatically. "Master Crafter?" The seasoned old carpenter wiped his rough hands on his breeches and lifted his gray eyebrows warily.

"I suppose I'll hang back and make war machines. Damn him."

At this unexpected remark, Michael's mouthful of ale erupted all over Jon. Still spluttering, and hopping off the table to apologize profusely, Michael pulled out a cotton rag to wipe off the jerkin of his master's son, but Jon lashed out, pushing him back against the wall.

"You take nothing seriously, you oaf, and you don't care a fig about anything. You can't even ride worth a pinch of salt! You're just a stupid coward, Michael, with no aims or goals or thoughts for anybody but yourself."

"That's enough, Jon," intervened Robert.

"There's more to life than planing boards, Father, why can't he see that?" Jon fumed out, not waiting for an answer. He didn't really want one. A moment of quiet shock passed. Robert let out a parental sigh.

"I'm afraid the boy has ambitions. And I'm afraid for him."

"That he'll be disappointed? I don't think you need worry about that, Uncle."

"I don't. I fear he will succeed." The apprentice shook his head. Position and politics had never held his interest. Robert stood to select a marking knife from the shelf and reached for the leather strop. He leaned over and gave his attention to the task at hand, but kept up the conversation. "So, nephew, what are yours?"

"My what?"

"Ambitions. You're too young to not have any."

A hint of a smile tickled the corners of Michael's crumb-laden mouth.

"Well…"

"Eh? Speak up, lad." Robert stopped honing his blade to look up with his eyes, not bothering to raise his head.

"I wouldn't mind marrying above my station, so I can spend my time crafting and not have to think about money."

"Got anyone in mind?"

Michael laughed. "Nope. Plenty of wenches around here, but a terrible shortage of ladies."

"Don't be too sure." The craftsman had lowered his eyes again. "A cavern full of bats can hide gold, further down."

"Maybe. But I'm too busy to go looking right now. Guess she'll have to come looking for me." He had picked up a file, but he put it down again and stood up reluctantly. "I suppose I better stay out of the gaoler's reach and go see that armorer. What a stupid waste of time."

Robert smiled, understanding how the young man felt. For a brief second he missed his old life in the isolated north; his former lord would avoid a battle at all costs. But the memory slipped away quickly. Some things were worth fighting for, he thought—though he certainly didn't consider the burgomaster's siege one of them.

Three days later, the armed citizenry huddled in the shaded woods just below the stronghold, a thick-stoned fortress set defiantly (or so it seemed to the burgomaster) atop a rocky hill. They stomped silently and blew into their hands, trying out numerous stratagems to ward off the pre-dawn chill. Siege towers lay on their sides, replete with wooden wheels and ready to roll into position. Catapults had been quietly cranked down and were already loaded with their first missiles.

No lights burned through the black slits in the gray walls. Frogs croaked; a lark began its song, but the tension in the air stifled it. At the moment the sun rose, so did the burgomaster's peasant forces out of the east. The command to attack sounded so thin to Michael in the wide-open morning air.

Besieged

What did he have against the reclusive knight who held this small plot of land beyond the edge of town? Nothing. He was merely a leather-clad pawn to be moved about on a real-life chessboard full of arrows and stones and blood.

The catapults and archers began to pelt the castle while the conscripted workmen strained to haul the towers up the crumbly slope. The stiff hauberk bit into Michael's shoulders. For a brief second he envied the unarmored David, facing a giant with only his sling and faith-filled aim. He changed his mind when a volley of fist-sized rocks assailed the group from above, pinging off his steel cap and thwarted by the hardened cowhide from breaking his ribs.

He sweated on, grunting with the others to raise a siege tower, vaguely hearing shouted commands to stabilize its base. The stones were a nuisance—the wooden wheels kept slipping over them. And the tower was a heavy one, because the fortress was tall. At last it was in place, and Michael ran to place a shim in its track to keep it there, close enough to the wall to allow access over the rampart but just out of the defenders' reach; Robert had built a small folding ramp at the top to close the gap when the breech was made. Other towers were in place now; all seemed to be going well enough. Then Michael glimpsed a stalwart man in a silver helm standing resolute on a parapet far above him, watching.

Deep down he knew the attack was futile and poorly planned, doomed to fail. Still, he kept to his post, steadying the tower's base while his comrades-in-arms climbed the giant ladder with speed and gusto. The defenders were ready, in spite of the sleepy appearance of the stronghold—metal arrow tips sliced through the leather armor, and men rained down around the wooden framework, landing smack-hard on the sharp scree.

Jon seemed to come from nowhere with a sudden inspiration. He hurled himself upward through the middle of the tower's frame, yelling to Michael to steady the downhill side. His words were almost drowned out by the clamor of skirmish and a hesitant call to retreat. He then grabbed the rope attached to the topmost ramp and leaped away from the wall, joining his weight with the force of a lever applied by the castle's defenders. He landed atop Michael, breaking his own fall, but an instant later the siege tower toppled over in a sickening crunch, pinning the apprentice underneath and sending Jon tumbling backwards and away.

An ax-stroke of pain fell on Michael's leg; blackness rolled over him like a thick velvet curtain while he pushed impossibly at the heavy timbers he had dutifully pounded together with his own hands.

Leaning against the battlements over the gate, the knight in the silver helm stretched and sighed.

"That didn't last long, thank God."

"Shall we take a small foray out, my lord, to put those poor losers out of their misery?" said his squire, already poised to go.

"No, no. Leave them for their kinsfolk to pick up. They did not fight willingly, I think." The squire nodded, surveying the mess. "Wait. See if that fellow under the tower over there is still alive. If he is, bring him inside."

The burgomaster's men had fallen back to reconsider the cost of overtaking such a mighty stronghold, but the poorer retainers slunk hastily back to their workshops and fields to abandon the whole fiasco. Stories circulated through the guilds about Jon's final brave assault. Michael was missed, but when the townspeople went back under flag of truce to collect their dead, his body was not among the slain.

He woke two days later, ravenously hungry. A leather strap crossed his chest and continued up, under his armpits, toward the head of the wooden bedstead—a novel way to tie a man, he thought. Something pulled his legs in the opposite direction. The room was close and dark and foul. He must be set up for torture in some dungeon. Rot. He made a quick attempt to loosen his bonds, but a sharp pain in his thigh overwhelmed his effort, and he cried out.

Light instantly flared from a curtained doorway to flood the turret room. A bewhiskered guard appeared and threw open the thick wood shutters. Michael could see only sky behind him as he approached.

"Whoa, there, soldier. Keep still an' it won't hurt so bad. There now, yer leg bone's broke clean through, doctor says. We're stretchin' you to get it mended straight. Now hold on an' I'll get you something to slake yer thirst."

The man disappeared, and Michael was left alone with his thoughts. His keen hearing soon caught hold of words spoken on the landing.

"It's a miracle he pulled through that fever."

"Wonder what the master wants of him. With armor like his, he wouldn't fetch much of a ransom."

"Well, you'd best clean him up. He's probably famished, but who'd be able to eat, smelling like that?"

Ten minutes later, he lay exhausted, but happy to be in fresh linens. Hot, spiced wine took the edge off the pain as well as his appetite until something more substantial could be brought. But before the promised meal arrived, the knight

Michael recognized from the battle strode in and peered down at him in concern.

"Hmm. You are younger than I expected. It's hard to tell a man's age when his eyes are shut. Sir," and here he made a slight bow, "you are welcome."

"Welcome's a strange word for a prisoner."

"You're no prisoner. You're a guest."

"Why?" Michael's forthright manner obviously pleased the knight, who returned the rough-edged compliment with a direct answer.

"Your comrade-in-arms almost killed you, then left you for dead."

"He did? That was my cousin..." The knight pulled a heavy chair out from its place against the stone wall and sat astride it as if it were one of his mounts, its back sticking up like a warhorse's neck.

"Did you want to fight?"

"No." Michael eyed him curiously. "Not many of us did, really. We couldn't afford the fine to refuse."

"Ah. Yet you obeyed your orders."

"I don't shirk a duty, sir," answered the apprentice carpenter, amused in spite of his discomfort that he had warranted the attention of so worthy a gentleman.

"Would you like to hear a story—a true one?" the knight asked. Michael laughed and said he had nothing better to do at the moment. "It's about how I came to own this castle instead of your town overlord. His father and mine were brothers, twins, no less, and to put a stop to any quibbling over inheritance, their father—my grandfather—divided up his little serfdom equally, or so he thought. The castle and its lands one way, the town the other. I'm sure he'd hoped to create a mutual love and dependency between the two, with the lord of the castle to protect the townsfolk in the event of attack, the town craftsmen supplying the castle's needs, and so on. But once he died—wouldn't you know it?—they two soon fell to grumbling. Each felt slighted. Naturally, they passed their grievances on to their children."

"So the castle was yours by inheritance."

"So was the quarrel, it seems. But I have enough. Wanting more than you have only makes you miserable." The knight had spoken without a trace of bitterness. His story aside, he turned to Michael's. "What is your trade?"

"I'm apprenticed to a master carpenter in town. I only had two weeks left before becoming a journeyman."

"Still an apprentice? Why so long? You're well over twenty."

"I started late...and I like to take my time," he added sheepishly.

"Do you do good work?"

"I try."

The knight smiled broadly.

"Then I shall make you an offer. Build me a chest worthy of a gracious knight, and you shall have earned your freedom—and your bed and board too."

"I think I owe you more than that."

"If I like the chest, then you can come back sometime and work for me as master carpenter."

"It bears thinking about." That Michael should feel so at ease with this man surprised him. "But you'll have to let me out of these trusses before I can start."

"That's the doctor's business," answered the knight, laughing lightly and looking across the room to where the consultant had appeared and silently waited.

"At least a fortnight," came the reply.

"That's a long time to have to stay still," protested Michael with a groan.

"I'm afraid you'll have to." His host rose to give orders. "Now get this man some victuals. He wants meat, I think." The patient grinned, shaking the knight's offered hand with a thankful and firm grip.

Lying still was by far the hardest thing he'd ever done. He tottered on a mental tightrope between boredom and despair, and only two things helped him. One was a dim echo of his mother's voice saying, "God gives us no more than we can bear, and he gives us patience first." The other was his concentrated vigil against bitterness; he would not let the sting of Jon's abandonment overcome his gratitude. He would conquer it with forgiveness. After weighing all the options, there was no other decent choice.

So, with nothing else to do, he began to pray. As he did, little by little and all of a sudden, the peace of God trickled into his soul, and he turned his thoughts more and more to the design of the knight's project.

The chest finished—warmly polished and beautiful beyond his host's expectations—Michael took his leave of the castle amid many fond wishes and sincere farewells. As he shouldered his modest bag and limped down the sloping path, the knight watched from the rampart just above the gate.

"Pity about his leg," he confided to his squire. "He would have made an excellent knight."

Ceaseless interior prayer is the continual yearning
of the human spirit towards God.

– A Russian staret to an inquiring pilgrim

IX

Moonlight and Firelight

The stars stretched themselves across the canvas of the night-heaven while Miriam stretched herself beneath the thick fleece cover to gaze upward, as if to place herself among them. Summers in the high meadow were a balm, soothing the sting of her frostbitten soul. The fire leapt up now and again to launch another spark skyward, though they never seemed to reach their destination.

"Papa."

"Hmmm?"

"Are you awake?"

"Almost. What is it, child?"

"How do you pray?"

"You've been praying for years now, Miriam. Surely you must have some idea what you're about..."

"No, I mean you. What do you pray? Besides the words in your breviary?"

Wide awake now, he thought a long moment.

"I used to pray lots of things," he answered with a touch of remembrance in his voice.

"But now—what do you pray now?" She was in earnest; there was no use trying to avoid her directness.

"Lord Jesu Christ, have mercy on me."

"Is that all?"

"It's more than it seems."

"Mmm. And where do you look, up or down? Or don't you—do you shut your eyes?"

He paused, took a breath to speak, then waited a second longer. "I don't even know anymore, Miriam. It doesn't matter. To pray is to go with your thoughts into the deep places of your heart. That's where the eternal Lord waits for you."

"I can't find him there, though, Papa."

"How do *you* pray then?" He sat up.

"It changes all the time," she answered carefully. "I look around and... tell God how beautiful he is."

"You tell him that, do you?"

She could hear him smiling through the darkness.

"Yes. Do you think he minds?"

"No—he probably likes it very much." The wind breathed into the birch leaves; they rustled, quivering with hidden music. Some of the sheep stirred.

"Sometimes I ask him who I am."

"Does he answer you, then?" Jacob wanted to explain, but he knew so little himself. And, as she'd never asked, he figured it wasn't for him to speak on God's behalf. This mystery was quite beyond him.

"I think so. Once, maybe more," she said. He leaned forward, attentive and eager, as she went on. "Just... just that I'm his. Somehow."

Jacob sighed with relief.

"There's naught better to be than that. You hold onto it, won't you now?"

"I don't think I'm strong enough, Papa. I only hope that he'll keep hold of me."

"He will, girl, he will." *Somehow.*

She slept almost at once, as secure beneath the dark canopy as if she'd been at home. In the smallest things, remembered Jacob, and even in ourselves, are hidden deep secrets beyond anyone's understanding. All the same, he wondered when he should tell her he wasn't her father. Perhaps he needn't; perhaps she knew by now. Well, as she seemed to have already found Another, he did not trouble himself any longer about it and drifted back to sleep.

It was getting late. Joan stepped outside to peer into the waning sunlight. Silhouetted against the horizon, Miriam walked slowly down the hill toward the cottage, absorbed in thought. Her shawl flapped loosely about her. The shepherdess winced and, wiping her hands on her coarse frock, went to meet her.

"Aren't you cold, child?" she asked, trying not to sound alarmed as she took her adopted daughter's hand in her own. It was ice-cold—as she had feared. "There's hot milk inside." They walked together, their feet flattening the new-born grass. Miriam did not so much as lift her head until the closing door shut out the dusk which had crept up behind them.

Joan admired the girl: really, no longer a child. She was not a born beauty, but she would grow into it, in time. The wise peasant woman foresaw a lovely bloom in the girl's troubled face, and marveled. Gaiety had given place to a sinewy drive, bravely hidden beneath a demure and downcast mien.

"What is it, Miriam?"

"I so like the evening light... it doesn't hurt my eyes. Do you think they'll ever darken?"

"Why?"

"It never bothers people with dark eyes, but the sun... it makes me squint." Though they were fair—of a silvery steel color, thought Joan—the eyes which rose to meet the mother's held the depth of a midnight sky.

"You've beautiful eyes, Miriam, no matter how different they are."

"They're cold."

"There's something else the matter, isn't there?"

Miriam bit her lip, nodding in admission. "Gerda says she's in love with the laird's son. It was all she'd talk about today."

"Why should that trouble you?" She'd never known Miriam to express interest in young men.

"I'm glad for her, really. But she seems so giddy over him, and she calls me a fool for not having a... a consort. She said I scare them all off by being so cold and faraway. But am I as without feeling as that?"

"Hardly, Miriam. You feel more than she'll ever know. Besides, a good man is something to wait for, not run after."

"There are far too many other things to think about, anyway," the brooding girl answered distantly.

"For you, yes." Joan was rolling up her sleeves to knead bread. "You have to remember that some sheep get to like the taste of clover, even if it does blow them up on their insides. They'll even knock over the ricks to get at it."

"They don't trust the shepherd; their appetites get in the way. But what has that got to do with..."

Moonlight and Firelight

"They don't know how to trust him. Thoughts are like sheep, Miriam—you have to pasture them where they can graze on what's good for them, and you have to guard them from nettles and cliffs..."

"And clover," Miriam finished. Joan smiled, knowing that her practical lesson had worked, miraculously, without invading the girl's guarded mind. She watched Miriam ponder while savoring the cream-skin floating atop the warm, thick milk in the wide wooden cup. "But what do you think? Has Gerda done well with that lanky son of the laird?"

"Only time will tell. Just because he doesn't suit your taste doesn't mean he's wrong for her. Right now, though, there's churning to be done if you want butter on your bread." Joan weakly tried to keep the girl from musing overmuch, knowing that Miriam's mind was restless as the inside of the churn, rhythmically pounding away at the many questions she would never ask aloud.

Miriam had gone to the tiny village to take the priest a cheese and some spun wool. Joan found her husband in the barn, weaving willow rods into new ricks.

"She's growing up, Jacob. You can't be sending her into town alone like this."

"No? And why not?"

"Her name, for one thing. People still think she's a Jewess. And there's too many lusty soldier types about. There's not a young lass safe in the country."

"She's no Jew, she's too fair," Jacob muttered. He put down the fence piece and stood, plunging his hands deep into mended pockets. The rumors had wafted up the slopes like black smoke: marauders were ravaging towns in the southeast again. The talk in the market square had turned from courtship and the price of pumpkin to plans for escape or defense; even country-dwellers were barring doors and shutters at nightfall, though no curfew had been ordered. To these things, Jacob was stubbornly immune. "We can't be shutting her up summer as well as winter, now, Joan."

"No, but there is the girl's future to think of."

He set his jaw, resolute, bristling.

"That's in God's hands."

"It's in ours as well. What if something were to happen to us? Who would—"

"It's God's business, woman. We don't even know who she is—we may never know. He'll have to sort it out." But the shepherd sensed Joan's need for a more concrete answer, so he added, "She would have the sheep."

"But she'd be alone."

"Would she now?"

He resumed his work, silencing her, so she went out, her eyes stinging. He couldn't be expected to understand: he wasn't a woman. Nor had he ever been raped.

"Holla, Miriam!" Gerda's voice called from behind as the young shepherdess made her way uphill from the hamlet. Miriam stopped to wait, happy for company. Her dark-eyed friend approached, panting. "Did you hear what they were saying in the market?"

"What?" She didn't often linger to listen to the gossip.

"An invasion! Just two days ago, and only twenty miles away. A horde of barbarians raided a village. They cudgeled a harmless old woman to death—a great aunt of Wilhelm's. It's horrible."

Miriam vaguely remembered Jacob telling her about a similar attack, years ago, before he had married. Funny how things happened over and over again...

"You don't seem to have heard me."

Oh, but I have, thought the shepherdess.

"Are they coming this way?" Miriam asked softly, unconsciously fingering the neckline of her muslin tunic and walking on without slackening her pace.

"No one knows. But everyone's keeping a watch."

"Oh."

"Miriam, aren't you afraid? What's wrong with you?"

"I don't know. I... I just want to be alone."

Gerda stopped short, completely baffled. "You know, Miriam, sometimes I think you're made of ice."

"So do I."

It was a fear she had, that one day she would wake up unable to move at all.

What she'd heard repulsed and confused her. How men, made in the image of God, could maim and pillage, rape and plunder, she couldn't fathom. The beautiful countryside now loomed full of monstrous shadows; the world had suddenly become a dangerous place. Miriam shuddered and withdrew to a secluded niche set against the ridge just above the rustic homestead, where she could let her thoughts roam free and where her fears would seem far enough away.

She stood on the brink of a precipice, leaning against the one steadfast tree that clung to the rock season after season, looking down at the glistening lake basin below. It was really a wide, stopped-up river, a resting place for the water tumbling down from the melting ice fields before it cascaded over the southeastern outlet on its way to the sea. The river channel formed the uppermost border of this region. Beyond it lay more rolling hills and valleys interwoven with small vineyards and grain fields, and beyond those lay the misted edges of the northern mountains.

From whence she had come, spoke an inner voice.

A gentle breeze mounted the ridge from the lakeside and played with her hair. Sunlight danced on the ripples of the water, interrupted only by the tiny wake made by a crossing ferry. She had watched the lake's placid surface reflecting the sky like glass, and, another time, seen its eddies swirl into torrents at the height of a summer tempest. She was drawn by its beauty and repelled by its power.

Power. Miriam likened the marauding raids, the sieges, the clashes of royal siblings to the storms on the lake. One minute chaos reigned, and the next, the sun rose sparkling on fresh-washed grass. A dog's bark woke her out of her chafing reverie. Her father's mastiff trotted up, squat and ugly but welcome, wagging its tail as she bent to scratch behind one bent, wolf-scarred ear.

"You came for me? All right, then, let's go home." No one would molest her in the dog's presence. Perhaps she should take him along to town next time. They raced each other down the hill to where the trenchers were being laden with supper.

The following Sunday's homily had been a somber one, with an apocalyptic eye on a coming holocaust, but Miriam walked home smiling. Joan noticed at once.

"You're not usually gay after Mass, Miriam." No, she wasn't, Miriam realized; she usually thought silently. Especially as of late.

"It was the baby, Mother."

"The one you made laugh aloud—by tickling, no less—during the *Gloria*?"

"It was sweeter than a carillon."

"To you, maybe. It may have kept others from their prayers."

"Oh?" She hadn't thought about that at all. "Did it bother you?"

Joan's sullen face melted.

"I thought it was wonderful." They two laughed, then fell quiet while the turf passed beneath their feet. Miriam now wore thick sheepskin boots that Joan had made for her.

"Have you ever held a baby, Joan—of your own, I mean?"

"Just you. I thought I'd conceived once, quite some years before you came to us, but I was mistaken." She had miscarried, actually, but Miriam didn't need to know this.

"Do you think I ever will?" It was a real question. Miriam had not yet come into womanhood, and she was nearing eighteen.

"I don't know."

"Do you think there's something wrong with me?"

Many things crossed Joan's mind, but none of them seemed serious enough to be called *wrong*. "Why?"

"Others do."

"Is it for them to say?"

"I suppose not."

"Having a baby doesn't make someone a woman, Miriam. Or a mother, either."

"No; you've shown me that."

"Have I? How?"

"You find peace everywhere, because you have it in your own home. You're... you're at home with yourself."

Joan understood perfectly. "It's taken me a long time."

"Is it... is it hard to be barren?"

Joan stopped to study her foster daughter, whose light hair had dimmed to an ashen brown, her eyes not so bright as they were when she was small, but still very penetrating.

"Barren? I might be childless, Miriam, but I've never been barren." They walked on homeward together, hand in hand.

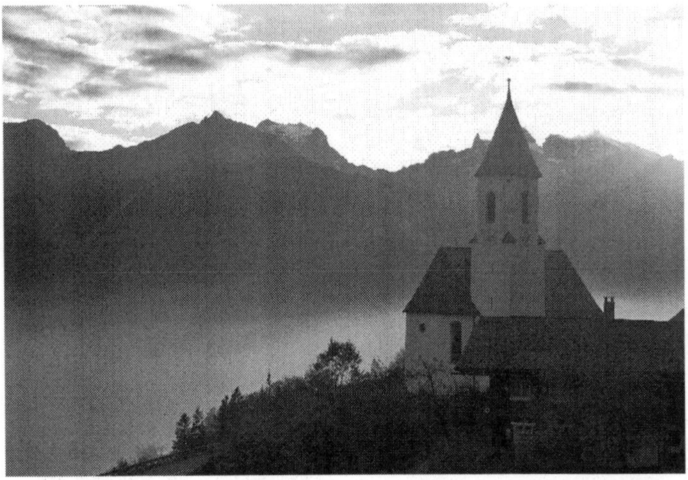

Self-knowledge must be seasoned with knowledge of God,
or it would end in confusion.

– Saint Catherine of Siena

X

Midnight

Miriam began to dream, at first only faint flickers, mirrored images of life as it should be—as she wanted it to be—with the added, blessed comfort that she had no curse to overcome: her hands were never cold in her dreams. Then they came more regularly, almost predictably, darkening, either feeding on or fueled by her growing fears.

The landscape was entirely changed from the one she knew, but she moved in it as if she'd been brought up there. The village people had misted faces, and cotton-ball sheep moved about listlessly in idyllic alpine meadows. When she wasn't tending them, she would climb nimbly up to the forested saddle to chat with the soldier on duty there and look out over the foothills, while clouds sat like nesting birds on the jagged mountaintops nearby.

Near the sentry's post there was what seemed to be a cleft in the granite wall. It was actually an opening into the mountain itself, a black shaft hewn by miners long ago when men imagined treasure hidden in every earth crack. It was far from useless, however, for after a bit the mining shaft met a large and winding natural cavern, which twisted downward right through the heart of the mountain, nearly to its base. Affixed to the roof of that labyrinth, in the ingenious manner of dream-machinery, stretched a cable linking the saddle to the palace, which lay like a jewel in the deep valley at the mountain's foot. And hanging on that cable was a cage, used as a carrier device by soldier above and palace servant below. Rations were hauled up for the sentries at the top; beef and mutton were sent gliding effortlessly down without the aid of a winch. The hours and miles saved on both sides were no small convenience.

For a long time in her recurring dream, the girl-Miriam begged the soldier on duty to let her have a ride down in the cage, and he always laughed. Even when she asked why not, in that persistent way of hers, no one ventured to explain to her why such a thing should be unthinkable. The scene played itself over and over, until one night deep in the dream, Miriam caught the expression on the guard's face as he peeked with her down the darkening shaft. Fear. Fear of some unnameable thing between there and the palace. A lurking, ancient fear taking the imagined shapes of hideous trolls, wraiths, misshapen goblins, and other formless but more terrifying shadows.

After that night, the dream was different: it went on.

She was her present age, tending the sheep in a high meadow fenced in by sheer rock walls, when a vague thundering vibrated nearby. Miriam cordoned off the flock with a few fallen spruce trees and stones, blocking the one exit out of the natural enclosure. She then flit past rock and tree to an open glade where dozens of saddled horses grazed, their armed masters discussing a strategy for storming the palace and overthrowing the vulnerable queen, who had been deserted by her crusading husband. The dream-shepherdess listened, horrified, as they finalized plans to overrun the sleepy summit village before plunging down the grade and besieging the palace that very day. They were between her and the town, so there was no way she could sound an alarm. But she could, by stealth, get to the sentry at his post—and perhaps send an urgent message down the hidden mountain chute.

The laughter of the remounting invaders ebbed away as she crept behind bush and boulder. When the charge was sounded, she made a dash across some sparsely-covered ground. She saw a look of unprepared shock on the sentry's face when he came into sight. She seemed to run far too slowly, tortured by the pounding of horses' hoofs and the rush of foot soldiers, their shouts blending with screams and crashes in the distance as scattered cottages fell to their onslaught.

Then, as she finally neared the lookout post, she heard a faint noise of pursuit behind her. Turning to see, something struck her hard against a rock ledge, and she looked down to where the bolt of a crossbow jutted from between her neck and shoulder. The stab of pain clouded her vision; she could just make out the archer closing in on her. She pitched forward, stumbling—then awoke, damp with sweat and clutching at her bared shoulder.

She told no one, but grew more distant in the months that followed, pondering the dream. And so distracted, she failed to hear the telltale twilight noises or see the pale glint of creature-eyes in the dark corners of house and garret. While she dreamt and wondered, other intruders had come, bringing with them a warfare of their own, against which steel helms and bucklers were powerless.

In their wake, death rolled over the countryside in a long, merciless, unsparing wave.

We are God's work of art...

– Saint Paul

XI

Journeyman

Wormholes. The wood was full of them. The board was fit only to feed the fire after all. The tree had looked so straight, so sound, so tall. He had been so careful to cure it... no. The worms were there when the tree was felled. It wasn't his fault. He checked it again, searching for hope. The close grain of the timber deserved to become more than a workbench or stable wall. But there was nothing to be done. You could take out the worms, but not the holes they left behind.

His thoughts were interrupted by Robert's arrival in the workshop.

"Michael, I'm missing my gauge."

"Here it is." The master noted irritation in his nephew's tone of voice and looked over.

"Woodworms, is it? Why do they ruin the best pieces, eh? And you can't see them 'til the bark's off." He flicked one out with the point of his knife. "Maybe you'll find a place with no worms."

Michael picked up a chisel and laughed. "There'll be something else. Fungus. Or rot."

"Always is. If not in the wood itself, then the climate, or the food. Or the women. But you never know. Michael, m'boy, you can wander the woods for a year an' not know which trees have the worms. Once I dragged home a dead log—I'd passed it by for three years. It was the most beautiful piece of wood. Perfectly cured, too. Fit for carving, it was."

The journeyman quietly gathered up his tools, carefully covering them with chamois before slipping them into his bag. He wanted to put them all away in the workshop, to tuck them back into the rough cabinet like newborn babies into their cribs. But his mind was made up. He wouldn't compete with his master's son. He just wouldn't. Robert's voice, softer now, broke into his packing.

"Where will you go?"

"Where a good carpenter is needed, I hope. Maybe north, where the cedars grow."

"Ye'll have to work up a reputation. They'll look at yer leg first off."

"It won't take long. There are so many that's been in the wars, it's rare to find a man that doesn't limp, anymore."

"Yer right, there. Here, I brought you a parting gift. Somethin' to remember ol' Robert by, maybe that'll bring you back now and then to tell us all about yer adventures." Trembling noticeably, the callused hands held out a polished tinderbox, a gift to the new journeyman. "Made it m'self, from that dead old log."

"I couldn't take this from you, sir," said Michael nervously. "It's a masterpiece."

"So are you, m'boy," returned the elder, cheerily clapping him on the back. "So are you. Now take it an' off with you."

"Yes, sir." Michael wrapped it carefully in a soft cotton rag and tucked it into a fold in his shirt. "And, sir... God keep you, sir."

"How can he help it? He's stuck with ol' Robert."

"Like a favorite tool in the hands of a craftsman."

"Maybe. But one that gets dull sometimes. Fare you well, Michael Carver."

But the young carpenter couldn't reply. He shouldered his bag to counterbalance his weak leg, turned his face towards the east, took a deep breath and a hard, longing look into the eyes of his master, and set off. The road wound upwards and beyond a group of sycamores; before he'd even got that far he was winded, so he looked back. There stood the craftsman at the door of the cottage, his arm draped over the solid, stately form of his wife of twenty-seven years. Time had worn them both into polished treasures—like Michael's tinderbox. He waved, and they waved back, their free arms moving as if they were one person instead of two intertwined.

The sunlight fell through a high canopy of leaves, pooling in bright mottled shapes on the ground at his feet. His path led now through a glade of saplings, their slender trunks swaying leisurely. Their lower branches had been stripped away by hungry deer and by cold peasants hunting firewood, leaving the spaces between them open and airy below their interwoven tops. Michael stopped to rest, drinking in the sylvan freshness. A woodpecker's tap hammered overhead. The tall trees dwarfed him, like gracious giants stretching ever upwards in their whispering dance with the wind. He liked being small, a moving fragment in a beautifully crafted world.

Like most lone travelers of his day, he warily kept his money pouch—light as it was—close to his skin, with his baggage weighted over it. As he sat down to eat his brown bread, he unpacked Robert's gift and held it up in the afternoon light. How many fires were held inside, he wondered. The wood had been worked smooth, then worn smoother by the craftsman's hands as he lit fire after fire for cooking or metalwork or nights alone in the forest. The journeyman looked beneath the surface grains right into the depth of the wood—it was like looking through the water of a mossy lake, but into browns and reds rather than blues and greens.

Two shadows fell across his lap.

"That's a fair piece you got there."

"It was my master's." He squinted up into the light to see who was talking. Two men stood silhouetted against the sky; they were decently dressed and friendly, judging by their smiles. The one speaking knelt on one knee to oblige him.

"Craftsman, eh? Where're you bound?"

"North, I think."

"Someone expecting you there?"

"No." The kneeling man threw a glance at his companion while he picked up a small stone to scratch in the dirt.

"Bless me, it so happens that we're headin' the same direction. Might be good to hook up and help each other along. The wolves can get thick at night." Wolves. Michael had only ever heard them howling in the distance; he never imagined meeting one. Here were two sizeable men, surly and confident. The kind of fellows wolves would be sure to dislike.

"Might be. Have you been this way before?"

"Oh, lots of times. Nice road, but not enough inns. Ain't that right, Giles?"

"'At's right. A man's not safe on 'is own 'less he likes to sleep in a tree."

"Doesn't sound very comfortable," admitted Michael, laughing away his misgivings.

"Nope. You git up all stiff an' cold an' walk funny fer a half mile."

"Well, there's only one problem," said the carpenter, rising to throw his pack over his shoulder.

"What's that?"

"I already walk funny. I don't move any too fast. Got a weak leg and a heavy load. I might slow you down."

"'At's okay, master. We're in no rush, an' we won't have any baggage to speak of till the trip back. We'd be happy to take turns with yer bag."

"In return for a pint or two at the nearest inn," proposed the older one. *Merchants*, Michael thought, and he wondered what it was they bought and sold. Tossing his head upward with a quick lift of his eyebrows, he fell in with his new traveling companions.

They soon left the shaded glen to trudge across open country where flies buzzed and the grass grew high. The larger man took Michael's pack as the path ascended and the afternoon crept on. Small talk was exchanged, mostly friendly banter between the two—he guessed it—brothers. He limped along, appreciating the distraction of their rough but harmless chatter. They weren't the kind of friends he'd tell his sorrows to, but that mattered little: he had few to tell.

The brothers were adept campers; an hour after they stopped to set up a lean-to, Giles had two rabbits caught, skinned, and turning on a makeshift spit over the fire Michael had gathered and lit. Conversation came quickly as dinner progressed. The elder brother did most of the talking.

"Belong to a guild, then?"

"Only a small one," answered Michael. "I'll probably have to join another chapter up north."

"Guess so. But if you do any work close to that tinderbox of yours, you won't have no trouble."

"My master carved it."

"Well, it sure is lovely. You being apprenticed to him an' whatnot, you're probably quite the craftsman too."

"I like what I do."

Giles yawned. The stars were coming out. Michael built up the fire and offered to take the first watch. He tucked his tinderbox into a deep pocket in his mantle while the two men settled heavily onto a mat of grass they'd piled up under the crude shelter.

"'Night, then, Master Carver."

"'Night." He sat with his back to the fire and a stick in his hands, trying to pick out a familiar constellation in the darkening sky so he would know when his watch was over. The only sounds were the rustle of wind in the trees and the quiet scurry of little night creatures prowling for food. He took a draught from his water skin and thought, feeding the fire and watching the sparks fly upward. Loud snoring soon came from behind him, keeping him easily awake until his time was up, three hours later.

He stretched, yawned, and shuffled over to Giles to trade places. The bigger brother still snored, but by now Michael was too tired to be disturbed by it any longer. He fell gratefully atop the warm mound of grass and was asleep before he could make himself quite comfortable.

Cold and stiffness woke him just before dawn. He reached beneath him to remove the sharp-cornered tinderbox. There was still a handful of stars overhead, but they were soon to be tucked sleepily into the covers of coming day. Michael crept out of the bivouac to discover a fire pit of cold ashes, his companions and his bag of tools nowhere in sight. He groped for the leather thong around his neck. It too was gone—along with his money pouch. There was no use in trying to overtake them: the embers were dead, and he had absolutely no knowledge of finding track or trail. He sighed and let the chill morning breeze stroke his hair. Robert's words about the value of mistakes rang in his ears. Well, this was a beauty.

He disentangled the tinderbox from his cloak and gathered some kindling. They had crossed a brook the evening before, so he wouldn't die of thirst, but it would be a longish day without breakfast. As he opened the carved treasure, he smiled in relief: there were his papers, and two gold coins he had begged Mistress Crafter to take back. What spark had prompted him to keep them there? He laughed and the sun rose. The little fire blazed up to warm him a bit before he started on to the next town. He would see the blacksmith first. A few months' work and the tools would be replaced. But the trees he wanted were further north, so he would go on.

Half an hour later, after a cold splash of water on his unshaven face, he was off, whistling with the meadowlarks.

Therefore I am now going to woo her;
I will lead her into the wilderness and speak to her heart.

– The prophet Hosea

XII

Soliloquy

Jacob was already eating breakfast when his wife descended the creaking ladder from their loft. The fire had burned ember-low and was just beginning to renew its yellow freshness from the fir cones he had piled upon it.

"Where's Miriam?" she asked.

"I thought you might know."

Joan sighed. "It's like this every spring. When the snow melts, she's gone."

"Can you blame her? She's shut up all winter."

"It's cold out still, before the sun rises."

"She's got that cloak now, and your boots and cap. She won't freeze in those."

"I'd still like to know where she is—I'm none too well this morning." Jacob looked up; she so seldom complained. Her face was pale, sweat beading on her forehead beneath wisps of graying hair. She smiled back. "I'd just like a bit of extra help."

"Done, woman," answered the shepherd, scrambling to his feet and reaching for his staff. "I'll leave the dog."

"Many thanks, Jacob."

Before he left he filled the kettle and put it on the fire to stave off her chill. Pulling on his coat, he called back, "There's pennyroyal out now."

"Bring some." The rough door closed softly, leaving Joan to shiver in the gathering light. She looked at the empty pile of straw near the hearth, envying Miriam's courage and ashamed of her own weakness.

Jacob had no doubts as to where Miriam would be. He labored up the hill to its rocky crest, where it fell away in steep cliffs towards the pent-up river. The sky to his right lightened imperceptibly from gray to steel-lavender. He leaned on his staff more than usual, his breath coming short and sharp. He'd had a fever too, just a few days ago, after he found a dead rat in the loft. Now his leg felt heavy. He was not a man who welcomed sickness, but from some hidden crack had come the unannounced visit of God's darkest servant.

Now, thoroughly winded, he saw her, silhouetted against the dark gray waters below. Her back was toward him; she sat perfectly still, eyeing the mountainous region beyond as if she knew she belonged there. Solitude was precious, even in these lonely places. Jacob sat down next to his ward—some nobleman's deserted daughter—in silence.

"Hello, Papa. I'm glad you came." She reached for his hand, to hold it with hers under the heavy folds of her cloak. "I wanted to ask you something."

"It's long since you called me that. You're a grown woman now." She was nineteen, and not a suitor in sight.

"Where did this cloak come from?"

"I thought I told you. From your own father."

"Why did he send me to you?"

"I... I don't really know."

She turned to face him, and then took out something that reflected the flat blueness of the dawning sky. "And this?" He started; he'd meant to give her the brooch another time, perhaps when she left home. She answered him before he found his voice again. "I don't want another father, I want you. But something's calling me, Papa. Away. And I don't want to go." He didn't answer, knowing that she could decide well enough for herself what to do. A moment passed.

"Come, Miriam. Joan's not well. She sent me for you."

She rose quickly, her face tense, while her eyes embraced the northern horizon in a silent farewell. She helped him to his feet. Turning their backs to the view, they started down the slope.

"You're limping, Papa."

"Getting old, I guess. Got a stiff leg." She didn't believe him. Her pulse quickened with worry. "Would you take a piece of an old man's mind, if ever you go out into the wide world?"

"Of course, Papa. Your words are always wise."

"Not always. I've made my share of blunders. Mortal sins included." She smiled at his modesty. "Miriam, you're young. And comely."

"Comely? Me?" she laughed, nervously.

"More than you suppose. Somebody's bound to see. Keep out of loud inns, child. You'll be safer in holy houses."

She took his arm. "If they're full of people like Jacob Hirte, I'm sure that's true. Look, there's some pennyroyal. Shouldn't we take a bit home?"

What more could he teach her? Her greater Father had already taken her out of his reach.

The inside of the cottage was darker now than the brightening spring morning outside. It took a moment for the two to see Joan lying on the earthen floor, groaning with fever. Instinct overruled words, and Miriam took off her cloak and folded it to make a pillow. The shepherdess' face was mottled, her eyes swollen shut. Jacob threw his coat over her and went for water, muttering fervent prayers for mercy.

"Hush, Mother, I'm come." Joan heard the low voice, but the tension stayed until Miriam's cold hands were upon her face. The woman's lips moved wordlessly. "Save your strength, you'll need it," Miriam said softly. She loosened the linen at Joan's neck, only to see the galloping pulse and the tiny red blotches. Plague. The storm-breakers in Miriam's inner seascape began to pound savagely at the small craft that was her.

Never had a day gone by so slowly. She would not leave the cottage, keeping watch at Joan's makeshift couch even while Jacob gave in to the gnawing pain in his groin. Outside, spring sparkled on virgin grass; the dog lazily guarded the gate. Miriam moved woodenly from hearth to straw, cistern to basin, unable to discern whether she herself was sick with plague or only with fear.

Sometime in the afternoon there came a timid knock on the door. She thought better of opening it and went to the tiny window instead. Gerda stood outside with a basket, anxiously glancing at the penned sheep, clearly wondering why they weren't out grazing. Miriam rapped sharply on the thick glass and motioned her friend away, shaking her head and forming the word "plague" with her lips in loud clarity. Gerda's hand went to her mouth; she turned and fled without once looking back.

Soliloquy

Miriam felt alone.

Jacob moaned pitifully from the corner. She took up his breviary, sat next to him, and began reading Compline, her voice a loud echo surrounded by four thick walls and the golden residue of a lovely afternoon. He grew quiet, his breathing still ragged and quivering. She closed the book in her lap and shut her eyes to pray.

A small noise jolted her head up. The light was nearly gone; dusky twilight seeped into the room's stuffy corners. Joan was sitting, wide-eyed but vacantly staring into the orange flicker standing sentinel on the grate. Miriam softly rose to lay more wood on the fire, though her neck and limbs were stiff. Then she knelt near the wan shepherdess, knowing with one look that she would not be better.

"Miriam," the woman whispered.

"Lie down, Mother. I'm here."

"Where's Jacob?"

"Nearby." Joan closed her eyes, relieved. They had always been together; what could separate them now? Miriam sponged her forehead. It was too late for healing measures but not for comfort. The sick woman feebly reached for her daughter's cold hand and held it, her face calm despite the pain tearing at her inside.

"There are two fires, remember that," she barely said, with effort. Miriam put her head close to listen. "Two fires, Miriam. One cleans, one blackens; one melts, the other burns. Only one can warm you." Joan stopped, spent.

"Yes, Mother. Two fires." It meant something, or might someday. "Sleep now. You'll be better in the morning." Joan's hand responded with the small pressure of a motherly pat. She took a sip from the goatskin held to her gray lips, then let her head relax upon the cloak, satisfied.

Miriam was right. When day dawned, they were both dead.

She closed the cottage door behind her and wandered down to the sheepfold, waiting for the fever to roll over her, to drown her. It didn't; the curse she was under kept even death at bay. After an hour, she went back to the sleeping house to get her cloak and cap. She noticed the breviary on a rough stool, and picked it up. It was a near mile to the thick-timbered church; the cool air might clear her thoughts. Her feet plodded silently down a road she knew well enough to walk in her sleep. Perhaps she *was* asleep, lying beneath the gnarled tree above. No, the smell of death still lingered about her. She hoped the breeze would rinse it away before she met the priest.

Her news was not the first he'd heard—his eyes were sad when she greeted him.

She sat in the dark nave while workmen hammered rough boards into coffins and loaded them onto an ox-cart with six others. Behind these sounds, she could hear the gravediggers' thick, thudding work in the churchyard. All were eager to bury the pestilence. Wakes were unnecessary and unwanted. Even the funeral rites would be said at a distance and in haste, priest and people alike half-veiled in vain protection.

Miriam climbed up the hill behind the cart. The Hirte cottage was the first stop because the old priest didn't think his animal could pull much of a heavy load up that steep incline. Once the coffins were sealed, the stone house was emptied. She wearily watched as straw and bedding, cloth and cupboard were piled high outside and burnt. *Two fires.* No one spoke. Miriam stood frozen while the workmen ebbed away to meet other tragedies. Puffy clouds collected above the northwestern horizon; the wind blew strong and cool.

"You can come stay with us, Miriam," a voice behind her said gently. Benumbed, she didn't turn around.

"I can't, Gerda. I might bring it into your house."

"It may come anyway."

"No. The children... No."

"You're tired, Miriam."

"Am I?" She looked listlessly about, seeing only gray columbines in the blooming fields. Then she turned, thankful that her friend kept her distance. "I can't stay here, Gerda. I don't belong. I don't know if I ever did. My... my real father's up north. Somewhere."

"But the plague could reach him as well."

"Oh, Gerda, I have to try. I can't stay, you must see that." There was no answer. There were no tears on either side. Just wind blowing through budding trees. "The sheep—you take them. The dog as well."

"But..."

"No, I don't need them. I'll go north, I have to. I'll... I'll die in the wintry north, where my body can freeze along with the rest of me." She turned away again.

"Miriam," the young wife began, pleading, but the other held up her hand. Gerda waited for what seemed a long time, but the shepherdess was marooned in her grief and would not be rescued. No one could talk sense into this strange friend of hers if she couldn't. She went home slowly, thinking to ask her husband how much the Hirte sheep would be worth and to contrive, somehow, to help this poor adrift creature. Besides, the children would be missing her; she had to be getting back.

Night closed in, thick and dark. Miriam huddled in the barn with the sheep. Strange that they had been spared. The same dream pursued her even now: she awoke with the gaping mouth of that mountain cavern staring at her. What must she face, after this? Jacob's voice stirred in her memory. She had asked him once how he could be happy with so little. "Nobody can, by trying," he'd said. "God has to empty the heart of all desires." It sounded so calm, so passive, so easy. Well, her desires had not exactly been emptied: they were pitched out the window by some almighty, invisible hand.

She roused herself slowly some hours later. Sheep and dog were quiet. The light of an early, gray morning sifted through the half-open door—how could she have failed to bolt it shut? A woven satchel hung on a wooden peg close by. In it, she found a skin of fresh water, a few oaten cakes, a cheese, and a small leather pouch heavy with coins.

God bless Gerda, the Practical.

She dragged herself to the cistern to splash stinging-cold water up into her face. "When my father and my mother forsake me, the Lord taketh me up." It was in Jacob's breviary, but she hadn't the strength to find out where—though she was painfully anxious to find God behind Jacob's shadow. Maybe if she found him, she would find herself. Dry and empty, she only wanted to do what she was supposed to do. If she did not know what it was, she would wander until she found it. Or until it found her, to restore or destroy her.

It didn't seem to matter which.

* * *

Hushed voices filled the empty corridor.

Soliloquy

"How is he, Sir Pieter?"

"He'll pull through, I think, my Lord Basil. I hope."

"I've never been so sick in my life," returned the counselor. "A quarter of the town has succumbed, and more than half the castle staff."

The knight hesitated, kicking at the pavement. "Will you tell him about the queen?" he asked, and under his breath said, "She was so very young."

"When he's stronger, not now. Sigismund's recovering?"

"Yes."

"Then he should be with his father when I bring the news," decided Basil.

Without a good-bye, the men parted. Pieter returned to his bedside vigil. Before he arrived at the king's chamber, however, he was stopped by a familiar woman carrying a bowl of blood-stained water across the courtyard.

"Sir Pieter," she greeted.

"Brigid."

"How is he?"

"Holding on," he answered.

"And my lady?"

"Dead."

"So many," she sighed. She touched his arm. "It makes me miss her more and more."

"Who?"

"The princess. She'll be back, though, one of these days. You'll see." He nodded curtly with respect and walked on, unable to speak. How she could hope for a miracle in such circumstances was far beyond his ken.

He stepped softly into the royal apartments. The pewter figurine on the mantel seemed to cast a pitying look at him as he approached the king. The fever had not left him, but its grip was loosening. He groaned from his bed.

"Isolde...cover the child, damn you. She's crying again."

"They're not here, my lord." Strange that he didn't call for his son.

"Oh, of course not." He struggled to sit up, grabbing at the knight's sleeve. "But she will be, Pieter. She has the last dragon, you know. It'll find its way back, through all the devils in hell. My God," his voice broke. "She's not dead, and still she haunts me." Pieter sponged his face. He lay back upon the silken pillow but remained restless. The fever broke that night, and the king never mentioned his daughter in Pieter's hearing again.

* * *

The storms drove her southward. When she set her eyes with longing upon the northern mountains, now hardly visible behind her, they sat in black shadow, the thunder above them rolling, threatening her away. Her pace quickened, but try as she might, she could not outdistance the coming squall.

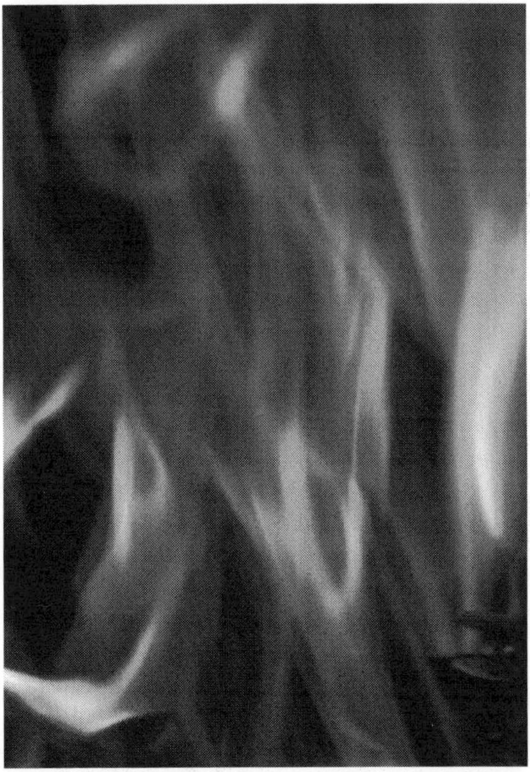

Blessed are those who mourn...

– the Gospel of Matthew

XIII

Encounter

Miriam pulled her worn cloak more tightly about her. The wind whistled through barren trees, suddenly changing direction to whip leaves and broken twigs about in a chaotic dance. She began to hurry. The coldness of the air bit and stung the exposed part of her face as she stumbled toward the town ahead.

On the outskirts, there was no noise apart from storm sounds; everyone had hidden behind closed doors and thick shutters. The dusty grayness blended everything together. She stopped, wondering which direction to go next. A busy murmur drew her toward the square, where the market was being hastily packed away as the sky darkened. Men grasped empty-handed at billowing awnings; makeshift tables blew over, spilling vegetables and housewares onto the narrow footpaths. Donkeys brayed, carts creaked. Irritated voices hoarsely shouted at boys who scrambled to pick up scattered goods, but the wind blasted words away.

A lone figure stood next to a rough stone wall, waiting for a break in the scurrying traffic. Miriam guessed it to be a woman, bent with age. No one else seemed to notice her presence. One hand held the wall, and the other a stick which poked out into the lane amid the murk and din of the disappearing market. Satisfied that the way was clear at last, she ventured out. The wind snarled like an uncaged beast, and the woman's mantle flew from her, pulling the stick out of her hands. She froze, scowling and braced against the chill air, her outstretched hand reaching.

Miriam plunged toward her, dodging laden carts and stepping over strewn rubbish. Blinking and squinting against a growing gale, she reached the old woman faster than she expected. She took hold of a thin arm, calling into her wrinkled face to come along. They slipped into a small walkway between two low earthen cottages, leaving the wind for a blissful moment behind.

"Stay here a moment, Mother," ordered the shepherdess. "I'll get your cloak." The old woman drew a long breath and found the wall at her back while the younger searched the deserted square. Running footfalls announced Miriam's return. "There," came the now-known voice, "and here's your staff." The smooth stick was laid against the open palm, the woman's rough woolen mantle replaced around her bent shoulders.

Bony fingers, but strong, grasped for Miriam's hand and followed her arm up past her shoulder to her face. The woman's eyes, white and darting, left no doubt in the mind of the shepherdess that she was blind as a stone.

"Bad storm coming. Sweet of you to stop. Don't know your face, but I like it. Can you take me home?"

"I don't know where you live."

"Well, I'll have to talk you there, then. It's due north of the market, up past the main road, then east five minutes' walk up a small hill and to your left. Just past a few young birch trees. Think you can get me there?"

"Yes, once I find north."

"Can you see the church tower?"

"Barely."

"That's east. Turn a straight left and you'll hit the main road."

They set out in haste, Miriam wondering how this poor woman could put so much trust in a total stranger. The dust had blown up to cloud her vision again, but the directions proved clear enough. Soon they were on a grassy track that wound upwards, bending around a hollow where a half-timbered cottage stood, its stone chimney rising guardian-like above thick thatch. A rich house, once, but now aging and unkempt. A clump of trees on the hill behind muted the wind from that direction. The blind woman rested her stick against the door and groped for a rusty key that hung around her neck. She found the worn keyhole in an instant, sent the iron in straight as a homing pigeon just let go, and bustled inside. Miriam followed, shutting the door and leaning on it to seal them into the sturdy refuge.

"Leave the shutters. I'll light a lamp," the woman said. A few faggots of wood burned low in the hearth; from these, the homeowner lit a long broom straw and felt for a candle atop the mantle. Either her aim was good or her memory accurate, for soon the place was awash in the little flame's glow. Miriam smiled while her hostess placed a few more sticks on the fire.

"There's a jug of milk in the larder—my neighbor up the valley's a dairymaid—and some dark bread. It's supper most nights, and I'd be pleased for you to share it with me."

"I would be most happy to."

"Of course you would. I daresay you're a far cry from home, judging by your speech, and besides, who could go back out into *that*? Come a long way, have you? Sit down a spell and tell me who you are." Many things crossed Miriam's mind, but few seemed to truthfully matter.

"I wish I knew."

"Well, you must have come from somewhere." The blind woman seemed neither shocked nor amazed. It became easier to talk, and before Miriam knew it, out tumbled what she knew of her story, haphazard and muddy like water from a broken dam. The elder listened, engaged and attentive, never once speaking until silence had blanketed them. She turned the silver brooch over and over in her wizened, exploring hands.

"This came from your father."

"That's what I was told."

"Then you were hardly born a peasant."

"I wasn't raised to be a nobleman's daughter, though."

"Perhaps a craftsman's... a jeweler's? Someone wealthy."

Miriam stood and went to watch the daylight ebb through a crack in the shutters.

"I don't know."

"It doesn't matter, now that you're here. You'll want more light, I think, so go find the lamp—there's one I keep for visitors, near the hearth somewhere—and I'll be along after I wash up. And no, you can't help, you've done enough of that already. You'll get to know the workings of the house better tomorrow anyway, when it's not so dark."

"Can I stay with you, Mother?" came the surprised voice in return.

"I hope you will. It's too hard to be alone and blind anymore."

Miriam had to douse the wick in the lamp's oil before it would take the little flame she offered it, it was so dry. When it stopped sputtering and burned evenly at last, she began to feel a little tired, and much more at home.

Dusk became evening. The firelight danced on the round stones of the hearth. Miriam stared wondering at the skilled hands of the blind woman, deftly embroidering a flower on the patched hem of her cloak.

"I haven't done this for ages. Thank you for threading the needle."

"Such a small thing, really."

"Do you sew, girl?"

"No. Not well, I mean. I've only done mending."

"Wouldn't you like to learn?"

The shepherdess winced, and was glad the old woman couldn't see.

"I... I've never been very good at needlework, Mother."

"Oh, saints alive, call me Chantal," said the lady, nearly laughing. "You make me feel old. Now, come sit over here next to me." Miriam acquiesced. "Now, I'll move the needle over a bit and find a new center—there. Always start at the center, and that way you'll know where to start the petals. But then again, you're not blind, so you can start wherever you want! The thread pulls away, like this—I think it's more fitting to sew them from the center, the way they grow."

A minute more and the flower was done. Chantal broke the thread with her teeth. "Saves me from having to hunt for the scissors," she explained. "Now you try." She reached down and felt inside her basket, pulling out a scrap of linen, while Miriam threaded the needle with a strand of soft azure blue. It brought a memory of the sky above the high meadow, which she had already begun to miss. The gnarled hands kept close to the young ones, checking the position of needle and cloth. For the first time since their meeting, Miriam felt awkward.

"I'd have thought you were the one without eyes, the way you keep jabbing your finger. God in heaven, child, you've bloodied yourself!"

"I'm sorry, dear Chantal, but I... I can't feel very well. My fingers go numb." Her voice quavered. The old woman took the scrap of cloth away and held Miriam's hands in her own.

"Why, they're so cold, that's why. I thought the fire was plenty warm." The fingers began a more fervent search, reading first the callused hands, then the troubled face of the shepherdess. "You haven't a fever, you're too cool. Why, I'm toasty warm, and I'm supposed to be the frail old lady. How are your feet?"

"They're cold, too."

"Put them by the fire."

"It won't help; they're always cold."

"Even in those sheepskins?" She was bending over, probing the soft boots.

"Yes."

Thought filled several empty seconds.

"You—you don't have leprosy, do you?"

"No."

"Are you sure?"

"Yes." There seemed nothing more to say.

"Hmmm. Better take an extra blanket tonight. That one."

"But you need it."

"I can use my shawl. Never use it at night anyway. Maybe you'll warm up a bit by morning. We can try again when there's more light for you to see what those cold fingers of yours are doing, eh?"

"I would like that," sighed Miriam, putting out the lamp. She settled down on the bracken pallet her hostess had gathered together, gazing at the ruby embers of the fire until sleep overcame the throbbing in her needle-pricked finger.

When the Beloved visits us in the night,
He makes our chambers to be the vestibule of His palace halls.

– Charles Spurgeon

XIV

Starlight

Sometime in the darkness of the early morning, the dream found her, closing in like one of blessed Anthony's desert demons, taunting, testing, gloating over her. There was no escaping it, no point in trying to shut her unconscious mind to it. She would have to dream it through.

The noise of battle savagery came first, with the scene taking shape at the point of her flight. She ran nimbly over the uneven ground, yet she could not outdistance her pursuer. The distance was greater than she remembered from dreams before. She saw the familiar sentry at his post, as yet unnoticed by the attackers and not knowing what to do against such terrible odds. Again, the crossbow bolt struck her shoulder—how many times had she dreamed it? She whirled and plummeted on, driven by pain as well as terror. She kept expecting to awake, as before, but this time she didn't. The dream dragged her on.

She plunged into the sentry's tiny keep, to be pulled down by him behind the low stone wall. Motioning to the chasm where the cable-hung cage awaited its next load, she clutched at his coat.

"You must... let me go down to warn them; they're going to besiege the palace, I heard their plans." He protested, but she tugged at him, undaunted. "They'll take me if I stay... it's my only hope... please, help me in." He saw the reason in her words, as well as the dark stain spreading on the shoulder of her tunic, and complied, but shook his head when she beckoned him to join her.

"This is my post," he said. There was blood on his coat when he closed the iron door upon her—her blood. Yet his eyes had more than fear in them when he waved a hasty good-bye. They had strength, and courage, and... hope.

As the cage began to descend on its cable, she looked back into his pleading, blessed face. And she knew, in the instant before she woke, that the face was Jacob's, and that the dream was her life.

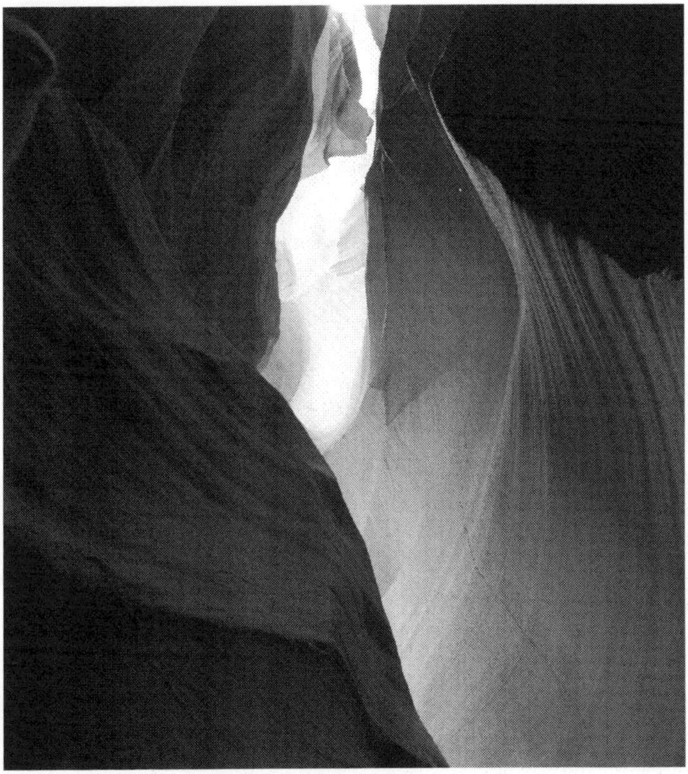

Prayer is my daily offering of fresh flowers and roses.

– Charles de Foucauld

XV

Embroidery

Miriam rose late, dressed hastily, and looked about for a way to be useful. She found Chantal in the meager kitchen, preparing a simple breakfast. A carved wooden vase on the table held fresh-cut flowers. The blind woman smiled and answered her new lodger's thoughts.

"I keep them for the smell. And I remember their colors. Sit down and eat."

"I'm sorry I slept so late."

"Shouldn't be, after a long journey to a strange town in a nasty storm."

"You must tell me how I can best help you."

"Well, now, I thought about that some, last night. Can you chop wood?"

"Yes."

"Good—that's a tough one for me. So's the laundry."

"I can manage that, easily."

"And, a few years back when I still had my eyes, I used to have a corner stall in the market for woven goods and embroidery. I thought maybe—after last night and all—I could take some of it up again, you helping me thread needles and get the colors right. You could take it to town to sell for us."

"You would trust me?"

"God save you, child, of course I would. Can't keep a young lady like yourself cooped up all day with an old biddy like me, can I now?" In spite of her clouded eyes, she winked. Miriam couldn't help but smile. "And there's one more thing."

"Yes, Mother—Chantal."

"I'd dearly love it if you could walk me to Mass."

"So would I."

She found the brook conveniently close, a quiet tumble of cold, fresh water that flowed down the hill a stone's throw away from the house. Miriam sighed as she poured another bucketful into the old barrel-bottom for a second rinse. It was taking her an awfully long time. Twenty minutes later, she hung the clothes on the jutting branches of an enormous fallen log, just behind the house. All the shutters were open on that side, letting the strong sunlight pour into the cottage. Chantal's face appeared, framed by the rough wood casement, soaking up the warmth like one of her flowers.

"They haven't been so clean in at least a year."

"How do you know? You can't see them!"

"No, but I can smell. And you've been at it awhile."

"I couldn't help it. My hands kept getting cold."

"Oh. You've got a problem there; that stream comes right out of the mountains. It never warms up. But we never run out of water." She pursed her lips, considering. "You said you could chop wood?"

"Aye."

Embroidery

"Look at that old log there. I keep bumping into it, but I can't afford to pay anyone to come chop it up for me. If water's no problem, and wood's no problem, what's to stop you from using this old cauldron to heat up the washing water? Your hands would stay warm and the laundry'd get cleaner faster. Well, maybe not faster, with the time it would take to get the fire going. There's never much to do, anyway."

"Oh, Chantal, that sounds wonderful."

"Then do it, for God's sake. And for your own."

"Thank you!"

"Shush. Thank *you,* Miriam. Oh, there's one thing I forgot to ask you," the blind woman ventured, leaning out a little from the splintery casement.

"What is it?"

"Can you read?"

"Yes."

"Of course you can, bright thing like you. Do you, by any chance, have anything you could read to me?"

"Just an old breviary."

"Hallelujah."

"It's in Latin."

"What else would it be in?"

Miriam stood on the brink of a lovely summer, of that she was sure.

* * *

On the prince's birthday, the northern castle was all alight with music and dancing. Basil, richly dressed in glowing silk, stepped up to congratulate the king who sat brooding behind the head table, chin in hand.

"An able-bodied young man, already! And a bright one, Sire. You must be proud of him." The king shifted in his seat, his eyes fixed on his son, gaily mingling with courtier and yeoman alike. His heir. And, he mustn't forget, grandson—and heir—to his most powerful neighbor.

"Yes."

"His education will soon begin in earnest. You'll encourage him to expand his horizons, no doubt."

"You mean send him to study at his grandfather's court."

"Of course, Your Majesty." The counselor's gold chain of office glittered as he smiled and waved at a lady across the great room. "It is expected that he have a balanced perspective..."

"Of both kingdoms. Yes, no doubt. Now, if you will excuse me, Lord Basil," he began, rising. "It's time for a speech."

"Certainly, Sire." As soon as the music ended its cadence, he clapped twice, and the gathering turned its festive attention to the host of the evening's celebration. But as the king began his address, a portly older woman motioned to the lute player, who gracefully slipped away to meet her at the moonlit well behind the lofty hall.

"Auntie Brigid, what is it?"

"It's a favor, an important one, Nigel. For the king himself."

"Sour these days, isn't he?"

"Shhh, listen. I've been thinking on it for ever so long. When I saw that you'd come tonight and heard that sweet voice of yours, I knew you'd be the right one to ask."

"Ask what? Really, you do build up the suspense. Worse than I do when I tell tales."

"That's it, Nigel: I want you to tell a tale."

"Tonight? Which one?"

"Not tonight, and one that I'll tell you. And not here, no—somewhere else. You'll have to go south."

"South? Why?"

"To find someone." He looked puzzled. "Will you?"

"Tell me this tale, first."

"Not until you agree."

He knew something of his aunt, and he liked everything he knew. It was a challenge, an adventure, a secret—and therefore, irresistible.

* * *

Summer business had slackened, and the growing chill in the air stirred the townspeople to prepare for coming cold. Miriam wore wool beneath her cloak these days. The merchants had been kind to her, allowing her a small corner table on which she set out Chantal's work and, when she felt brave enough, some of her own. Their hands were not idle; the blind woman's old customers came back quickly to order colors added to their workaday kerchiefs and tablecloths. People were, on the whole, pleasant and soft-spoken, taking pity on strangers such as Miriam with tolerance and asking no awkward questions.

She had sat at their stall all afternoon, taking in now-familiar sights: the hills embracing the little town, the church tower, the road meandering toward Chantal's. The sense of belonging was temporary, but it heartened Miriam nonetheless. It was coming to be late afternoon, time to think about going home. She should finish the embroidery in her lap and pack up.

"Why do you not wear your hair more loosely? It is not so becoming to hide it beneath that dour cap." The voice, spoken in a song-like, friendly tone, startled Miriam out of her reverie.

She scarcely moved her head as she lifted her eyes to meet the speaker.

She saw a woman twice her age—but beautifully dressed and more free in manner than the others in the market square—standing in front of her little table and eyeing her curiously. A dancing smile enlivened her face, and Miriam could not imagine what should amuse her so. Perhaps she was tipsy, Miriam thought. Then to her surprise, the woman leaned over the table and said softly, "You'd sell more if you were more careful about your looks. You're very pretty, you know." She straightened up suddenly and folded her lithe arms in front of her dark dress, which was trimmed with silver thread. "Are you from here?"

It took a moment for Miriam to capture her breath; she was hardly used to such direct immodesty, and from a complete stranger.

"No." Her eyes were down again, but she could not concentrate on where the needle should go next.

"Mmm, thought not. You're not dark enough. Come from up north, do you?"

"Yes." Why was this woman asking so many questions?

"Your family still there?"

Miriam looked up quickly to meet this strange woman's over-friendly gaze. "They're dead."

"Don't seem to want to talk about them much. Did they upset somebody, is that it?"

"No—it was the plague."

"Oh!" The lissome woman crossed herself hurriedly and with, thought Miriam, a hint of mockery. "Aww, how sad for you." She shifted her weight and looked around. "I'm a stranger here too. Just come now and again to do some business." Miriam wondered, irreverently to herself, what this *business* might be. "Really, you should let me work on your hair sometime."

Miriam's heart pounded and the color rose to her face at this, but somehow she found the presence of mind to be polite.

"I'd rather not sell anything by my appearance," she said softly.

"That's obvious. Well, a little warmth on your part wouldn't hurt." The words stung. An awkward pause followed; Miriam again felt scrutinized. She set the needlework down in her lap. The woman was simply not going to go away.

"What is your trade?" Miriam asked, curiously enough.

"Oh, medicinals, mostly. Herbal remedies, a few trinkets and bangles, philters for beauty. Wouldn't you like to see some?"

Miriam began to feel embarrassed and declined. "I'll look next time they're on display." Most of the merchants had packed up by now and were exchanging farewells.

"Fine. And with the brisk trade you're doing, you might even buy something for yourself, for a change."

"The profits aren't mine."

"No, probably not. Well, perhaps I'll see you again, next market day? It's two days from now."

"Yes."

"It's been my pleasure, then, fair Mistress..."

"Miriam."

"Miriam. And I am Barbara." The woman made a little bow as Miriam nodded and gathered her linens. She couldn't help watching the beautiful "herbalist" stride out of the market—and notice that she glanced behind her with a twinkle in her eye just as she disappeared from view.

Barbara had been watching this thick-booted sales girl all day while hidden behind her booth and carefree conversations with other merchants. The brief visit had paid well, for when she had bent over Miriam's rough table, she had caught the glimmer of silver and the flash of a red stone on the inside edge of the fraying cloak. Her suspicions were confirmed. An old debt would be paid—in full. Perhaps even with some nineteen years' worth of interest added on.

Miriam clutched her basket tightly, her eyes fixed on the path ahead; she nearly walked into a small herd of goats being driven across it. The evening breeze cooled her. Fading light settled over the little vale where the cottage nestled among the birch trees; their leaves rustled, beckoning and comforting. The puzzle of her origin had stirred itself up again; the brooch pricked her mind like a thorn. It, too, seemed to want a home, to get back to wherever it belonged. Somewhere in the north. How far?

She stopped stone-still, holding her breath—someone or something was following her. The sensation was new and frightening to one who seldom felt even noticed. Not followed—pursued. But whether by something outside of herself or by her own thoughts, she didn't know. The passing days had been so sweet; she had been so content. How had this thick cloud stolen over her tiny ray of sunlight?

She pulled open the door, pausing once more to listen. With a sigh she stepped inside; the lamp was already burning. Closing the door softly, she barred it carefully against the whatever-it-was that made fear leap up like a spark.

"Ah, Miriam, welcome home." Chantal appeared out of shadow to give her a kiss—she made her way so quietly and ably about the house, silent as a cat but with no stealth. Always a pleasant greeting, yet tonight it was somehow unsettling. "How was the market today?"

"Slowing down. But there were still some orders."

"They'll have to come to the house soon. No one wants to go to market once the snow falls."

Evening fell, too quiet, upon the meal.

"What is it, child?"

Miriam carefully chewed and swallowed before answering. "I met such a strange woman this afternoon. She sells herbals; I'd never seen her before. But she was very free with the townsfolk... Chantal, I don't see why she needs to sell anything. She was dressed more like a countess than a traveling merchant. She asked me so many questions."

"Maybe she's lonely."

"She guessed I was from up north."

"Oh?"

"She said my features gave it away, and that she was from there, too. But—oh, she seems too sure of herself to come from anywhere."

Their conversation turned to other things, but Miriam slept poorly that night, reliving her dream over and over again.

Market day dawned crisp and cool. Miriam was in no hurry to get the washing done. The water steamed into the autumn air, catching the sunlight in little golden clouds. Dew had settled dust, and by the time the morning mist lifted, she could even see the flash of a sluggish river beyond the low, velvety hills.

She settled back, her legs folded beneath her. The brook trickled music behind her; a few birds called their secrets back and forth. Winter would come—there was no holding it back. But here in the bosom of the hills and comforted by her blind hostess' warm hearth, she could stay forever.

The clothes hung dripping on the tree branches when Chantal came with warm, dark bread. Miriam packed her basket and ate, lingering.

"Beautiful morning, isn't it?"

"Yes, Mother."

Chantal no longer objected to the title: her lodger had lost too much in the way of family.

"You might meet that strange lady again. Don't be troubled by her. She might have a sadness of her own and just hides it behind her forwardness and fancy dress." Miriam somehow doubted that, but she kept quiet. "And who knows but she might be of some help to you, if she's indeed from up north."

"I'll show her the brooch—if I feel sure she won't try to steal it."

"You do her a disservice, child."

"If you could only meet her, Chantal. She wants something. From me, I think. And I don't know what it is."

"Let God at her, then, Miriam. If ever we see a fault in someone, we should be as sorry about it as if it were our own. Perhaps what she wants has nothing to do with you."

"Perhaps not," her lodger answered in a faraway voice. "She may not come at all."

As Miriam's footfalls receded down the path, the blind woman went directly to a worn woolen rug and knelt to pray protection over the troubled girl.

But *she* was there, milling about and conversing with salespeople as they blew into their hands and set up their stalls. She wore a deep blue garment of some length, gathered up at the waist; her linen blouse and petticoat were white, new, and dripped with lace. Silver dangled from her wrists and fair neck. *She's so friendly with everyone,* thought Miriam, who—there was no denying it—was very plain in comparison. Barbara put some finishing touches to her own display before greeting the embroidery seller with the air of an old friend who hadn't seen her for a year.

The chill ascends from feet to knees,
The fever sings in mental wires.
If to be warmed, then I must freeze
And quake in frigid purgatorial fires
Of which the flame is roses, and the smoke is briars.

– T. S. Eliot

XVI

Danse Macabre

"Well, my dear, be good to yourself," Barbara said grandly. "It's all you have, you know."

Miriam thought surely not, there had to be more. There was... her hand went up to the brooch fastening her rough cloak from the inside. All of a sudden, the darkness of the dreamscape yawned like an open chasm before her. Something unknown, more cautious than afraid, prevented her from touching the silver clasp.

"It's been a pleasure talking with you," she found herself politely saying.

"That it has, my dear. And if ever you do go north, you're welcome. I'm on the way—near the top of the mountain pass east of here. It's the only way over, you know. It's a lovely spot, straddling two kingdoms (but who knows how many there'll be by this time next year, eh?). The house is only a bit off the road—it's dressed stone and I daresay cozy enough when the wind whips through. Miriam, au revoir." Barbara parted as easily as a wave sliding back seaward from the beach, leaning over affectedly to give the girl the formal kiss of a high-bred lady.

With great relief, Miriam waved farewell and set off home with a much lighter heart. The world was full of strange and wonderful things, but the most marvelous of all were the endless turnings of people like Chantal and Barbara. Trudging up the hill, she was suddenly choked with homesickness. Grief flashed lightning-sharp; she waited, ached, for the refreshing splashes of tears to wash the sorrow down her cheeks and away.

But they would not come.

The moon waxed, and waned again. The market, a social lake freezing in the town's center, slowly stilled as a cold wind began to cut through cloth and cloak. Merchants boarded up or carted away their stalls for a few months' respite. Yet Miriam, for all her modesty, could not help noticing people staring at her, and in passing she perceived whispers in tones cutting and sharp. Why should they only now begin to notice her odd dress and demeanor?

Deep within the lining of her cloak, she carried a hand-carved comforter, a link forged long ago to the high valley where she had herded sheep as a child. She reached for it now, drawing it out of hiding at the door of the cottage. The smooth wood, discolored with the handling of lanolin-coated fingers, brought sweet memories. Caressing her neglected treasure, Miriam entered the shelter of the house to find its mistress seated by a smoldering fire, sewing. Chantal smiled while her young helper lit a lamp—her movements had betrayed her.

"You're feeling better tonight."

"Aye." Miriam went to the wood box and eagerly placed a knot of scrub-pine on the coals, tending it carefully and blowing the flame into warmth and light. "It won't be long before I can stay home with you during the day."

"You've done well, Miriam. I have you to thank for a full larder and my warm feet. But there's more to it than that, isn't there? There's something in the marketplace troubles you."

"Yes, Mother. I've been so self-conscious lately. Everyone seems to notice me these days."

"And why not? A woman of worth in a world like this one? Why shouldn't they notice you?" She dropped the cloth in her lap and put up her hands in an elderly gesture of surprise. "Lord have mercy, child, they envy you."

"Do they? It doesn't seem like it. They whisper when I go by."

"Sometimes jealousy comes out in strange ways. Let them talk." The fire popped and crackled as the heat broke the knot.

"I brought you a present."

"Why?"

"No reason. To thank you. Well, God has been kind to both of us." Miriam nervously put the wooden flute to her lips and took in a deep breath, the next moment filling the room with a tune so wild and piercing it hung in the close air—an eagle in search of food for its young.

"Oh, Miriam, that's lovely! It sounds like... like a mountain brook—with trout!" The erstwhile shepherdess laughed, and then played a sweet, wandering air until her listener yawned, shaking her graying head.

"Shall I wake you, Mother, or let you sleep?"

"Oh, wake me, after a morsel. It's dark out now, I think." There was fresh butter, and the women dined lavishly in a royal dining room embannered with warm stone, sheltered by thick, dry thatch. Chantal settled back and sighed. "Now, play something happy."

"Do you think I can?"

"I know you can. Go on." Pressing the flute against her lips, Miriam considered. Then she lifted it and drew out a reel, steadily picking up the pace until it a gigue followed close behind. Chantal's spotted hands began to tap softly upon the arm of her chair. She unexpectedly stood up. "Don't stop, sweetheart. You make me young again!"

Miriam watched, intrigued, as the joyful rhythm bounced against the walls—a perfect invisible partner. Chantal gingerly took up the skipping steps of a country dance with what were once very light feet. Her patched and mended, faded and embroidered skirts swished in the firelight, and only when the tune ended did she grope breathlessly back to her chair. Miriam laughed faintly, then louder, and the older woman joined her.

"Eh, but it's been a long time! I'd forgotten."

"But your feet remembered."

"And so did your fingers."

"Then there are parts of both of us wiser than our heads," Miriam conceded, relaxing her shoulders.

"Child, that's the first nice thing you've said about yourself. But there are many more. I'm glad you came home with me."

Until that moment, Miriam had not known that the blind woman delighted in her company. She lay the fife down on the stone mantel and knelt by the chair. Words were needless; Chantal reached out to place a trembling hand on her head. Thus they sat together as the pine knot settled into its nest of glowing embers, until the forest scent lulled each of them off to their respective piles of straw.

Something woke her with a start—a crashing sound nearby. The cottage was black, floating amid a moonless night; not a gray shadow anywhere.

"Chantal?" A heavy sigh, then fast, shallow breaths. "Chantal, are you alright?"

"Just thirsty," came the hasty reply.

Throughout her stay, Miriam had never known Chantal to stumble even once.

"Let me get it." The sounds stilled as she felt her way to the skin bottle and back again. Somehow she managed to find the waiting hands of the blind woman, who drank greedily. *Maybe she's had a bad dream,* thought the younger, *and isn't quite awake.* The breathing slowed.

"Ah, that's better." Chantal tumbled back into her straw bed while a concerned Miriam tucked the woolen shawl about her shoulders. "Just like when we first met," remembered the tired voice.

"Yes. Good night, Mother."

"Good night."

But it was some time before Miriam slept again, and when she did it was fitfully, awaiting the cock's crow.

She woke late, donned her boots, and rushed searching through the cottage. She found Chantal in the garden, kneeling to weed the flower bed; at the sound of Miriam's approach, she lifted her head, her wrinkled face rosy and bright.

"Why, Miriam, child, what is it?"

"I... I thought... that you mightn't be well."

"On such a lovely morning?" Chantal closed her clouded eyes and drew the air in deeply. "I can almost smell the colors!"

Her deft fingers resumed their search for things that might choke next spring's flowers. "There's a hot kettle on the hob. The apples you brought yesterday are really nice. I hope you don't mind that I already ate," she said, her head cocked to one side in mock embarrassment.

"No, not at all." Retracing her steps—slower this time—Miriam admired the tidiness of the little house, the steam rising up the squat chimney, the crisp freshness of the linen tablecloth, the sunlight streaming through the kitchen casement, the apples placed like an artist's still-life in an earthen bowl. She sat, bewildered by her own misgivings, eating her breakfast and listening to the lark's morning song.

Minutes passed, and Chantal came in wiping her hands on her smock and blowing. "We'll have daffodils in spring, Miriam. And lilies. Were you able to get some of Carmina's cheese? It would go so well with those apples."

"No." She didn't want to go anywhere, not today. "Would you like me to go to her house and see?" she asked nervously.

"Oh, would you? It's not so very far. But wear your cloak, sweetheart; the air's a bit nippy." Chantal waved her off as Miriam ascended the golden ridge. For a second she almost turned round. *I'll be back soon*, she thought, and forced herself onward.

She had just stepped inside the dairywoman's chalet when Carmina's oldest girl, braids flying, crashed through the gate.

"Mother! Mother, it's Mistress Chantal. She won't talk to me—she just lies there. What shall we do? Hurry!" She pulled at her mother's dress.

"Run to the monastery and fetch the old monk. He knows his herbs. Now!" The girl disappeared down the ridge. "We'd better go, Miriam," came a calm voice from somewhere, but

Miriam stood unmoving, her fears gathering around her like a blackening cloud. Carmina led her down the path. Together they arrived at the gaping doorway just as the sun reached the valley and ricocheted off the glistening slates of the richer houses in town. The dairymaid went first, while Miriam followed in hushed silence; no one was home.

Chantal had gone, leaving her crumpled form lying atop the straw. The sightless eyes of the corpse were open and staring, but the eyes of the blind woman were unseeing no longer.

All this Miriam knew in an instant, and she turned and fled eastward, through the dairy meadows and beyond, driven by a thorny prod of guilt—and unknowingly pursued by whispered rumors of sorcery and the coming of the plague.

The friar knelt to close the milk-white eyes and place a roughly fashioned cross in the cool, ivory hands. "Set forth, O Christian soul, from this world in the name of God the Father, who hath created thee; in the name of Jesu Christ his Son, who suffered for thee; in the name of the Holy Spirit, who was poured out upon thee..." He spoke in the vernacular, musing in his head as to whether or not Latin was for the living, or the newly departed, or only for the officials in Rome. The words went on, citing prophets and saints, martyrs and apostles and all the company of heaven, and at its conclusion there was a mumbled "Amen" from those who had crept up and gathered behind him. He stood, lean and tall, looking around searchingly. No one stepped forward.

"Any family nearby?" he finally asked. There lingered a nervous pause.

"No, Father, just a girl who sold embroidery for her in the market."

"Where is she?" Pairs of eyes exchanged glances or stared at the floor. No one knew. "So who will bear this good woman to the churchyard, then?"

"Father, none of us would rather touch her. They say her servant girl's brought the plague."

"This woman did not die of plague."

"Then it were bad magic," came a woman's voice from the back. "I heard the devil's own music coming from this very house after sundown, just last night." The old friar looked up sharply but could not identify the speaker. He sighed; these people feared everything they didn't understand.

"No. She was old, that is all. And she of all people would not have tolerated any kind of evil under her roof." They did not believe him; he hadn't seen the steamy clouds rising from the back of the house, or the strange way the young woman crept to and from the market, trusting herself to no one. He hadn't heard the whispers spread by the apothecary woman, nor the murmurs that crackled like wildfire across a dry field.

"Brother Bernard and I will take her in a cart, then. Back to your homes, all of you."

He found the iron key still in the lock and took it, leaving the cottage last and locking the door behind him. He marked the lintel with the sign of the cross and set back down the hill toward the monastery, stopping only by the carpenter's to order a coffin.

* * *

Miriam had long since abandoned the path and shot into the shadowy woods; all sense of direction was lost. She ran, her cloak fluttering behind her sail-like in an endless ocean swelling with grief. A glade opened suddenly before her. The high sun glowered down upon her like a searchlight, blinding her, piercing her. Turning on her heels, she sought shelter beneath the twisted arms of a gnarled oak, collapsing on the ground between its roots and trunk.

She was shaking. Shaking, and sweating and panting. Her hands went to her face but jerked back when she felt their chill. She gathered her mantle about her, held her knees, and caught her breath. Thoughts came creeping back as sorrow gave way to fear. Where would she go? Winter was coming apace. She would have to go further south—for now. There was no compass to go by, so she studied the movement of the tree's shadow for some minutes; she had to make marks in the dirt to track it as she no longer trusted her own eyes or mind.

She would have to go through the town. Had anyone seen her? It didn't matter; she would soon be away. She would stop at the beautiful parish church and light a candle for Chantal, and perhaps also find comfort in the dim coolness of the sanctuary and the patient, listening ear of the priest there. Yes. He would help her know what to do.

* * *

Brother Bernard sat in the copy room, laboring over his vellum. He felt so at home here—more than he did even in the monastery chapel—with the smell of ink, his stained fingers, even the hard bench beneath him. He never hurried. No: he considered the text far too sacred to mar with a careless mistake. Sometimes he wondered if he thought too much about what he wrote, whether his questions would distract his careful copy-work, although he always checked it again at day's end to make sure the words matched the original perfectly. His pen dipped and scratched in disciplined rhythm, pumping out the words of life to minds searching through the mist of a fallen world.

It was his call, his mission.

The prior, Cyril, seldom visited the copy room while Bernard worked. The novice needed privacy and thick silence: his keen young senses amplified minute noises into roaring distractions. Copy-work required peace of mind, and Cyril knew that Brother Bernard's concentration could so easily break into fragments at the smallest interruption.

The prior remembered well his own need for the sweet silence, during his youth when he sat for hours painstakingly bringing unseen saints to human sight—though he worked on wooden panels, with crushed hues and gold leaf. The icon-painter from the time-hardened east found disdain and even scorn when he came to the "progressive" monasteries of the west, a refugee from barbarian invasions. Cyril's beloved handiwork was smashed and burnt, and then, when he came here, laid silently aside to take up the more practical duties of gardening and hospitality. Besides, his hands shook too much nowadays to form either image or letter clearly; words would shimmer on the page before him. So one day he rubbed his eyes and lay both brush and quill down, never to pick them up again.

But he would have to interrupt. There was just enough daylight left to pick up the body and prepare it for burial tomorrow in the priory's small graveyard. Chantal, God rest her soul. He sighed, knocking as lightly as he could on the rough-boarded door.

"Ave."

"Bernard, excuse me."

"Yes, Father, certainly," said the young man, turning to face him with keen eyes.

"We'll need to take the cart into town. There's been a death—a widow, with no relations." Bernard looked puzzled. "It appears no one wants to take her to the church."

"They don't have the money for it, I suppose," answered the novice with a wry smile, and rising. Cyril lowered his head, mostly in silent rebuke. "Yes, I'll gladly go. But you look tired. Can I manage on my own?"

"She wasn't a large woman. Yes, I think so."

"Who was she then, Father?"

"Mistress Chantal."

"Oh." The younger man crossed himself, his heart pricked.

When they came out of the stable with the cart half an hour later, they were met with the smell of smoke. Looking up, they both saw it: a black, cloudy pillar ascending heavenward from the other side of town.

* * *

The parish church was empty. Miriam scarcely dared breathe as she crossed the transept, her soft boots making no sound on the wooden floor. Through a side door, she caught sight of the priest in the courtyard. When he saw Miriam emerging from the church, he drew himself up, a rigid marble column with wide, flaming eyes.

"What do you want here?" he cried, clutching at the crucifix on his breast. She saw the terror in his ashen face as he lunged at her with it. "Be gone, evil woman!" The words went home, along with the realization that she was the cause of his fear. But why? It must be the curse. Of course—he could see it breaking out all over her, like the plague. Her uncleanness drove her from him, from that holy place where saints in incense-dusted niches kept constant vigil against spiritual lepers like her.

Someone began to follow her as she left the church grounds. She started to run again, while shouts multiplied behind her. The hood of her cloak had fallen back, her hair undone: lashing about her face, it obscured her vision. Her cap. Her cap and fife and... and Jacob's breviary. They were all she had, and they were at Chantal's. She must get them! Perhaps there, she could close her pursuers out with shutter and key; she could not outrun them much longer.

Gathering up her skirts, Miriam veered north toward the half-timbered house she had come to know as home. As she breathlessly mounted the hill, she stopped in despair, aghast at the sight before her.

"Kyrie eleison," she heard her voice say. The little cottage was wrapped in leaping flames, the thatch a giant torch. Around it gathered a score of the townsfolk—she knew many of them—either watching or containing the blaze they had started. She tried to call out with strength enough to stop them, when a merchant from the marketplace saw her, and pointed.

"There she is!" He didn't need to say more—the small crowd followed his gaze and words as if they were a battle cry. Dazed, Miriam let the slope add speed to her descent, as she plummeted down a goat path toward the main road.

"Don't let her get away, or we'll all be dead!" came another cry in a voice Miriam thought she recognized. West. It was all downhill, and there was a small monastery at the edge of town. Jacob's voice: *"Holy houses... you'll be safe."* Maybe there... Trying to elude the mob behind her, she stumbled against a wagon track and fell, pulling herself up again as a stone whizzed past her ear.

"Christe eleison," she whispered as she hurtled forward. A hammer-blow struck her in the back and another in her side, knocking her off course. She gasped sharply but dared not stop, pointing her feet once again westward. The gates of the enclosure were in sight now, but they seemed such a long way off. Her pace was slowing. More rocks fell, with accusing shouts, from behind her. She could try to plead with them… no. There were too many, and they were far too angry for reason or pity. She would never be heard. In that instant, something struck her head, and she covered her face in feeble protection just before a red-hot flash seared her arm. "Kyrie eleison!" she cried aloud, whirling round again to see the blurred opening of the monastery engulfing her. Her legs gave out then, and she squeezed her eyes shut as a stone wall appeared out of nowhere to break her fall.

O Comforter, draw near. Within my heart appear,
And kindle it, Thy holy flame bestowing.
Oh, let it freely burn, till earthly passions turn
To dust and ashes in its heat consuming.

– Bianco da Siena

XVII

Exile

"Father Cyril, there's a mob at the gate," Bernard reported, having abandoned the cart to investigate the noise outside.

"Is that what it is?" asked the prior, leaning on his staff.

"Please hurry, Father. They've stoned a girl." Bernard was distraught. He lifted his coarse habit to run back.

Miriam lay where she had fallen, crumpled and dazed at the foot of a low retaining wall, inside the enclosure. The crowd just outside the gate waited with ready accusations. Cyril appeared, his expression unruffled by the waves of fear and anger in the sea of faces before him. Quietly he took in the scene, perceiving the truth.

"There's a woman needs dealing with, Father," said a spokesman, pointing.

"Aye," another man said. "She's a witch. Should be burnt and right away." The noise rose violently in assent. A storm wind stirred from the north; the air grew cold. An obvious omen to confirm their views.

"And who among you has examined her?" Cyril demanded. Silence. As he thought: she was the victim of an unfounded rumor. He turned to the novice. "Take her inside, Bernard. Then off to Mistress Chantal's, before the storm gets here."

"That house is burnt—it were cursed," a woman called in a loud, victorious voice.

Cyril's eyes blazed, though his face remained calm, his voice steady. "Go anyway, Bernard. These people will not harm you." Then, to the crowd, "You have dealt with this woman enough. You must leave her to Holy Church now."

"Not for pardon, surely, Father."

"For examination, my son. All will be done that can be done. Or is your justice better than God's?"

Cyril moved resolutely to close the gate, ushering the crowd away with further assurances that the matter would be resolved, by exorcism or trial if need be. In his shadow, the novice hurried to gather up the crumpled woman. She had no strength to resist him, and blindly grasped at his cincture as he supported her, her feet dragging over the stone pavement. She was bent nearly double by the time they stopped at the low lintel, he to push open the heavy door, and she to pitch forward onto a low bedstead within the dim cell. *That long cloak must be hiding some wounds,* thought Bernard, and he sucked in his breath when he saw her hair matted with blood, a crimson rivulet trickling behind her ear and down her neck.

He'd only just placed her in the most comfortable position he could when the prior entered, carrying clean cloths and a bowl of water from the well.

Miriam tried hard to open her eyes, but the room spun and tilted, so she left them closed and tried to slow her breathing instead. The dust-dry air came in shallow through her open mouth.

"Before you go, Bernard, please bring me the shears and some silk thread." The novice withdrew reverently. Cyril knelt to remove Miriam's cloak. She winced and groaned as his hands gently searched for broken bones. Two wet streaks gleamed on her back and forearm; although most of the stones had been hurled as threats, at least one hand had been intent on ending the girl's life. But the blood was not coming fast, so he turned his attention to her head wound. It was jagged and long. He would have to cut her hair. He uttered a soft thanksgiving when unconsciousness rolled over her, the pain-knit brow giving way to empty calm.

The oil lamp cast faint, flickering shadows on the wall and the low beams of the ceiling. Miriam's eyes opened with effort against the throbbing in her head. She was lying on her side, growing slowly aware of enclosing warmth: a poultice upon her back, a coarse woolen covering, the comforting glow of the lamp set on a table before her. The soothing smells of comfrey and clove drifted by. Her inner forearm burned; she raised it slightly to catch sight of a clean dressing spiraling from wrist to elbow. She swallowed and tried to take a deep breath, but a grabbing sharpness in her back cut it short. Closing her eyes again, she vaguely heard the door scrape against the threshold. A cold wind shook the lamp flame; the scent of coming snow made her shiver.

An old monk carried in a steaming basin and some linen, closing the door to with his foot. He smiled a faint welcome and, without a word, went around the narrow bed to change the poultice on her back. The sound of dripping water brought with it the recollection of how she had come to be in a monastery cell. He was at her side now.

"Good evening, Daughter. I've brought you a drink."

"Father," she murmured, her voice thin, "thank you." The mead warmed her throat but left a bitter taste. She must have made a face.

"There are herbs there against the pain. Here." He continued to support her head, his hand shaking mildly, and a sip of sweet water followed.

"The crowd—will they be back for me?"

"No, you're in safe refuge here. Isn't that why you came?" the prior asked. The edges of her pain began to fray; her breath came easier now, though still shallow.

"I didn't mean to bring danger," she said, slurred and apologetic.

"You needn't fear them. They are mistaken about the old woman. Their fear of the plague brought them to blame you," he added thoughtfully.

"Forgive me, Father," murmured she. "I meant the curse."

He was quiet for a short, full moment.

"There is no danger, child. You have come to a place where curses are undone." Cyril stood, bent over her to remove the warm poultice he'd applied moments before, and gazed again at the gash the rock had torn in her back. He wasn't sure whether or not she'd heard him as she drifted off to sleep, but he found himself wondering at his own presumption.

She slept through Terce, and Cyril proceeded to weed the herb garden. The curious Bernard sat close by, mending the woman's torn cloak. In the boundaries of their rule, talking came alongside work more comfortably than at any other time of day.

"And how is our guest this morning, Father?"

"Asleep and quiet." His look told more than any amount of words.

"But something is bothering you about her."

"It's very strange. Wounds like hers usually become angry and hot," he began to explain. Bernard nodded in agreement, needle in mouth. They'd tended other patients together, hurt in the odd accident or occasional fight. "She should have a fever, yet she needs extra covering, though she shivers not."

"Loss of blood, maybe."

"No. There was so little bleeding. I'm glad you didn't send for a leech. To bleed a woman in her condition might be the death of her."

"He wouldn't have come, anyway. He always puts off coming to the poor."

"Bernard." Cyril eyed him reproachfully.

"Forgive me, Father, for my rash words." But the prior seemed to not hear. The novice held his hands still so as not to interrupt his superior's thought. Cyril sighed and resumed the conversation.

"She mentioned a curse."

"Odd—that's what the townspeople said. They're afraid of everything: dark clouds on the face of the moon, a stranger who speaks little and dresses differently... they said something about her bringing the plague, didn't they?"

"Chantal didn't die of plague. I told them that."

"They still fear it."

Cyril sat back upon his heels. "A curse could be at work."

Bernard held his breath; a sparrow chirped in the courtyard. He answered, unintentionally loud and speaking quickly, "In a woman like that? Why would she come here for shelter then? No, Father, I don't think so. Look." He reached beside him to present the scorched remains of a worn book. "I found this breviary in what was left of the house. It wasn't the blind woman's, pious as she was." Cyril took it in his earth-stained hands, turning it over and wondering. "There's some mistake, Father. That girl's more saint than sinner."

"How do you know, my brother?" For some moments, the only movement was the shadow creeping across the sundial. "It's time to be quiet now, so God can have his say." Cyril stood slowly and turned toward the refectory, burned book in hand. Bernard stayed, respecting the prior's solitude. There was more to be said, and he, an obedient novice, would wait.

Her eyes opened heavily. She lay on her back, a dull, crushing pain in her side making breathing an act of forced labor. Propping her strong hand beside her, Miriam sat up, leaning forward over crossed feet to take the most weight off her chest. She then dragged her bandaged forearm into the shelter of her lap. Her breath came easier—a little. She couldn't discern the time of day: the light falling through the cell window came from a cloudy sky. Her head hurt, badly.

A small knock preceded the scraping of the opening door this time. The prior was obviously pleased to see her awake.

"Good afternoon, my daughter."

"Hello, Father," she answered politely.

"Is it easier for you to breathe that way?" She nodded as he set a tray down on the rough table. "I'm not sure if your ribs are cracked or broken, but they'll mend." He sat down and felt her forehead with the back of his hand. "Perhaps this will warm you up."

"It smells nice."

"Standard fare for monks: vegetable soup. Are you hungry?"

"A little."

"You'll need some help, I think." He took up a wooden spoon and fed her with an experienced hand. He then helped her lie down again, now on her side.

"Chantal—my blind mistress. They burned her house down."

"I know."

"She was in it."

"No, Daughter, only her cast-off garment. Brother Bernard gathered it up for burial." He noticed the pale dullness of her eyes when she looked up at him.

"Did you know her?"

"Yes." He smiled, savoring a memory. "She always brought us flowers, fresh-picked from her garden, for the chapel. She used to scold us for our 'herbal practicality', said we didn't have enough color around this place. That was after her husband left her. Then she went blind, and almost mad, but that passed. I would meet her poking her way about town, and she would squeeze my arms and tell me I was fasting too much, that I could use some nice fat mutton between my teeth once in a while." He paused in his happy eulogy. "She dragged one of the brothers home with her one day to mend her thatch, and she gave him a whole jug of sweet cream in thanks."

"She was very good to me."

"And you to her, no doubt."

"I helped a little, only enough to earn my keep."

"How long did you stay in her home?"

"Little more than six months." Miriam bit her lip. "She was so good to me, always so cheerful. She never treated me like someone who was…"

"No. She would only perceive good in someone who helped her. And, Daughter…"

"Yes, Father?"

"It is not usual for one who is evil to do so much good. Chantal knew that." She winced at the probe.

"Surely you've noticed the coldness, Father. It won't go away. I've always had it, ever since I can remember. You… you don't think I'm under a curse?"

"We are all of us under a curse."

"Yes, Father," she replied, remembering her catechism.

"You'd best sleep some more. I'll bring something hot later." She nodded gratefully, closing her weary eyes. Healing was hard work. The aging prior pulled the mended cloak over her before tracing the sign of the cross on her forehead. She smiled modestly. He knew that if she were cursed, it wouldn't last much longer. *Only what has died can be resurrected,* he thought. She was well on her way—whether she knew it or not.

Cyril walked across the courtyard, looking at the softened edges of the flagstones placed there by who-knew-how-many monks before him. The monastery was an old one but not famous, its founder's name forgotten, while the work of love remained. It attracted very few pilgrims, having no notable relic or miracle-working grotto. The prior liked it that way; he would have preferred the life of a hermit. As twilight embroidered the sky, he went to the chapel to light some candles for Vespers. Bernard would lay down his quill presently and join him for the nightly reading of the Psalter before they shared a simple meal in the silence of their discipline. Bernard was a good novice, even though his idea of saints with upturned, wondering eyes wasn't anything like Cyril's icons which would look you in the face—or straight through you. He tugged at the heavy chapel door and stepped inside.

He noticed it at once. Something was there, among the stone pillars. A presence he could only think of as a gnawing hunger penetrated the sacred spaces. A deep, longing ache filled the darkened room. It captured his breath and quickly tossed it back to him, an invisible will-o'-the-wisp. His tension died when he perceived that the void was one awaiting Light, not the suffocating presence of evil as he had first thought.

He entered softly and lit a taper, glancing aside as spark leapt to wick so as not to be blinded by the flame's sudden brightness. Sighing inaudibly, he straightened himself to survey the room. In the corner of his eye, he caught the shadowed form of the woman bent nearly prostrate in the back. His guest. Strange, that she should be driven here accused but turn out to be a penitent or pilgrim.

He had seen it that morning, when she took the brown slice of bread from him, her hands reaching graciously to receive it as if it were a fine jewel from a sweetheart, or the host itself during Mass. *Holiness comes in many shades,* he mused. Why, the saints were canonized only after their deaths, and many more, he was sure, had never been brought to the attention of the Holy See.

Taking up his breviary, Cyril pulled at his mind like a reluctant donkey to return to the present. He caught himself thinking how he would paint the icon of blessed Mary Magdalene, out of whom had been cast seven demons, using Miriam as his model.

By the time Bernard had come in, summoned by the little bell, she was sitting, still in the back, composed and silent. She listened impassively while the psalms echoed against the vaulted ceiling, the monks' voices blending in chanted unison. All were absorbed: Bernard in the words, Cyril in the purity of tone wafting heavenward like incense, and Miriam in the greatness of the hovering presence of God, comforting and covering her like no cloak from any weaver's loom.

She sat next day by the well in the herb garden, soaking up the afternoon sun like a sponge.

"Care for company?" Cyril's brusque politeness brought a nod of her head, the thick bandage serving her well as a cap.

"Please. But I thought you kept a strict silence here."

"Not for visitors, unless they require it."

"Sometimes I do. But not now," she murmured, her expression unreadable. "There is too much of it, now." Cyril noted that she said so little of what she thought, and sat a respectful distance away, just close enough to talk.

"Brother Bernard found something among the ashes when he went back to the house. I thought it might be yours." Tenderly, he held out the ruined breviary, too blackened to be of further use.

"Oh, Father." She took it, turning the frail pages. Then looking up again, she added, "This belonged to the shepherd who raised me. He taught me to read from this. I think he used to be a novice somewhere." The prior smiled, ruefully.

"Jacob."

"Why, yes," she said, amazed. "How did you know?"

"Your accent, and this." He gestured at the book. "He was my charge once. Then he met a woman, and his true calling. He must have made an excellent shepherd—all the animals here loved him. He's your father?" Something seemed amiss—there was no resemblance.

"No, but he was all I knew of one."

So, he is dead, Cyril deduced. Probably the plague, if the rumors had any seed of truth in them, as rumors often did.

"His sufferings are over now."

"Yes."

But yours remain, he said inwardly, looking down into the mint growing near their feet. He knew by her haunted demeanor that she could no longer stay in the town, or return to her former abode. "Where will you go now?"

"I don't know. I wanted to find my own father, but he might be dead too. And I've little strength. And it's soon winter…" Yes, it all made sense: she had great difficulties with winter.

"Have you any idea where to find him?"

"North—beyond the mountains. But I can't go north now." She fumbled in the recesses of her cloak. "I have only this—I think it belonged to him, but I'm not sure. I found it in my pocket." The brooch appeared dull and dusty in the sunlight, though the ruby still shone. Cyril's old eyes squinted in an attempt to recognize it.

"I've never been any good at heraldry, but I would think it came from a great house." He had a sudden idea, and risked asking. "You seem at home here. Have you never thought of taking the veil?"

She laughed—softly, modestly, sadly. "I did once, Father, but it takes more courage than I have to be betrothed to the very King of Heaven. No, I couldn't." She looked piercingly at him. "What could I give up, not even knowing who I am?"

"This curse of yours, perhaps."

"It won't leave me; I cannot shake it off or pray it away. I've asked God, I've done penance a dozen different ways..."

"You wouldn't be aware of it unless God meant to break it."

"How then, Father? What am I to do?" She faced him now, her eyes growing desperate.

"Nothing but wait. That's the hardest thing to do, isn't it? Let him show you in good time... He's already shown you something, I think." He became silent, waiting for her to fill in the story—if she so chose.

She drew as deep a breath as she could with the pain tightening in her back, and told him that she dreamed. "But Father, God doesn't send someone a dream about... herself."

"You are mistaken, child. The patriarch Joseph shared his prison cell with two who dreamed about themselves."

"One dream was good, the other bad," she recalled. "Mine is a nightmare; I'm afraid of it."

"God is able to bring good out of evil, and I am certain you are in his hands. You will only gain if you follow the road ahead of you, even if it is the one the devil intended to destroy you by. But no one likes to enter the valley of the shadow of death."

"I feel I'm already there."

"So is the Good Shepherd, right beside you. Just belong to him; give yourself over to his care. It is his curse to break." Long seconds passed. "As are all curses." She took in his words, biting her lip. The afternoon shadows lengthened. "Let me help you back. You require some rest, I think."

"Body and spirit both, Father. Thank you." She leaned on his arm as they ambled back to the warm cell. Bernard, at the prior's direction, had placed a charcoal brazier there an hour earlier. Cyril wished her a peaceful evening and retired to the chapel, where he could pray and puzzle over the odd guest the Lord had brought to his hostel.

It was there he remembered. He should have known, days ago. He would have to tell Bernard. *But not yet*, he reasoned. *Not yet.*

The prior stood alone in the copy room, leaning over the parchments. He admired Bernard's conscientious hand and was pleased with his carefulness. The young novice had plunged into his work so eagerly after breakfast— he missed the others, who were out preaching and had been for several weeks. The door burst open, and in plunged Bernard, shattering the quiet.

"I think I have it, Father," he announced jauntily.

"Eh?"

"Sister Giuliana's abbey, a day's ride south of here. They would gladly take her."

Cyril paused a moment. Bernard had a habit of beginning in the middle of a thought.

"Who?"

"Our guest, Father. The lady Miriam."

"But she is not yet recovered from her wounds."

"She won't be, if that mob comes back to drag her off. It's happened before—they don't always wait for an inquisitor." There was no immediate reply. Cyril's eyes were back on the vellum. Bernard went on, "That's the passage I copied yesterday, that's what gave me the idea. 'Thou shalt hide them privily by thine own presence from the provoking of all men; thou shalt keep them secretly in the tabernacle from the strife of tongues.' A holy house. She belongs there, Father. A woman's house."

"She does need a place to winter..."

"And she can't stay here. We could secret her away—tonight. I've already spoken to Amiens. He goes there anyway, and his cart usually passes by here in the evening. He can take her along, with a gift for the sisters."

"And arrive by morning."

"It only awaits your consent, Father."

Cyril smiled. The written Word was taking on flesh in the virgin soil of Bernard's fertile heart.

"So be it." The novice spun on his heels to finalize the arrangement. "Oh, Bernard."

"Yes, Father?" he said at the door.

"I don't think her name is Miriam."

"The Lord Mayor is asking to see you, Father." Cyril looked up from his Vulgate, sighing. He was of the firm mind that temporal powers should not reach into the realm of the sacred—he had observed the problems it caused in both East and West, pitting emperor against priest, king against pope, time and again. His countenance was therefore harder than usual as he entered the refectory to greet the distinguished visitor who waited there.

"Ah, Father!" gushed the heavy-set gentleman, bowing serenely, his many rings a-sparkle. "How well you look. Though how you maintain your health in such an austere setting stretches my admiring imagination."

The prior grunted and motioned the mayor to the only chair in the room. He himself took a bench opposite.

"You are welcome, Lord Mayor. But you haven't come on retreat or pilgrimage."

"Alas, no," he answered, blustering slightly. Why did these holy men have to be so frugal in their speech? He had hoped for more small talk to quell the stringent atmosphere. He leaned back judiciously. "My presence here concerns your guest, Father. I have had some complaints from the townspeople, and the parish priest..."

"Did they tell you they burned her house down? For no reason?"

The mayor fidgeted. "They had cause to believe there was a health hazard, that they were preventing the, ah, contagion from spreading..."

"There was no such thing."

"And a spiritual danger as well. Surely, Father, you recognize the seriousness of the matter. There are charges of witchcraft brought against the young woman." Cyril detected a hint of alacrity in the visitor's tone.

"Have you forgotten that I am qualified by my order to act as inquisitor, sir? I have examined her. She is no witch, but an orphan who mistakenly sought refuge in our town—and found hospitality with the most pious laywoman I ever knew."

"Your qualifications, worthy as they are, do not come with papal authority, however." The mayor rubbed his hands together; he had not expected to debate with this frail, soft-spoken monk.

Cyril went on. "She has received the 'justice' of the mob, who noticed her grief and made up stories. Do you see further need for justice—for examination, even—for an outcast with deep scars on her body now, as well as her soul?"

The Lord Mayor shook his head; there was no reasoning with this man. "May I at least ask her some questions, to satisfy myself as to the accuracy of your, ah, impression?"

Cyril rose decisively, slowly. He folded his hands in front of his cincture and walked the short length of the room before turning to answer.

"I'm afraid the Lord Mayor cannot. The woman has been sent to an abbey for convalescence. She'll not be any more trouble for you there—it's far enough away."

"I see," the official said, deflated. It seemed sensible enough, even satisfactory, though he would have to return empty-handed to some angry, powerful people. The matter was out of his jurisdiction. "Then I won't take any more of your time. Good day, Father." Cyril merely bowed his head, then led the dignitary out the door and escorted him to the gate. The gentleman took his leave hastily, glad to be out of that too-quiet place.

Bernard rejoined his prior in the courtyard.

"Do you think he'll try to bring her back?"

"No."

The novice breathed out sharply in relief, his arms crossed and rocking back on his heels. "Then she is safe." He was so pleased his plan had worked, that an innocent woman had been rescued from the stake.

Cyril gave him such a look that no spoken word of rebuke was necessary. "It is time for our office, my brother. Then I believe there are preparations to be made, tomorrow being the feast of Saints Simon and Jude. Some of the brothers will be returning."

"Some, Father? Didn't you tell them all to be back by then?"

"You forget the plague." Cyril continued toward the chapel, but Bernard paused in realization. Death. Of course. No one was safe.

They sat before the kitchen hearth following Compline, huddled in silence against the growing wind outside. Bernard burned with a question.

"Speak, my son."

"Why didn't you say good-bye to her, Father? You're in charge of hospitality."

Cyril stoked the fire meditatively. "I don't believe in farewells, not with people like that. But it was good of you to see her off."

"People like what, Father?" probed the novice.

Cyril leaned forward, elbows on knees and hands folded together. Bernard listened eagerly as the prior drew out his words with an intended effort to keep them simple.

"If you recall, just last season I went with Brother Simeon to convocation, held three days' journey west of here... It was my custom to watch and listen to the people around us, to find out what they thought important. Such a habit has always helped in my preaching, though my brother thought it terribly worldly of me..."

Bernard was taken aback; he wasn't expecting a confession, and he had never known Cyril to ramble on like this.

"There was a minstrel in the square, telling a marvelous story about a princess from the far north, under a curse and sent away from her father's court until it should be broken. Not an uncommon story, really, but this was the only one I've ever heard without an ending. There was merely presented a mysterious hope that she would return and the bard's promise that, if ever he found out, he would come back to tell the rest of it. It made one wonder..." He stirred the fire.

"And you wonder, Father," ventured Bernard cautiously, "if our guest was that castaway princess."

"I know she is."

The novice felt at once queer, bewildered, and jaded. "Are you certain it is not a mere story?"

"Absolutely certain." The fire crackled demurely on the grate.

"Do you think she wonders it herself?"

"No. She has not yet heard the tale! She carries a secret she cannot understand. Understanding would be of no help to her, anyway. She will draw closer to God in the darkness of not knowing."

Bernard bristled and rose, agitated. "But was it not our duty, Father, to help her? To tell her who she is?"

"No, Bernard. Only God can show her that."

The novice began pacing. "Then why did he bring her here? To be freed from that curse, maybe—if you'd had the sense to tell her what you just told me." He stopped abruptly, and turned to confront the prior. "It's a curse to not know who you are, Father."

"No, my son. It's a blessing, if one is not ready to know."

"We have erred, Father, I know it. We could have…"

"We did what we were supposed to do: shelter her, pray for her. Such a person's soul is God's and no one may touch it—not even us. Attacks on her body, her honor, or her possessions are allowed by him, and they will somehow bring him glory. But her soul, Bernard, they may not attack, for he will protect it from the whole world, and indeed from all hell." All this he said slowly, letting the words sink into Bernard's mind like pebbles in a lake. "It is for us to serve all such blessed wanderers, not to tell them what we think they should know."

"Blessed, Father?" came the frustrated reply. "*Blessed?* You said she was cursed. How can someone be cursed and blessed at the same time?"

In silence, the prior lifted his eyes to meet Bernard's. The young man shook his head and withdrew to his cell, where he spent the darkening hours of the stormy evening grappling with things he couldn't understand but wanted to. He knelt, he paced; he sat on the sharp edge of the bed frame, holding his head in his hands, trying to dispel the question, aching to solve the riddle. In desperate frankness, he stood to ask aloud, "How can something be cursed and blessed at the same time?"

His eyes were drawn magnet-like to the crucifix over his bed. He heard the distant cry of Jesus from that tortuous cross, "Why have you forsaken me?!" It seemed blindly heroic, achieved at the very moment he was most annihilated. Then he knew. The question melted away as a morning mist. Cursed by men and seemingly abandoned by God. Accused, wounded, mocked, killed. Yet, blessed by God to endure with patient joy someone else's suffering. Many someones. Even his own.

That night, the sweet darkness held for Brother Bernard the holiness of a suffering God; it rent his heart in unlooked-for ecstasy.

"O sweet Jesu!" he cried, falling to his knees upon the stone floor and burying his face in the rough woolen blanket, to muffle his sobs and sponge away his many tears.

* * *

The gritty taste of dirt had taken his appetite away. Michael breathed through a linen cloth, tied behind his neck, as he stood chest-deep in a long pit, leaning on his spade. Three days of digging a mass grave. Strong as he was, his arms and back ached. The late rains had soaked the fields and mud was heavy to sling... Still, the work kept him warm.

He'd lost all commissions when the town had dispensed with coffins a week ago; there weren't enough people left to chop down the required trees, haul the wood, bury the dead... They hurried only to the most essential tasks, holding kerchiefs in front of their faces. Many had fled, and crops went unharvested. Tempers were short as hunger crept upon the heels of the plague, and theft was on the rise.

Michael slept in a woodshed, upon a low wooden platform under which he kept his tools. The peasants who shared the hovel next door gave him food in exchange for his guarding their fuel supply at night. During the long evenings he would sit by any hearth he could, whittling and carving animal-figures on throwaway bits of wood, mostly to divert his attention from the incessant cries of mourning surrounding him. People were going mad with fear, grief and hunger; he didn't want to be one of them. In the mornings he would give his work away: children wandering in the streets would seize the carved wooden birds he held out to them, smiling for the first time in days. But he was tired. He hoped the winter would slow the spread of the scourge, so that he could trade grave-digging for something more satisfying—like chopping wood.

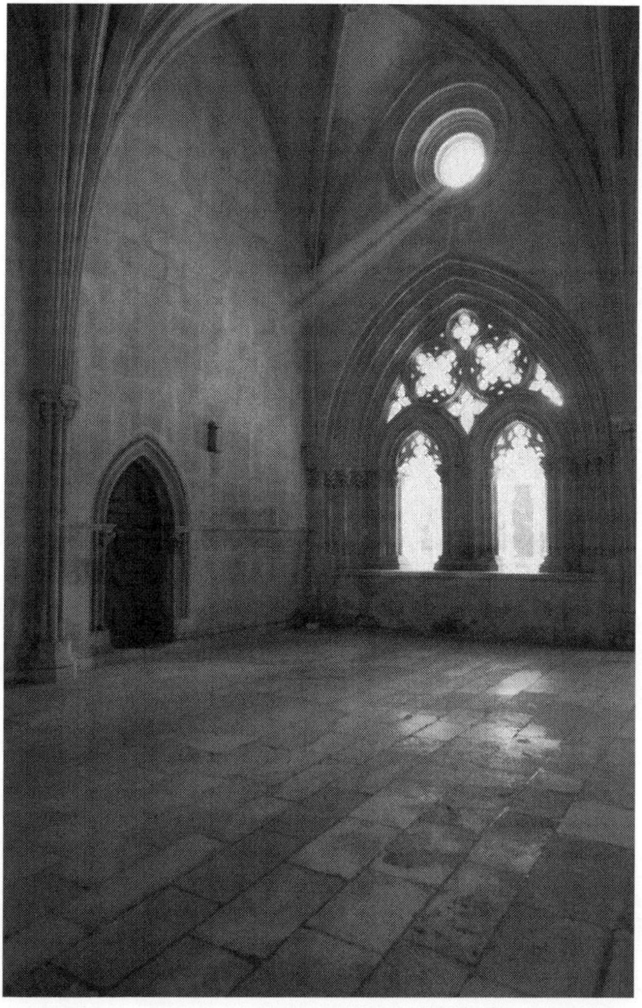

Peregrinatio est tacere.

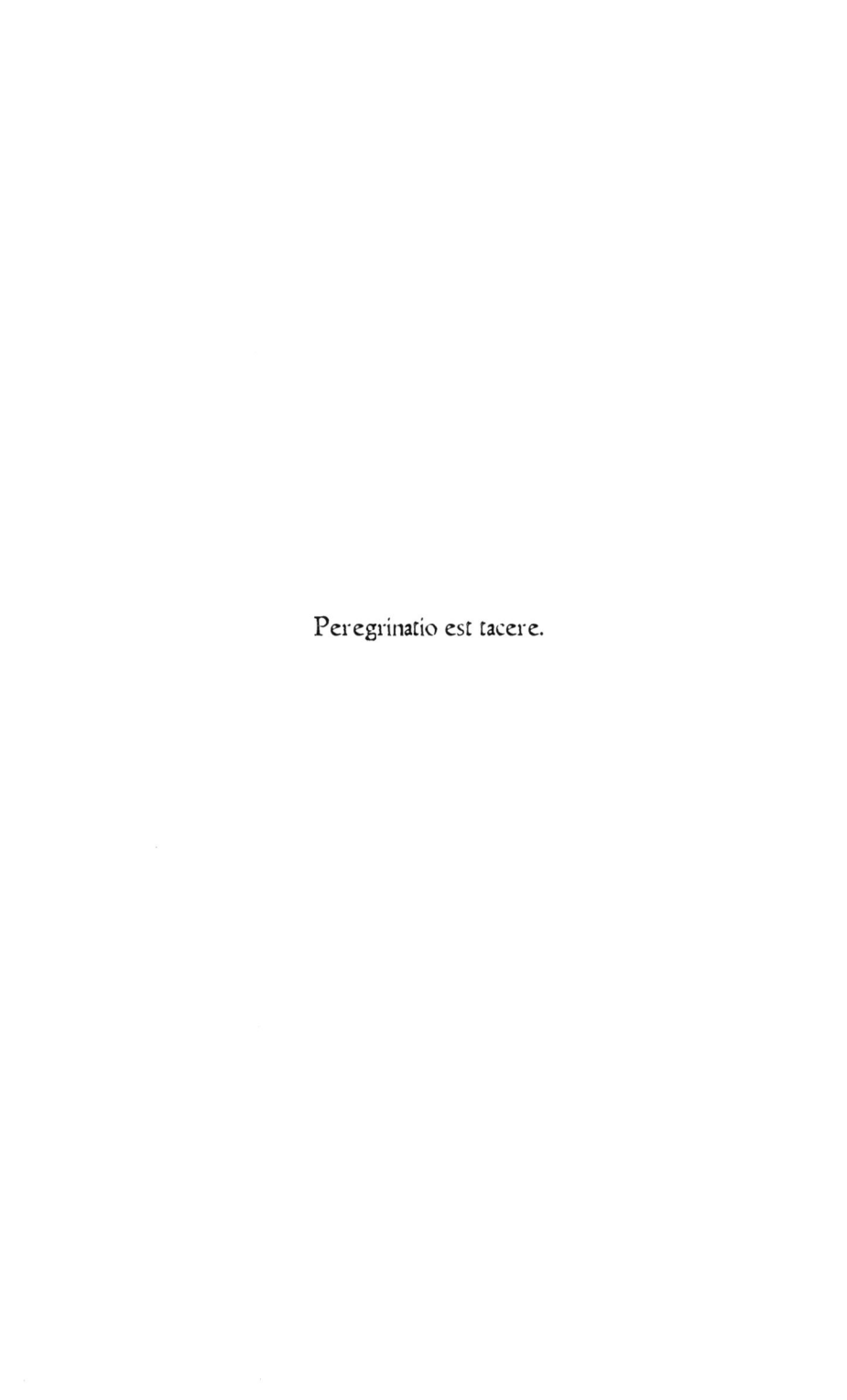

XVIII

Winter Haven

She had ridden in the back among the hay bales until the light faded and the town lay some distance behind them. A harvest moon shone from the far side of the trees on their left; its silver light fell across the road in blue stripes. Her back ached with stiffness when she climbed onto the bench seat, where she sat huddled beneath her cloak and hood for the remainder of the night's journey. Wolves howled in the distance but were not hungry enough this time of year to approach. Miriam was glad—she hadn't strength enough to stay alert, much less fend them off.

The dry night air gave place to a piercing cold just before dawn, when she found herself suddenly wide awake. The farmer had stopped at the trickle of a stream to wash the dust from his face and forearms. He said it was a river to ford when the mountain ice melted in the spring. She believed him—she had seen how watercourses could change. Even from here in the dim morning light, she could see her hills in the distance, where

Jacob's sheep would be re-growing their winter coats... She longed to be beyond those hills, after the winter was past.

She would have to wait.

A bright green sward rolled up to the enclosure of the abbey. The chanted *jubilate deo* filled stony recesses with the sweetness of women's prayer, spilling over the walls and stealing through the narrow gate. A few minutes more and her driver stepped down, leaving Miriam to sit in the cart while he spoke with the sister who kept the door. She glanced at Miriam and nodded, opening a rusty lock to let them inside.

Sister Giuliana, the abbess, had just emerged from the side-chapel, her clean, flowing habit giving her a rather angelic air.

"Why, Amiens, what brings you so far from home at such an early hour?"

"Come on business from Father Cyril, Abbess."

"An all-night journey? It must be urgent." The seasoned Giuliana eyed Miriam carefully. "You must be tired. Please come inside and sit down." They followed her measured step through the hushed cloister into a room with several ancient books and a few wooden benches. The farmer doffed his cap and handed her Cyril's letter, which she unfolded with care and read attentively, with a slight, endearing scowl. Miriam had no idea what it contained, but it seemed to inspire confidence and magnanimity. The eyes of the abbess met Miriam's with pity and softness.

"There's breakfast in the refectory, Amiens. You're welcome to it, as the sisters have already been dismissed."

"Thank you, Abbess, most kindly," he said, exiting.

"What is your name, child?" the abbess asked after the door closed behind Amiens.

"Miriam."

The sister of Moses, recalled the Abbess. *The mother of our Lord.*

"I am sorry for your many losses. May you find some comfort here from the Lord, under whose wings you have come to take refuge. You'll be here through the winter?"

"Yes, Abbess."

"I do not expect our guests to follow our rule. However, you should become familiar with our daily routine so as not to interfere with it. Cyril wrote about work; he said we should find you something indoors. Why is that?"

"I get cold easily."

"Well, he seems to think it important." She thought a moment, tapping the bench with long, graceful fingers. "The cook will be only too glad for some help. There's a small garret room over the kitchen. If you could be quite comfortable there, the guest quarters would remain free for other visitors. We do get snow sometimes, and there are people who go on pilgrimages, even in the winter," she added hastily in explanation, trying to be friendly. Miriam smiled patiently, suppressing a yawn. "Sister Martina will prepare your room, then, while you eat. Don't refuse—I know you need your strength. Then you can rest and get used to the place."

"I thank you, Abbess."

"Not at all. It's not my house, you know. I just live here. You're entirely welcome. And Miriam," she said, catching the gaze of the new lodger with the very Hebrew-sounding name, "my door is never locked."

The garret room was pleasant, cozy, and quiet. There was just one thing the abbess had failed to mention: Sister Martina, the older nun who stayed in the cell just below her, snored terribly. But Miriam soon got used to it and after a while, found it a comfort.

Two nuns sat weaving in the community workroom.

"She's running from something."

"What makes you say that, Sister Irina?"

"That haunted look in her eyes. And her cloak hood is always up."

"Is it kind to suspect her? She works so hard, and..."

"And is always at services, Sophia, or hadn't you noticed? She knows the office better than any novice here. She doesn't talk to anybody—maybe she's afraid of being caught."

"Caught?"

"I think she's a nun herself, trying to escape Holy Church. Maybe a heretic, or fleeing a charge of immorality." Sophia gasped, which only fueled Irina's fire. "Where would be the best place for someone like that to hide? In a convent, of course!"

"Sister, you do her an injustice. I..."

At that moment, Giuliana entered the room, and the two sisters resumed their work.

Sophia wore a deep blush on her round face; Irina's expression was taut.

"What's troubling you, my daughters?" There was no answer, but the pause was brief: it was of no use, trying to hide from the abbess.

"Oh, Mother, we were just wondering what brought our kitchen girl to us."

Sister Sophia looked up nervously at such a banal confession.

"God did, Irina."

"Is she doing a penance, Mother? She's so quiet."

"No. Her life is a penance right now." Guiliana sat down in patient understanding. "She doesn't need more than that, especially from you."

Sophia blanched. "Forgive us, Mother."

"She is in the best disposition for prayer, according to the blessed Augustine: desolate, forsaken, stripped of everything…"

"We didn't know, Mother."

"No. It was not your business. How glad our Lord must be when each of us—every one of us—gets to know herself and realizes her own poverty! Do not steal this precious gift from your little sister, my daughters."

Irina's hands lay quiet in her lap. "Is there any way we can comfort her, then?"

"Yes. Pray for her. Respect her. And do not press yourselves upon her. She doesn't need your consolation."

"How can you say that, Mother, when it is consolation she so sorely needs?"

"Because consolations do not always awaken us to God's love. And love is the only cure for all our sicknesses." She said this rising, then left softly. Warp and woof met in silence as the two sisters sat, each weaving threads of compassion into her heart's tapestry.

Miriam loved to slice onions. The hot stinging that overspilled her eyes reminded her that she was not unable to cry. She would try to think of something sad enough to keep the tears flowing, but they always stopped. That curse had put a cap on her well, bottling them all inside.

She stayed in the chapel nave one morning after Prime; Giuliana caught her nodding. A concerned sigh escaped her as she sat down.

"Miriam."

"Oh, Abbess, I'm so sorry."

"You sat up all night with Sister Martina. How is she?"

"Her fever's turned."

"Why didn't you come to one of us for help?"

"I would have had to leave the building."

"Miriam, there is no rule restricting you to your quarters."

"The snow was falling..." her voice faltered.

"You need to rest, child."

"I thought there would be rest for me here, Mother. But I can't find it."

"Stay still, then; let it find you. Remember what the psalmist said when he couldn't find any: 'My soul truly waiteth still upon God...'"

"'... for of him cometh my salvation.'"

"Yes. You have been through much, my daughter. Someday God will add all our trials to the great ones he himself has suffered and make something beautiful out of both. But, for the present time, these interior battles are harder to fight than any other, are they not?"

Miriam nodded. "Isn't there some penance I could do, then, to silence all the doubts?"

"No—you need God's guidance, not a penance."

"Where will I find it, Mother? He seems so very far away." Her eyes wandered to the rood above the chancel. "And yet I want to find him so badly."

"You would not be seeking him so hard, Miriam, if he wasn't already calling you to himself."

"Then why does he keep me in the dark?"

"He must have a reason. Perhaps... perhaps it's easier to rest, in the dark?"

"Yes," she answered, deciding to keep her dream to herself.

"Go to your room then. And sleep." Miriam unexpectedly reached for her hand to kiss it. The abbess was touched by the gesture, but as Miriam rose to leave, Giuliana wondered why her lips should be so cold.

The cook found her peeling potatoes.

"Didn't you notice that the wood box is empty? The bishop's coming today, and he'll expect something hot when he gets here. Don't gawk, girl—go get some wood!"

"Let me get my cloak and boots."

"There isn't time for that. It's only a bow-shot to the shed, across the paddock. If you hurry, you won't even notice the snow. Go on!"

Miriam swallowed and opened the door, sucking a whirl of snowflakes into the kitchen. Her heart beat fast as the door slammed to—she could hear the bolt sliding into the lock. The storm had been interspersed with sunlight, which got mixed up in the falling snowflakes. Covering her eyes with her hand against the glare, she propelled herself toward the gray outline of the woodshed, keeping the paddock fence on her left as a landmark. She moved stiffly across the powdery snow, feeling the path below through her thin shoes. The wind blew into her face, obscuring her vision. She clutched at the fence-rails hand over hand, and slipped onto the frozen step before the shed, trembling.

She could not feel the cold—she never had been able to. It was the numbness she dreaded. She couldn't feel her hands now, or her leather-clad feet. Her breath came and went with the snatches of wind. She fumbled at the latch, groping to fill her arms with dry logs and sticks. Hugging as many as she could carry, she let the door close itself behind her, set her sights for the corner door, and pitched forward into a cold cloud.

"What was that?" asked Irina, who had come to help the cook with the preparations. A crash outside the kitchen door had startled them out of conversation.

"Probably that fool of a kitchen girl Abbess give me. I sent her to fetch some wood—fire's burnin' down." Wiping her hands, the cook bustled to the back door and drew back the iron bolt. The wood lay strewn before the threshold, with Miriam fallen, prostrate and motionless, in a soft pool of whiteness.

"Sister! Come help." Together, they dragged the snow-sodden form over to the hearth, and the cook scolded on. "Look at her! She's gone and..."

"She's blue with cold and hardly breathes. Mother of God! Build up that fire. Where's a blanket? We've got to get her dry!" For the next few moments, the place bristled with activity. As the rough cloth of Miriam's dress fell upon the dusty flags of the kitchen floor, Irina caught sight of two jagged scars on the white skin. She covered the girl quickly with the thick wool cover, then she wrapped her arms around it and lay down close at Miriam's back, joining her own body's warmth to the fire's, straining to hear the labored breathing return. The cook appeared with a rough towel.

"No, don't rub," ordered Irina sharply. "Get a basin of warm water—not hot, you'll burn her." *So unlike a sister*, to order her around like this, the cook mused. Before she obeyed, however, the cook went to the bell and struck a call for help.

Giuliana had to push past a small group of postulants tugging a straw pallet toward the kitchen hearth. She stood aghast to see Irina lying on the flagstone floor with the kitchen girl.

"What happened?"

"I just sent her out for some wood, ma'am," the cook stated angrily. "We found her outside the door. Just a fainting spell; she'll soon warm up." She resumed her meal preparations and left the sisters to do their life-saving bit.

The abbess knelt beside Miriam's head, nodding in approval at Irina and praying in inaudible whispers. Together they watched pale color creep back into Miriam's ashen face. Giuliana put her slender hand on the girl's cool forehead.

"Mea culpa," she murmured, stroking back the damp hair.

The birds were back. Sister Martina found her charge feeding them from her hand in the courtyard. She looked softer now that her hair had grown out some.

"The sisters have tried preaching to them, Miriam, but they can't get as close as you do." Martina held an odd respect for her, ever since she'd heard the girl groaning in the darkest hours of the night.

"Maybe that's because I let them preach to me," answered Miriam, rising and dusting her hand off on her skirts. "Besides, I don't have anything I could say to them."

"I think you say plenty, just by listening. You listen so attentively, not just at services, but to the wind, even. Oh, I came to tell you that the abbess is ready to see you now." Miriam nodded, biting her lip and looking down. "Come." The older nun picked up the girl's cast-off cloak—the day was sleepily warm—and led the way to the small reception room. She stayed, sensing that Miriam needed some support.

"Here she is, Mother."

"Come in, my daughter. You have been happy lately. Why so quiet on such a beautiful day?"

"Because I'm leaving, Abbess."

"Oh, Miriam. You fit so well here. The cloistered life suits you."

"But it's too easy... You've told us to always strive after what is the more difficult, the more unpleasant, the things which mean harder work. Leaving you is the hardest path for me, Mother. Besides, I'm not called."

Giuliana had been looking out the window, but at these words her head turned eagle-quick. "You *are* called, Miriam. It's obvious. But maybe not to stay here."

"I'll go north... to find my kin."

"Alone?"

"I'm not alone, Abbess."

Every sensible argument against this flew in the face of the faith Giuliana had given her life to, to set aflame in herself and the others in her care. She recalled that she had no authority over Miriam's life. Neither God nor Miriam had given it to her.

"Then I will pray God to shelter you in your travels."

"I shall not forget your kindness to me." Some calm resolve had seeped into Miriam's will these past few months. She didn't even know where it had come from. She had grown aware of a tiny flicker of fire burning deep in the recesses of herself, and that she must follow it. She had no inkling whatsoever that the flame worked also in Giuliana's soul; they were two sisters unknown to one another. The abbess took Miriam's cold hand in her own.

"I will also pray for God to warm you through the chill nights." In spite of all the noble thoughts, Guiliana was afraid for her.

"Thank you, Mother," she said, smiling at Giuliana and Martina and reaching for her cloak. Martina helped settle it over her shoulders.

A hush fell over the abbey as Miriam stepped through the gate, fixing her sight on the northern horizon. Wimple-framed faces peered out of casements and through latticework to watch her go. Perpetually shielded from the base tales told in the outside world, none of them had ever heard of the Ice Princess.

It is safe to tell the pure in heart that they shall see God,
for only the pure in heart want to.

– C. S. Lewis

XIX

Flint

She was alone again. No, not alone. But under the broad sky with only a footpath stretching before her, she had never felt so alone. It was a spring rather than a winter restlessness she felt. Everywhere she turned, the ache was there, always with her, that bittersweet longing. Under the smooth surface of the river-lake which was her soul, a surging current pulled and flowed—she must go north.

It was nearing evening. She had wandered right through the day, not even stopping for food—she hadn't been hungry—and she was tired. She should find a place to sleep before dusk gave way to night; the moon would be almost full, but it would rise late. Up over a little knoll, she found a glade of blossoming dogwoods encircling a small patch of soft grass dotted with crocuses and asters. The wind blew warm, a foretaste of the coming summer. She wouldn't need a fire tonight; her cloak would be cover enough.

Lightning flashed in the distance, so far away that she didn't hear its thunder. Overhead, pinpoints of starlight peeked through heavy mottled heaps of layered cloud. Chirping crickets and the rustling of young leaves lulled her to the verdant bed. Before she settled down, she scanned the perimeter of the valley for a faint candle glow coming from a cottage or hut that might be nestled somewhere among the larger trees, but her search was in vain.

"'My help cometh even from the Lord, who hath made heaven and earth. He will not suffer thy foot to be moved; and he who keepeth thee will not sleep... The Lord himself is thy keeper; the Lord is thy defence upon thy right hand, so that the sun shall not burn thee by day, neither the moon by night. The Lord shall preserve thee from all evil: yea, it is even he that shall keep thy soul. The Lord shall preserve thy going out, and thy coming in, from this time forth forevermore. Glory be to the Father...'" The words of the psalm sounded hollow in this lonely, open place. As the graying shadows blended with the growing darkness all around her, she found herself adding, "And I beg your protection, please, on this long walk home. Amen."

Her eyes closed as she pulled her cloak over her head. When the moon rose, bright and orbed with a ring of mist, she was asleep.

* * *

He was itching to get among the tall trees that covered the hills in the far distance like short, soft fur. The blacksmith had helped him make some fine tools, but the guildsmen were more interested in wrestling power from the nobility than in building quality furniture. Then the plague had overrun the town... He looked up sharply from his reverie—it was a beautiful morning. He would take his leave before sunrise, skipping the awkward good-byes with people who had never made more than a crack of room in their lives for a stranger like him.

He left a hand-carved stag on the table in the rented loft room as a thank-you to the preoccupied landlady, shouldered his bag, and softly closed the latch behind him. It took some concentration climbing down in the dim light, to keep his pack from banging against the steep stairs or the wall, but he managed it. Then he slipped out of the village and away, breathing more freely and full of excitement at the wide stretch of world that lay between him and the fragrant timber at the end of his journey.

The sun rose on his right, and clouds floated overhead like wooly sheep as he entered a wide meadow. A clump of trees rose up ahead; he could see white stones among them. A good place for breakfast, he thought.

He was just mounting the little knoll, looking for a good spot to set down his bag, when his feet became entangled in something. Knocked off balance, he lurched forward, his hands spread in front of him to break his tumble on a soft patch of grass. He looked back, puzzled, to find the cause of his fall. It was a woman.

She sat up, blinking. Several strands of dusty hair had wandered from her short plait and now framed her sleepy face in drifting wisps; she brushed them back with her fingers to no avail. A worn cloak lay rumpled in her lap. Her eyes widened when at last she saw him, sitting there staring.

"I'm sorry, my lady," he stammered, remembering to be polite, and rising to his feet. "I didn't see you." She nodded—graciously, he thought—and averted her eyes. She had no companion, and he wondered if he had used the correct title in addressing her. It appeared that she needed some time to awaken, so he bent down to pick up the scattered contents of his pack, pausing only to rewrap the twine around the chamois covering his favorite mallet. Then he picked the burrs from his wool breeches. While his hands were thus occupied, he absent-mindedly noted her features, small for the wide face with its troubled eyes. The strong curve of cheek and jaw somehow reminded him of the grains in mahogany. It was a face more sad than noble, faraway but far from empty. Becalmed.

She had noticed his limp.

"I hope, sir, I have not caused you any hurt." Strange, she thought, to reply in such a formal tone. But she had been so addressed, and perhaps it was wise to answer in kind. It may also have been Giuliana's perpetual insistence on good manners.

"Hurt? No, that's old." What was a woman doing out here all alone? He was about to ask—the silence was turning into an awkward impasse—when he noticed the length of her hair. "What are you doing outside the cloister?"

"How would you know I came from there?"

"Your hair's not the usual length..." *for virgins, anyway,* he finished to himself. Women set apart cut theirs, and young women unspoiled left theirs long. Didn't they?

He certainly had an eye for detail. She laughed and then drew her knees up to her chin, her arms crossed in front, her cloak covering her legs, to answer. "I don't like to wear it long." He looked puzzled. "I left the abbey only yesterday," she continued to explain. "I was wintering there after... after the plague took my family."

A widow. That explained her mourning dress. He should offer condolences. "I'm sorry. It's been everywhere." It was true, but he saw that it brought no comfort. "You must miss him."

"Who?"

"Your husband."

"I've never been married."

"Oh, pardon me." Well nigh twenty, and still unmarried. It was very strange. "Do you mind if I have some breakfast?"

"No." She made ready to leave. Early sun shone on dew as the morning shadows shortened: it would be getting warm soon.

"Where's yours?"

"My what?"

"Breakfast."

"I haven't any."

"Well, then, have some of mine." He offered her a fresh apple, and her hunger sparked at the sight of it. She accepted it gingerly, savoring the juice when she bit into it—the crisp tartness helped her wake up a bit more. She tilted her head and ventured an observation.

"You're a tradesman?"

"Carpenter—journeyman. It'll be ages before I'm a master. Have to settle down first."

"Where?" She nursed a strange little hope.

"I'm heading north."

"So am I."

"Alone?" She didn't answer. He squatted down to be at her level but kept his distance. After all, she might be mad. "Look, my lady..."

"Miriam."

"Lady Miriam. I'm not a swift traveler, but... How far are you bound, anyway?"

"The mountains, at least." He was very entertaining, she thought.

"You'd be safer in a man's company."

She blushed and swallowed another bite of apple, afraid of hidden motives. But she soon came to see that he was right—

and decent. Though how safe she would be, she didn't know. He was no monk. But hadn't she prayed for an escort, practically, the night before?

"Yes, I suppose so," she finally answered. He was shaking his water-skin and distractedly looking around. "There's a spring just over that rise."

"Oh, good," he said in thanks, and set off in the direction she pointed.

While he was gone, she re-plaited her hair, covering it with a muslin kerchief. The only companions she'd ever had outside the shelter of a house were Gerda, Jacob, the dog, and the sheep. Everyone else had stayed away. She wondered, wistfully, how it would be.

He followed her lead so as to let her set the pace. His first impressions were making room for others: her slight but sturdy frame, the way she cocked her head to listen to the weather, the fairly broad shoulders—she looked less and less frail to him as her stamina showed itself. When the path climbed up a hill, she rarely slowed down.

They stopped to rest at a shaded brook amid some laurels. The bubbling of the stream and the endless dripping of ferns blended with bird song. He answered it with a whistle, then he bent over the water to splash some on his sun-stained face and neck. *How carefree he is*, she thought. *How simple*! How she envied him.

"Where's your home?" she asked.

"Used to be down in olive country. I moved further north to be apprenticed to my uncle. Got to like the mountain timbers, so I thought I'd look for a new home there."

"You didn't want to stay with him. Why?"

He found it unsettling, the way she looked past the surface. His eyes darkened, but not much.

"His son needed the family business. And I didn't want to be the competition." He picked up some stones and tossed them into the water. "I'd like to find an open glade halfway up a mountain, with big trees and rushing water..." his voice drifted off for several seconds.

"Sounds nice."

"I'd build a waterwheel and some sort of sawmill, maybe set up a water-powered lathe..." His practiced hands were already planning how to get the gears carved and fitted.

He went on for a moment longer, but she didn't hear the rest. She was too busy watching his hands dream.

The day rolled on as they walked, engaged in little conversation. He would stop now and again to shift his pack to the other shoulder and kick his leg out in front of him as if it were stuck. His short, brawny arms showed his age rather than his youthful face. On second glance, she noted that his beard was thick—though neatly trimmed. He was older than she, but it was well-hid beneath leather jerkin and a workman's loose sleeves.

The sun was sinking behind a low hill when they came to what looked to be a popular inn. Firelight and raucous laughter poured out into the darkening lane. The moment Michael crossed the threshold, he felt out of place with his modest new companion. While he took in all the activity, she was glancing about nervously and drew her cloak more closely about her frame.

"Ho, sirrah! A guest! Bring a brew then, for him and the lady," the innkeeper called above the heads of the seated crowd. They sat at a corner bench, and Michael stared at the mud on his boots wondering what to do. This role was new to him. A sallow-faced, bristly-cheeked man eyed them from a nearby stool. The moment Miriam lifted her head to look around, he winked at her with a ravenous eye—in spite of her cloak.

"Trade you me 'orse for a night with that there wench o' yers, mate." The sallow man said it loudly, drawing attention from the whole room. Michael flared inwardly, but he leaned forward, placing his elbow over his knee.

"Wouldn't trade her for a hundred purebreds, *mate*. 'Sides," he added, leaning back, "we just come for a bit o' supper. Got better lodging up a ways."

"Where?" the innkeeper guffawed, appearing with a pair of brimming mugs. "This is the last inn for miles, man." The whole room seemed to still, waiting for a reply.

"At a friend's," answered Michael, standing now with one foot upon the bench. He jutted out his chin, visibly curling his strong hand to look at his nails. "He's expecting us." The answer seemed to satisfy the onlookers, so he sat again as two pewter mugs of frothing ale were set noisily on the rough table; a trencher of soggy potatoes and venison was brought soon after.

The evening's noise resumed while the innkeeper sidled up to comfort his rejected customer, steering him to other female possibilities in the stuffy room. "Leave off 'em, Jack. We got better entertainments for you right over here..." He guided the embittered fellow toward the blazing hearth, calling back over his shoulder, "Better get an early start, sirrah. There'll be wolves out tonight."

"There seem to be a few in here as well," said Michael coolly. He pocketed some bread, and sopped up the thin gravy with another dry hunk. He looked for a consenting nod from Miriam. She gave it gladly, deciding that one sip of the ale was as much as she could stomach anyway. Michael tossed a coin to the innkeeper on their way out. In a moment, they were once again in the cooling air, walking briskly northeast.

"I'd like to thank you, sir, but I've yet to learn your name."

He stopped in his tracks. "Bless me, what a fool I am, pretending to be a gentleman. I'm sorry, lady, but it's Michael Carver, and happy to be of some small service." He bowed his head sheepishly. She smiled politely, but she looked troubled, her suspicions rising.

"You lied to them."

"About lodging? What, did you want to stay there?"

"What friend did you mean, Master Carver?" she asked, ignoring his tone.

"Look, my lady, I'm no priest, but I don't have to read Holy Writ to consider God my friend. And he's never let me down yet." She was silenced; a mile passed, and one by one the stars came out of hiding above them.

Imagine. Having God as a friend.

"I'll build a fire, over there." Michael began picking up kindling and sticks as he headed off the road up a slight incline; they had seen a small plateau silhouetted in that direction as twilight crept along the horizon. Miriam followed, and when they reached a tiny clearing, she gathered up a small pile of sharp stones.

"What are those for?" he asked, groping for his tinderbox.

"Wolves."

She hugged her knees with her arms and sat staring into the dancing flames.

"Two fires," she said dreamily.

"My lady?" Her gaze was fixed and faraway, straying among the coals.

"I'm always warming up at someone else's fire. No one comes to mine. Maybe it burns and blackens. Maybe I haven't one at all—only ashes." She was talking in mysteries. Well, what did he expect? She was practically a nun.

He built up the fire and said he'd take the first watch, alert as he was with the talk of wolves ringing in his ears. He even thought he heard howling in the distance. She seemed totally unconcerned and nestled in the bracken as if she slept outdoors every night. He heard her murmuring something in Latin before she settled, her back to him, into a still sleep.

A nearby rustling jolted him awake. The fire was still high; he must have dozed for a mere few seconds. Miriam was sitting bolt upright, straining to hear and squinting into the surrounding blackness. Suddenly she cried a sharp, "Yah!!" At the same instant, something whizzed past him. She was kneeling now with her head tilted, listening, and another rock waiting in her hand. A twig snapped behind her and she whirled, hurling the missile at fire-reflected eyes. There was a dog-like yelp and scrambling, then quiet closed in upon them. The fire crackled an "all safe" while Michael's heart pounded in his head.

He looked at the slight woman kneeling there, his mouth open, his early impressions of weakness shattered by what he had just seen. He shook his dazed head in dismay—she was a fell warrior!

"I'll watch now," she said, rising. He obeyed obligingly and traded places. With an arm and aim like that, she must have been a shepherdess, a position in life for which he had no respect—until now. It seemed she had something to offer him after all.

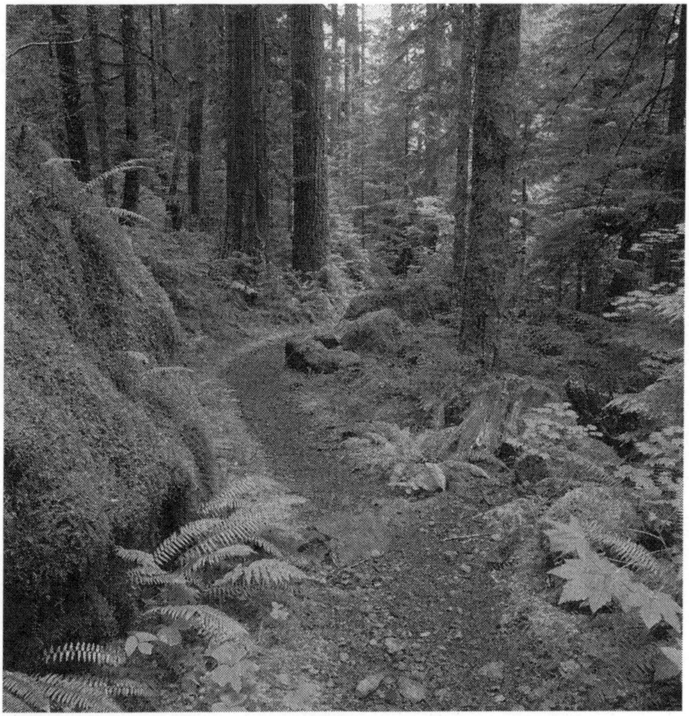

"By Jesus," cried a prostitute. "I will go with you, Piers. You can say that I am your sister!" She looked round, and she saw that she and Piers were alone.

– William Langland, 14th century

XX

Pilgrim Pas de Deux

The mist turned to drizzle as the pair ascended northward. Soon there was nothing to do but seek out a thicket under which to wait out the passing rain. Miriam explained that these summer storms were always short, but that brought little comfort to them when lightning flashed directly overhead. The thunder-crack fell like a giant axe stroke.

Soon after, sheltering in a wooded vale, they huddled back to back beneath a twisted willow, her thick hunting cloak held above their heads to deflect the fat drops that slipped through the tree's green fingers. Miriam studied the patterns of pebble and grass around her, holding her arm around her knees and soaking in the warmth at her back—afraid to even wonder what he felt at his. This new companion, this 'escort' of hers, would probably be more comfortable at a family feast—perhaps turning the spit, joking with the cooks.

The rain lightened some. Its sound gave way to a steady dripping all around.

"Why haven't you married?" His words came out of nowhere, with no particular tone of passion, only a driving curiosity. He wouldn't even wait for an answer before shooting out his guess: "Did your suitors die in the plague too?"

"I had no suitors."

"Why not?" Well, she wasn't the most eye-catching of women, but she wasn't quite plain, in spite of her dress: of an average height, neither buxom nor scrawny, neither thick-boned nor delicate. Well-proportioned, he decided. What must frighten people was her face, the way she wore her soul on it.

"They stayed away. I looked... acted... different. There were rumors."

"Oh." He stifled an urge to continue, *Is there something wrong with you?* He had wondered himself how he could be alone with so young a woman and feel no inclination to have her. But she was weary of his probing.

"What about yourself, Master Carver?" It surprised her to be so forthright, so forward.

"Nobody good enough. I always thought I'd marry a princess."

"Really."

"It happens all the time, in stories." His voice took on a narrating tone: "'Woodcutter's youngest son defies all odds and wins heart of king's daughter.' How's that?"

She laughed, lightly. "Not all stories have happy endings."

"Mine do." Incredible as his optimism was—it would have been arrogant if he weren't so ridiculously naïve—she ached for a morsel of it, and sighed.

"Your leg doesn't bother you?" she asked, changing the subject again.

Pilgrim Pas de Deux

He didn't see any connection, but it didn't matter. It was her turn to ask questions.

"Not very often. Slows me down some, but I can still work."

"What happened to it?"

"A battle. No, nothing so gallant. A siege tower fell over on top of me."

The rain had stopped altogether, but neither of them had noticed when. Michael rose to his feet, kicked his leg out in front of him, and continued in a lofty, put-on voice, "There are always thorns on the way to the palace." He bowed slightly, smiled boyishly, and offered his firm hand to help her up. His eyes widened at her touch.

"My God, your hand is cold."

The air rose shimmering from the grain while the rhythm of scythe and song paced the harvesters in their gathering and tying of the sheaves. Michael was laughing loudly as he worked, his sun-dusted face blooming beneath his beard. *He is so at ease with everyone,* thought Miriam, who worked a stone's throw away. The heat had made her slow, her cloak long ago cast aside and tucked away in his bag. She straightened up and looked across the furrows; the glaring light cut sharp, short shadows beneath the peasants—dark, misshapen imps playing about their feet. The smell of sweat mingled with those of earth and ripened wheat, acrid and warm.

She rolled up her sleeves to resume her gleaning. How pale her forearms were against the tawny field! A minute later, she was conscious of someone watching her. Michael stood a few yards away staring at her, and she smiled a greeting at him. Then she saw the silent horror in his eyes and lowered her own, turning her back toward him and quickly covering her arm. He had seen: what would he think of her now?

Wordlessly he picked up her meager bundle to carry it to the threshers. She followed at a distance, miserable and afraid.

That night they slept with the reapers encircling a wide fire, the stars and fire-sparks woven in a dark fabric above them with the sliver of a new moon. Michael tossed fitfully before opening his eyes to a barrage of prying thoughts. How had she come by such a brutal scar? And the shame with which she'd covered it—as if it were a brand, marking her. His stomach turned at the possibilities; some of them would account for her odd behavior. He told himself it was a holy wound, and though he longed to know what had made it, he would not ask her. He would not consciously add to her pain.

He sat up to watch the orange light flicker on the face of his sleeping companion, who lay opposite him on the other side of the fire circle. It was late; he alone was awake, sandwiched between deep breaths and grunting snores and therefore free to think.

She was too refined to be a peasant; there was a sort of gentility about her, deeper than her aloofness. Then he caught himself: she camped so easily... her shame about that scar... her callused hands—there was nothing ladylike about them. Her hands reminded him of well-worn leather gloves, but there was something about the way she held them...

His imagination drifted to a slim-fingered, willowy princess gliding across a landscaped terrace. Try as he might, he couldn't picture himself at such a lady's side, limping and bumbling along. He didn't exactly stand head and shoulders above his brethren, nor was he a fitting match for a well-dressed, tall, and gracious gentlewoman. And to ask a king—even a nobleman—for the hand of his daughter, well! That was beyond him, surely. Why, he was little better than a beggar! He laughed inwardly at himself and his fanciful notions, then he reminisced about Mistress Crafter and the sparkle in Robert's eye when he watched her knead bread. Then he took another long look at the form on the other side of the fire.

Perhaps she was a princess in disguise.

The morning dawned clear and cool. The reapers stirred as flies began to buzz around them, and several straggled off for a wash before Mass. Miriam followed other women to the farmer's well. A brown-eyed girl of eight scrutinized her dress, taking special notice of the hunting cloak and thick boots. She disappeared within the farmer's half-timbered house, only to emerge again with a steaming pitcher. Miriam softened as the girl offered it to her. Time bent backwards, to the sheepfolds on Sunday mornings, snug and secure while she dressed in the chill before the church bell tolled its summons... the steam rising from Chantal's laundry...

She smiled down at the girl and up at the mother who stood framed in the doorway, and then she reached gently to accept the gift. The water bathed her dusty head in a cataract of warmth—and gratitude.

Michael's tunic was still damp when he crawled into it to obey the relentless call of the lofty church. It was nice to be clean, though, and the day was warm. He would be dry before he reached the gothic portal. He shouldered his satchel and joined the ambling herd of people, keeping a sharp eye out for Miriam. She had not yet appeared by the time he was jostled through the door, so he settled himself onto a bench and tried to quiet his insides—being in a church sometimes made him a little nervous.

Although the responses were ingrained on his speech from years of repetition, his Latin was scant. The readings and the homily sent his mind wandering among the colored window glass, mentally measuring the circumference of a pillar or calculating the curve of an arch; now admiring the architecture, now studying the carved lectern, occasionally stealing a glance at his fellow worshippers murmuring and bowing in a reverent awe.

Sometimes a phrase would catch his ear and occupy his mind for days. "He descended into hell"—now that was a good one, and he wondered what manner of people the Lord had actually met there, what he said or did during that time. His was a wandering mind, free of speculative clutter. Michael's faith was grounded on simple, everyday things, and for him they were back-lit with an eternal smile. Pain was a passing thing. Tomorrow was ever bordered with a golden hem. Whenever he found himself troubled by life's ironies, he would pick up his tools and go contentedly back to work.

But today he fidgeted, unable to focus on the Mass. He'd lost his place twice before giving in to just be himself with his friend, Holy God. He discreetly reached into his bag to carefully unwrap his tinderbox from his mantle and quietly extract it. During the Sanctus he turned it over in his hands, noting the way the polished wood grains absorbed and reflected the hushed light. Three years it had sat in the woods, an ugly stump defying attention. Then Robert Crafter took pity on it and brought forth a work of art.

The drama up front continued: the host was elevated for all to see.

So many times he felt unprepared. But today he hungered for it, for something that holy, and regretted that he didn't come more often. He slipped the tinderbox back into its cushion, closed his satchel, and rose to limp forward. His eyes fell on the long shadows cast on the uneven floor; the sun had sliced shafts of light between the pillars, reminding him of prison bars, but the chancel was inviting, more spacious. Soon, he'd turned back, the taste of unleavened bread in his mouth, to find his place.

He sidestepped his way to where his bag was tucked under the bench, but before he sat down, he caught sight of her at the back, almost indistinguishable from the other poor folk. For one fleeting second he saw the Blessed Virgin herself—he had always imagined her in blue and white, holding a lily—superimposed upon this very ordinary woman who stood with covered head and steady gaze on deep or distant things he would never be able to see. Mary of Nazareth... a simple carpenter's wife.

A few minutes more and the Mass was ended, but still the journeyman lingered, head bowed, thinking of all the fallen, neglected stumps awaiting the notice of a master carver, thanking God for the one he'd stumbled over in his own path.

She'd left the church before him. He looked for her down the brown track ahead to find her in that tell-tale cloak. Her hair hung free for once below her kerchief, and the morning sun had got mixed up in it, glinting auburn and burnished copper lights from below its plain surface. Like the wood of his tinderbox.

It would only take a tiny puff of wind now, he thought, *to blow this spark into flame.*

It is not a refreshing and peaceful fire,
but a consuming and searching one
that makes the soul faint away and grieve at the sight of Self.

– Saint John of the Cross

XXI

Torchlight

She dreamed again. The dark cavern stretched before her—a hungry void waiting to fill her, or be filled by her. The earlier scene had played over and over against the borders of her mind. It was as if she were reading a story in a book when the pages swallowed her whole, the story now hers to live out, unknowing, at the mercy of some distant author spilling words from his pen. And she could never turn the pages ahead to read the ending; she couldn't untangle the images enough to make any sense of them upon waking.

It all happened, all over again. The marauders terrorized the mountain village while she cordoned off the sheep in the hidden canyon, to stealthily make her way toward the small stone keep, where the sentry kept watch in tired, late-afternoon light. There was the twisting turn to see her pursuer; the angry stab of the bolt as it pierced her shoulder; the stumbling, breathless race over rock-strewn grass; the words with the aging guard about the need to warn the palace more than a thousand feet below, on the other side of the mountain. There was the hasty pulling-to of the suspended cage, the last sickening farewell and wordless plea from the eyes of the soldier with Jacob's face, the cold metal closing of the gate, and the moving into inky blackness within the recesses of the ancient mountain, with no hope of moon or stars to light the way.

This night, though, the dream went on, terrifyingly sharp. The still, dark inner-mountain air rushed by, taking her shallow breaths with it. The fear was strangely mixed with relief that she had eluded the marauders; then a spreading sense of shame. She was a coward, leaving her people behind to be ravished and slaughtered—she should perish with them. The daring escape was prompted by selfish thoughts for her own safety.

The cage squeaked around a curve, and its speed grew greater and greater while the air grew thicker and the darkness smothered her. She so wanted to lose consciousness, but she couldn't—she wouldn't, not until she had come to the end of this journey with her message intact, or else the cage crushed into twisted metal bands upon a hidden rock wall in the mountain's hollow vein.

Time fell hammer-like, in seconds or years, before the speed slowed and the cage sped around another corner, knocking her against the bars. Light shone ahead, gray and dim, framed by the jagged outline of the lower cave mouth. The pain in her wounded shoulder covered everything in a pounding mist; with her other hand, she clutched at the bars in front of her, straining to look ahead.

Suddenly, and yet in a dreamy slowness of pulling away, a fir forest blanketed the foot of the mountain below her. The cage had emerged into late daylight and slid calmly down the slope to its bay in the palace kitchen. The dream-Miriam forced her eyes closed as the metal box halted abrasively, with a loud clang which told the kitchen staff that something had arrived from the mountaintop—usually the not-yet-butchered meat for a coming feast. She groped for the gate latch and fell against it, the metal door opening to spill out its passenger onto the scullery floor.

She steadied herself for a moment, holding tightly to the swaying cage, then with a determined will thrust herself forward toward the open door which led to the courtyard.

The scullery maid, coming to see what had been sent down, froze with horror-filled eyes at the disheveled figure plummeting toward her. The maid spun and flew, screaming, out into open air while Miriam stumbled after, trying to get the message to someone—anyone—who would hear it.

There was a group of men clumped ahead, and their heads all turned, following the screams as the kitchen girl rushed past them. Miriam's footing gave way, and powerful hands gripped her, breaking her fall and ending her journey. Even in her dream, her own voice sounded a faint echo; she had to strain to catch her own whispered words.

"Danger... coming siege. Cavalry, more foot soldiers... coming down the pass. Defend queen... hurry." It was all she could manage between broken breaths, and it came out fitfully. During this halting proclamation, her dream-sight pulled back: she surveyed the scene from a different, outside vantage point. She lay on the pavement, surrounded by soldiers of the queen's guard. The sovereign herself approached from some near distance, a puzzled look of worry on her face. A man-at-arms escort preceded her, pushing through the circle to the fallen messenger. Words collided in midair.

"What did she say, sir?"

"I couldn't catch it, Captain," answered a tall guard in the cluster. "Something about a siege. She just appeared from nowhere—apparently rode down the mountain chute in the kitchen cage!" He straightened, bemused. "She's drunk."

Miriam moaned aloud. Michael awoke, climbed the hayloft ladder, and lit a candle. He watched her sleeping face contort as her dream went on mercilessly. Her lips quivered; he tried to make out words but couldn't. He slowly reached for her cold hand and held it quietly, not knowing what else to do. Outside, a nightingale sang.

The dreamer listened to another voice, relieved to find a hearer.
"No. She's hurt." She watched the queen's man-at-arms bend searching over the crumpled form that was her, supporting her against his kneeling torso. The others drew back, aghast at the uncovered sight of the silk-red wound. The sound of voices dimmed, and the pages of the dream-book closed fast around her once again. Now she was lying on the knobby cobblestones, supported by someone while others strategized siege defense. She could vaguely make out the queen's low voice among them, ordering the physician to be summoned and the messenger to be borne straightaway to a guest chamber. Effort failed, and she felt herself being lifted up as the dream slipped away, leaving Miriam to sleep through the dim, early morning hours in a blissfully comfortable hay-bed, with Michael keeping a wondering vigil close by.

The sun had not yet risen, but was about to, when she woke to the rhythmic falling of an axe. Pulling her cloak about her shoulders against the dew-damp air, Miriam pushed open the shutters of the little hayloft. She could just see her escort chopping a thick stump of wood into kitchen fuel. His breath blended with the mist to soften the contours of his arms. When the sunlight reached him a moment later, she thought of a dwarf at his forge, pounding glowing metal into some useful shape. His torso glistened with the sweat of work; she marveled that he could be so warm on such a morning. The chips flew up like new-fallen snow, and the logs tumbled out neatly split and oven-sized.

So this was how he paid for their lodgings. He wasn't at all impressive on first sight, this southern journeyman, but here in the waking stretch of a new day, she found herself smiling in the shelter he provided. She liked him very much indeed.

Seeking is as good as seeing,
all the while God allows the soul to suffer.

– Julian of Norwich

XXII

Exposed

They descended a little hill to where a harvest festival glowed bright with color and noise. Banners fluttered, silks billowed, and cloth spilled out of looms with the brilliance of polished jewels. Eyes feasted on woven emeralds, embroidered sapphires, spun topazes, dyed amethysts; ruby cherries sparkled on linen-covered tabletops, persimmons glowed like fiery sunsets, and lemons glittered gold. And intermingling with all these sights was the music of marketplace sounds: friendly sales banter and friends from time-out-of-mind exchanging news, laughter twinkling like moving glints of sunlight on water.

Michael went off in search of refreshment, but Miriam was drawn to the shade of a spreading chestnut, where others were gathering to rest or sample the ripe fruit. Hidden from view, a musician played some string instrument near the tree's sturdy trunk; a fife picked up his air and juggled it into a merry gigue. A few happy feet began to dance on the trodden grass. At the tune's end, the fife was tucked away while the lute player—she could see him now—began to sing a love ballad which set the eyes of the young ablaze and the old to dreaming. A little girl tugged at her brother's sleeve in front of the crowded circle, and the very instant the song was ended, without granting so much as a well-earned breath to the singer, the boy cried out in a nervous voice, "Tell us the story of the Ice Princess!"

A murmur of agreement rippled through the audience and stilled to a hush, like a breeze flowing through a field of wheat and leaving it to sway expectantly in summer air. The minstrel looked up suddenly, his bright eyes dancing. He took in the crowd and answered the boy in feigned surprise.

"But you heard it only yesterday."

"We want to hear it again!" the little girl explained, her luminous eyes rapt and pleading. Nonchalant, the troubadour shrugged, positioned himself in practiced storytelling stance, cleared his throat, and began.

"Some long years ago, when you were either fair-haired instead of gray, or children instead of grown-ups, or not yet born at all, in a tiny kingdom on the other side of those high northern mountains," and here he gestured with a theatrical sweep of his lithe hand, "a king rode in search of a gift for his beautiful queen, who would soon bear him a child. As he cantered through a thick forest, he by chance met an old, poor woman, her hand outstretched for alms.

"'Please, sir,' she beckoned, 'a penny for bread.' But the king pretended not to hear, so taken up was he with thoughts of the future—and having no acquaintance with hunger, he passed her by. When the hag knew him for her lord and sovereign, she cursed him by all that is precious in an icy voice:

"'For your coldness, Sire, may you freeze in hell, while all around you are burning!'

"He laughed and rode on. But the cold breath of evil fell upon him from that day forward. The crops blighted under an early frost, and the gracious queen took to her bed with a chill. When the child—a girl—was born, she came forth not in the warmth of a woman's womb, but..." The minstrel leaned forward, lowering his voice just enough to woo his hearers toward a mystery. "...Covered all in ice. The fire on the hearth died to embers in an instant, flickering up again only after quick and careful tending. And the same was true for the princess: she was wrapped in the warmest wool straightaway, while warming-bottles were got for her silken nursery bed. The queen, her mother, lingered shivering for a fortnight more, and then she slipped silently through the fingers of night from this world to a better one, leaving behind an embittered husband and a baby whose little hands and feet would never warm.

"The king could not bear the sight of his child. He turned himself to his country's affairs with a vengeance and ignored her. He even contrived to have her vanish from his castle, his kingdom, and his life, so much stabbing pain did the very presence of the infant princess bring to his grieving heart."

Here the bard paused, his brow knit, his fingers moving to invisible music as he raised them to his pale lips in ponderous thought. Then he resumed, as suddenly as a drop of water falls from a melting icicle.

"But deep, deep within his hardened heart, there was more pity and affection for his child than ever he would admit. Of course, the king reasoned, his child would be gone for only a little while, until he discovered how to undo the curse of the old woman in the forest. And so, after a disguised servant crept away into the night with his baby daughter, he consulted sorcerer, wizard, necromancer, and priest—but all in vain.

The enchantment was so powerful he never did find out the secret by which it must be broken. Before a year had passed, he found himself hoping that somehow, by God's grace, she would never return..." The troubadour stretched and smiled in mock conclusion. "That was nigh twenty years ago."

Miriam's hand was at her throat, her face pale as death; she stood in a pillar of frozenness, thinking of Lot's wife, and hoping to God that nobody saw. A child's voice, hoarse with trepidation, came as if on cue from somewhere nearby.

"But what happened to the princess?"

A rippling murmur arose, which the minstrel silenced with a compliant gesture before he answered in a more normal voice, "No one knows. The one who carried her off was never seen again; he probably met with some ill fate. But the princess, now..." Fifty pairs of eyes strained for his speculation, fifty heads bent closer to hear. "Oh, she's out there, somewhere, and she knows that there's a king in the north of the world wants his daughter, and to him she must go. Does she feel his loneliness, or her own, the more? Perhaps she is blissfully unaware of her royal blood, perfectly happy..."

Sounds of disapproval were heard from the audience. How could she be, when such a rift awaited mending?

"No. There is something at work, something stronger than a moment's curse—something that will bring her back. And when she does return, the frozen north will feel its first real thaw in twenty years." He paused no more and granted no time for questions, though the story's unfinished ending drifted above them all like thick smoke. He picked up his lute and nodded to the fifer. They began a light *ricercare*. Tension eased as the crowd disentangled itself to return to the business of buying the many offered wares, though a handful of very country folk, their money spent, stayed to dance.

Michael stood behind her, but she didn't even see him. Instead, she turned to walk numbly toward the hill country, her back to the colors and gay sounds, her face set upon the shrouded gray mountains.

Miriam was wounded, in her soul. For in that timeless moment, she knew beyond certainty that the owner of the silver brooch, the unnamed king of the minstrel's tale, and her father were one and the same.

Michael followed silently, but he was perplexed. It was one of her fits of melancholy, he guessed; it would pass. But he would much rather have stayed to enjoy the harvest fair.

* * *

The torchlight cast long shadows in the empty hall where Basil and an armed knight stood in late-night conversation.

"Where are they coming from?"

"All from the south, my lord."

"They're getting stranger. Three now. The last one was all in gypsy clothes—she had a wild story! It's a wonder he doesn't have them thrown into prison as imposters. He's getting soft," the counselor decided as the other considered.

"Anyone might, who's lost two wives. Why, what would you do with these girls?" There was no answer. "Some of them seem so sincere…"

"Sincerely deluded, Gustav. They heard a faery tale told by a vagrant. They made it their own story, their own dream. Who wouldn't want to be the daughter of a king, no matter how small a kingdom he rules?" He paused. "I've never heard about this 'lost princess'. Have you?"

"Pieter remembers her. So does Brigid."

"Brigid is old, and senile."

"But Pieter is still a worthy knight, the only one left from the old retinue."

"He doesn't fit in so well with the new one," scoffed Basil.

"He suspects the girl was sent away."

"Why would a man send away his only child?"

"Perhaps she was in some danger," ventured Gustav.

"She'd be in worse danger by leaving than by staying here."

"She reminded him of the queen, then."

"All the more reason she should stay. No, she was taken for a ransom. Or else something was terribly wrong with her."

Gustav risked offering, a little abashed, "They say she was cursed."

Basil's learned eyebrows raised. "Cursed? First I've heard of it. Well, Sir Gustav, I wouldn't send my little girl away if she were cursed. Would you?"

"I don't know, my lord. If a man is desperate enough, he might do anything." The counselor shook his head and walked away, while the knight removed the torch from its sconce on the wall to begin his nightly rounds.

* * *

The smell of dust and sage hung in the air. They were walking due north, across a bare, treeless country stretching slowly upward to the nearing mountains. Somewhere eastward a river ran, but they couldn't hear any sound of it. It was a dismal land; the grass was sparse, parched and brown, the stubble of an earth-giant's beard. A damp wind blew over them, and when next they looked up, it seemed a sea of cloud was rolling to meet them from their left. The air grew palpably colder.

Michael glanced about, looking for shelter. Seeing none, he turned to the woman who trudged silently behind. The loneliness of the moor had stripped words away, and it only required a nod from Miriam to move steadily on. But before the fog overran them, a chasm opened before them, deep and dark—and wide. The cloud had already filled the bottom of it; Michael wondered if he could just hear the river rushing far below. The edges of the chasm were stony, sheer precipices. He stopped, baffled as to the direction they should take. Miriam had arrived at the edge and was looking down. Her eyes darted from side to side, searching.

"I can't see the other side," he said, peering ahead, then glancing at Miriam. Now she was looking west. He followed her gaze and squinted. "Can you see anything?"

"No."

He picked up a heavy stone and tossed it into the chasm. It bounced against hard rock once or twice, but he never heard it land or splash. Fog-colored silence.

"There is a bridge, Michael."

"Where?"

"This way." She had not moved.

"I thought you'd never been this far north before."

"I haven't."

"Then how do you know there's a bridge?" Her mind could be playing tricks on them.

"I don't know. But it's there all the same."

She must have strange eyes, he thought. "We should wait here until the mist grows lighter."

"It won't get any lighter." The sky had become heavy and thick; vision shrank as the cloud engulfed them.

"Well, my lady, it seems you have the compass. I don't. But let's stay far from the edge." He took her hand and pulled her back.

"Only we must keep to the side of it." She edged closer than he was comfortable, so he let her walk on that side but did not let go of her hand. It was cold as ever, and rough; the touch of it once again gave him a shock. They walked slowly, haltingly, Miriam keeping the steep gorge on her right and the journeyman straining hopelessly to see into the murky dusk ahead.

"In this light, it's almost easier to find the path if you close your eyes," he muttered. She didn't answer. Half an hour later, Michael's patience was exhausted. "There's no bridge, Miriam. Who could build one over *that*?"

"It's just ahead. Please."

Well, he would have to humor her. Soon they might come to the edge of the moor and find a bush or rock overhang to shelter under. There was no point in going back—the gray light was fading now.

"Here."

"What's that?"

"The bridge."

Two posts had been pounded into cracks in the aggregate at the edge of the cliff, a rope-something supported between them. Michael incredulously touched the hemp. It was far from new, but it didn't seem dangerously frayed on this end. He looked down a narrow, boarded pathway but still could not see the gorge's other side.

"We can't cross this."

"We have to. Besides, it's safe enough."

"What proof do you have of that?"

"I knew it was here." There was a tense silence. "What other proof do you need?" The bridge was no imagining; it was there, real, and had been long before they had begun their travels. What other proof indeed. This woman—she could see through mountains. He'd thought she held a secret, but he knew better now: she *was* a secret.

He was about to offer to go first, but he saw her outline already between the posts in front of him.

"Coming, Michael?" The wind billowed up from below like an angry wave; he felt the vibration of it in the rope railing.

"Right behind you, my lady." How did he know she smiled?

The walkway was flimsy, though, and the wind was strong. His hands grew stiff clutching at the rope rail on either side as he shuffled along. How long this lasted he did not know. Every now and again they would both stop and crouch, storm-tossed as a ship on the wide sea, and Miriam's fear rose up and rolled over her like the gusting fog under her feet, stealing the confidence out of her steps. Pieces of the boardwalk were missing; through the holes they could see a blackening, swirling grayness and nothing else.

I would hate to fall into that, thought Michael as he groped his way along. But the old boards held and the rope railing began to slope upward, and after a few minutes more the two opposite posts stood sentinel before them. Michael grasped the wind-worn top of one gratefully as he passed, turning around to see the darkening mist close in on his heels and even the boardwalk swallowed up in twilight shadows.

A few scraggly junipers were silhouetted ahead by a dirty yellow light. It was toward this they walked at a faster pace. They reached the tumbledown enclosure of a weathered inn, a low building with walls of thick planks, the chinks between them filled with brown mortar, its door wide open. Smoke from a peat fire spilled heavily out of the mud-plastered chimney. The master of the place, a toothless old man, greeted them in nervous surprise, bade them come in, and set two low stools in front of an ash-strewn hearth before disappearing into a back courtyard to rummage around for something for them to eat.

The only other light shimmered from the far corner of the room, where a pine knot burned in a rusty wall mount, revealing several straw pallets piled together. Miriam noticed a number of little black crawling things there, which she knew were not shadows.

"If I can get a chair with a back, you shall sleep by the fire tonight," Michael asserted. Only too glad to let him take charge, she nodded sleepily, her eyes raised to thank him.

"And you?"

"I think I'll, uh, stretch out on one of these here benches."

The landlord returned with some sort of brew, strong cheese, and stale bread, grinning at the couple who, despite their tattered appearance, looked to him like nobility. Michael made the most of the moment, and with a dramatic flourish he produced a silver coin, which the old man received with a happy bow and mercifully retired, leaving them some privacy.

"Miriam," Michael said, his mouth full of crumbs. Her responding look told him to swallow them. He did. "How did you know that bridge was there?"

"I don't know. It—it told me." The wind began to howl outside; the gloomy peat fire faltered, then regained its flicker. "I just knew. Chantal knew a lot of things."

"Chantal?"

"The blind woman I stayed with, after I left home."

"Oh." He swished the ale around in his mouth meditatively. "Miriam," he said directly.

"Yes?"

"Miriam—my lady—I do not know your story. I may never know it all... but I want to be part of it." She looked up suddenly, terrified. "Would you please consider..." But his words were stopped as she reached quickly to lay her cold fingers against his stammering lips.

"Ask me nothing, Michael, until... until I know more about myself. I cannot give you what I don't understand, nor can I give what doesn't belong to me."

"I thought you were your own mistress."

"No."

"Then who can I ask for your hand?" He was so eager, a frustrated child. She held her chafed hand up in the dim light.

"It's cold," she said.

"Not all of you is cold, Miriam."

"No." The woman's voice had lost its naiveté, her admission deep and soft in the closed room.

"You're *her*, aren't you?"

She couldn't answer—she wasn't sure. She felt, she thought... but now she didn't *know*. She looked at him, pleading, and then her eyes sought refuge again among the peat embers.

A torrent of realization flooded his thoughts, and he went on. "That's why you're going north, isn't it? To find this little king who somehow lost you years ago. It must be a royal emblem, that brooch you keep trying to hide—not even a nobleman could get a ruby that size..." Her sudden look silenced him.

"I can't go back until this curse is broken."

"What curse?"

"This coldness."

"Oh, that. Did you call it a curse before you heard the minstrel's story, or after?"

Her eyes flared in angry confusion. "Before. Years before."

"Oh." His tone changed from chiding to concerned. He leaned forward, slowly so as not to startle her. God, she was like a fidgety mare. "Any idea how this is supposed to happen?"

"Not a clear one." The fire whistled low, as if on cue. "It involves fire."

"It scares you, doesn't it?" Her eyes widened; she nodded almost imperceptibly, biting her lip. He stood and drew her to her feet, up to himself, putting his lips to her cool forehead as she continued to gaze at the fire. "Maybe it won't be as bad as you think." He wanted to say more, to crack and dissolve this ice-hold of Coldness in his warm embrace, but nothing happened. She did relax against him, though, her face warming.

Maybe it would be a gradual thaw.

But he must get that chair before she fell asleep. He took her hand and kissed it, briskly, without searching her face any more for answers he wouldn't find. Then he excused himself to seek out the landlord and settle her in for the night.

The Ice Princess. He suddenly felt very small.

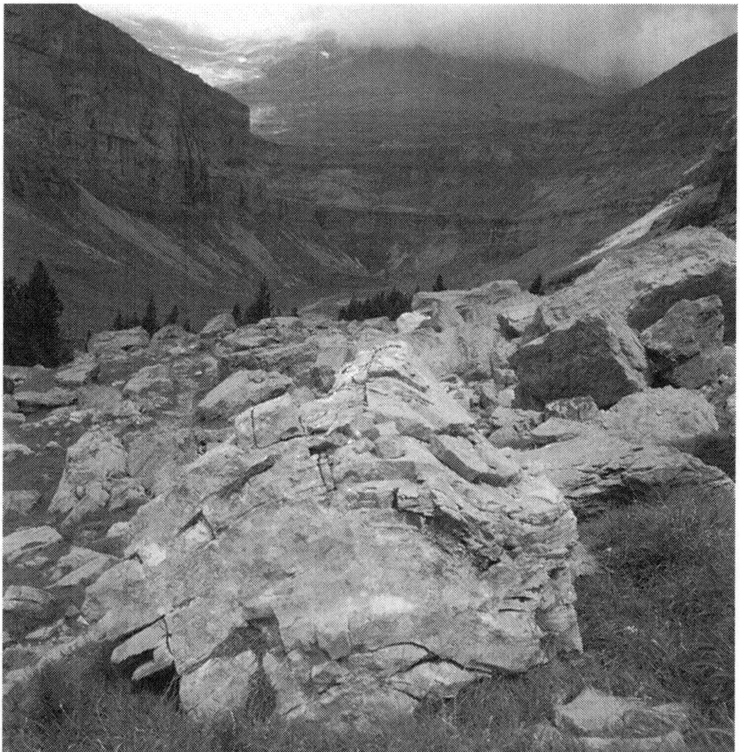

There are many ways of 'being' in a place.

– Saint Teresa of Avila

XXIII

Seduced

She was outside, washing her feet. He'd never seen them, as they'd always been hidden inside her thick boots. Now he knew why: the warm water trickled off dusky skin, mottled indigo-blue and faded purple—not quite gray enough to be death-colored. He grimaced. But she didn't try to hide them this time.

"Good morning, Michael." The mist had lifted; he hadn't realized how close they were to the mountains. They practically rose skyward from the inn's back door. "It's a lovely day for a walk." A walk, maybe. He certainly wasn't ready to lug his bag up *that*.

"I don't know, my lady," he said, scratching his chin and scanning the folds and clefts of unyielding granite. A few scant clouds drifted over the top.

"The poplars are just changing; there'll be colors. And it's so warm. Please, Michael, just to see the view. The innkeeper says there's a good path—even horses use it."

"Where does it go?"

"Right up to the pass. But we needn't go all the way. You could leave the baggage here."

"As my lady wishes," he acquiesced with a polite bow. Deep inside he felt they shouldn't—not today—but he couldn't explain this and so said nothing further.

Their conversation the night before had lightened her. The terrible fate she dreaded was nowhere in sight. What lay before them was only alpine beauty and fresh air, making her gladly homesick for a place she'd never been. For once she would leave off wandering, pressing forward... and just enjoy the lovely day.

The path wound in a leisurely traverse upward, bearing east across the rugged face of the mountain's foot. It meandered in and out among clefts and water runoffs, morning sun and sylvan shadow a glowing latticework of light. As the grade grew steeper, Michael panted, his leg growing heavier with the added work. Miriam walked ahead of him, humming. She steadily plodded on around corners where more beauty hid. He had never seen her so happy.

He was relieved when he came around a sharp bend and found her waiting at a spring. The moor and valley lay spread out below them, a world away. He could scarcely believe they had come such a distance. He caught his breath while she rolled up her sleeves to splash crystal-clear water over her face and arms, shaking the drips off her fingers and lifting her face to let the sun dry the rest.

"Winter will be here soon," he said with some concern.

"It's hard to believe, Michael. Today is so like spring. I could go on and on."

"Not much further, Miriam."

"Oh, but we're nearly halfway up already. Wouldn't you like to see what's on the other side? You could wait for me here, because I'd like to."

"No. I'll go with you. But we must turn back by noon."

They were making their way up an exposed switchback. Michael's pace was slowing; he had to lock his weak leg under him at every step, which took measured concentration. The mountainside fell steeply away beneath him. When he looked up from his feet he felt giddy, and he didn't know whether it was from the sheer height or the thinning air of the severe altitude. Only a few large trees stood proudly above—the rest were scrubby and wind-blown pine brier bushes. The fragrant scent he'd longed for wafted around him, mixed with another smell he failed to recognize: coming snow.

She was well ahead of him. The clouds flowed over, thicker and faster now, but she didn't seem to have noticed. He grew more alarmed as the light faded and the wind blew down upon them, colder now than at daybreak.

"Miriam!" She didn't hear him: the wind blew his voice down the slope. It was all he could do to limp faster, so as to catch her up. *We have to turn back*, he insisted inwardly, knowing that storms gather quickly in the high mountain skies. She should know better. Her cloak was open, flapping behind her. Didn't she feel the cold? He began to run, a stitch growing in his side. It seemed to take ages...

Finally, he was just behind her and caught her by the hand. She turned to face him with such a wild, longing look, the wind catching her hair in a frenzied dance. She glanced up over her shoulder, through the dancing air to where the pass must lie.

Oh no, he thought. It was calling her to come.

She smiled soothingly at him.

"Just a little further, Michael. Please," she said in the crisp wind. A few tiny snowflakes drifted past them. At first he mistook them for blossoms, but no, it was too late in the year. Perhaps she knew something he didn't, so he let her go. In less than a quarter hour, the flakes were falling heavily. He could see less and less of the path ahead. He had lost all sense of time: it must be noon by now. Still she went on, unyielding, while he doggedly followed, his eyes upon her boots, the distance between them growing.

"God, we can't see. Take us by the hand and lead us—lead us both—not where we want to go, but where it's best for us to be," he prayed aloud, though he could hardly hear his own voice. His feet were stinging into numbness, his leg an iron weight. The soft, cloudy curtain shimmered above him, throwing a white aura upon the woman now well beyond his reach. He wanted to lie down, to sleep under the downy coverlet of snow that he no longer tried to shake off.

Miriam walked on in the purity of falling whiteness, tasting the drifting flakes as they settled upon her enraptured face. When the wind began to swirl the snow, she felt herself caught up in its dance step. The inner whirl and call grew stronger. She was oblivious to danger, and all the time the wind grew fiercer and piercingly cold, cold as frost. The summit of the pass must be just ahead.

She came through a small hollow, around a bend and up over a short rise, hearing the silence hidden in the rushing storm and churning snow. But something lay ahead, off the path. She could hear... was it music? The horizon fell to nothing before her; she must be nearing the top. A vague, shadowy form stood against the gray sky—some sort of stone building. A tower loomed up over there, warm light spilling out of a doorway below. It *was* music. And such a hearth it must be, to make such a bright light! She drew toward it. Michael must be just behind her; she could hear his teeth chattering.

A silhouetted form appeared on the threshold.

"Hullo! Can it be you, sweet Miriam?" a woman's voice called. "Mon dieu, what a day to be out walking! You're welcome, my dear, come in!"

Barbara.

She lived up here, in a house of dressed stone, near the top of the mountain pass between two kingdoms... Miriam remembered the invitation. The luring firelight seemed to fill the whole house, drawing her in. Another echo rose from somewhere inside her, holding Joan's voice amid the swirling snow: *"Two fires, Miriam. One melts, one burns..."* She stood stone-still, her heart pounding now with uncertainty. Barbara—it must be, who else would expect her?—stood back-lit in the doorway, her bare arms held out in beckoning hospitality.

"Someone there with you? Bring him along, then—it's warm in here, and soon a blizzard out where you are. Hurry up, Miriam! You'll freeze out there!" The plea had become a rebuke, with an edge of unmasked impatience in it.

Freeze, or burn: that was her choice. Two fires...

She had already chosen—it was too late. All the warnings, the counsel, the dreams, Michael... She had listened to none of them. She was a fool, a cursed fool, and now the curse would devour her. She knew now what Barbara had wanted: *her.* Barbara would have them both.

No. Not Michael. She couldn't have him, he didn't belong to her. An unearthly cry rose up through the cold cloud of blowing snow as Miriam pivoted and fled, crashing into the man behind her. His face was speckled with white flakes that clung to his brows and beard. His breath was short, his eyes dazed. He was so pale! He hardly saw her: his sight was fixed on the warm firelight ahead. All this she saw, even while she seized his arm to pull him back down the path with her, away from one kind of death and into another.

From the stone building behind them, the hearth fire flared and sparked, and with it came the harsh, taunting laughter of the sorceress.

"There is no pit so deep that He is not deeper still."

– Betsie Ten Boom, Ravensbruck Concentration Camp, 1945

XXIV

Into the Abyss

Michael flopped weakly against her, so she threw his arm over her neck and grabbed his thick leather belt. How could she cover any distance with him in this blinding storm? The ground was uneven here, just below the summit—solid, glacier-worn rock. There were no vertical cracks to squeeze into to escape the howling wind. She squinted for a low bush, even, all the while tugging and pulling; thank God for the little slope to help propel them downward. But even that grew slippery as the snow settled upon it.

He was wet to the skin. They tumbled over the side of the path she could no longer see, into the small hollow she'd passed before, its banks shielding the drifting snow and its floor soft beneath the cold carpet. There was a young fir tree: she would take him there. It was the only cover in sight.

She had to drag him, and he was so very heavy. What a failure she was—his blood would be on her head.

"Lord Jesu Christ, have mercy..." She couldn't finish, she was beyond his reach. She would never arrive on the other side of that mountain; some demon had seized her in the dark tunnel to drag her down into blackness.

But Michael! He lay with his head propped up in her lap, unmoving, while the wind whipped snow flurries beneath the meager branches. Was he even breathing? God, he must be cold! She took off her cloak and spread it over as much of him as it would cover. She could lie next to him, as Irina once had… No, it wouldn't help—there was no warmth in her to give away. She had nothing. Her throat tightened as she watched his tanned face become an ashen gray.

No.

A guttural sound escaped her lips; she couldn't hold it back. Her eyes stung as the choking cries mounted, erupting from an inner chamber of molten feeling she never knew was there. Her face burned, and hot tears rushed down to fall over his hair and neck. She leaned over him to shield his face, her body racking with sobs that sounded inhuman against the wind. There was nothing she could do for him. That revelation tore at her insides, clawing its way out of her in the dripping form of tears.

She couldn't watch him die, knowing that she was the cause. She eased Michael out of her sodden lap and crawled away from him, a desolate Hagar in a freezing desert. Only this time, no miraculous warm fountain appeared out of nowhere to deliver them.

She couldn't even go very far; the wind hurled ice into her eyes. She knelt and wept, crouching in snow-covered duff. She looked up among the sparse, scraggly trees to search for she didn't know what, but their shapes dissolved into a bluish whiteness. Deepening color ran into the blurring scenery on all sides: the phosphorescent blue of moonlight-on-snow gave way to a dimming lavender, and then velvet-red overtook her vision. The warmth of flowing tears permeated her, growing to a ravaging fire.

Light faded and fell; pure, smooth black overcame all sensation, and Miriam, still weeping for him, slipped away into vast nothingness.

Michael laid still, a warm waterfall-trickle spreading upon his face. He thought he was lying in the warm, salty surf near his boyhood home, letting the little waves caress him as he basked on sunlit sand... He'd never known that freezing to death could be so comfortable. He vaguely saw a mist rising and a reddish glow somewhere above him; perhaps the ancient mountain hid a volcano. Miriam was gone. It didn't matter. He would see her soon enough. All he wanted to do was sleep.

* * *

The storm had passed right over the valley and now lay raging on the mountaintop. Brigid stepped outside her makeshift hovel in the courtyard to look at the angry sky. Southward, the ridge was overcome by snow-borne shadow, but a faint red glow colored the cloud that covered the narrow pass.

The castle itself sat brooding in the wake of the storm. A bolt of lightning flashed upon the forested ridge, and, at the same moment, Brigid heard something shatter close at hand. She looked back toward the king's apartments, from whence the sound had come. Faintly, against the sky, a rainbow streak of light flew out his window toward the tall trees.

"At last," she murmured, and she hitched up her skirts to run and tell Pieter.

* * *

Michael woke to the song of a thrush. The air breathed warm around him, and fresh. Swallows scooped the sky in perfect arcs, and above them eagles soared. He felt a bit damp, but otherwise he was comfortable and at ease. In a remote part of his mind lurked the memory of danger. A battle? No, that wasn't it. He hurriedly threw off the blanket covering him and stood to look around.

He'd never seen the place before. A path wound upward around short, wind-blown trees; there was a small sound of water flowing over rock. He should take his mantle... no, it was on him already, the lump of his tinder box within its folds. He bent down to pick up his blanket. An old hunting cloak. Miriam's. Where was she? He called her name into the empty echo of the hollow. Grabbing her cloak, he clambered awkwardly up the bank, driven by a growing sense of alarm. A wisp of black smoke curled above the ridge.

He came around a bend to confront the terrifying sight of a newly-charred ruin, black ash turning its doors and window-holes into sultry cavern mouths. The roof was gone. He couldn't go in—the stones still held the heat of a furnace. There was no sign of anything that breathed or moved or lived. In spite of the warm breeze moving now through the gap of the pass, Michael shuddered, chilled to the bone. Shielding his face, he stretched up to peer through a blackened casement. The shimmer of heated air distorted the few recognizable objects in the house: seared lamps, broken tables, and tapestries hanging as incinerated shreds. He stumbled around the outside and heard a familiar sound.

A horse's whinny. Against a rock wall was fenced a paddock, untouched by the fire, where a cream-colored horse stood frozen in fear, its flanks trembling and its nostrils flared in spite of the smoke. Michael pitied it and searched for the latch. The iron gate was too hot to touch, but with short tugs and a stick he was able to open it. The creature jerked its head at the sound and fled toward him, afraid of the house. A wet rope halter hung from a post; the horse made no resistance as he slipped the device over its arched neck and led it out, stroking its velvet nose. It paused patiently when Michael bent over to keep from fainting, nausea covering him in waves.

His memory could not fill in the blanks of the day before—the night before—he didn't even know which it was. Or where he was. Or why. He staggered on, his breath coming in little gasps. A pillar of cloud glowered at him from the west, the promise of another storm rolling in to drench the mountain in winter. He leaned against the crooked trunk of a wizened fir tree to steady himself. The hollow was below him—he should take another look. After loosely draping the end of the halter rope over a low branch, he slid down the duff-covered bank, then glanced back. But the horse did not move, so sure was it of its savior's return.

Michael's eyes darted from the spot where he had lain to a tiny hillock to his left, not twenty paces from the path. Something lay on the coarse grass. Blinking and panting, he made his way toward the place, only to find the limp cloth of Miriam's dress crumpled and damp, her thick boots besmeared with mud beneath it. The clothes were intact—no tears in the fabric, no blood. No creature had done this... He called again, but there was no answer. And he was not well enough to search any longer. The sharp pine air stuck in his throat. When his breathing came quicker of a sudden and a whirring sting of dizziness clouded his brain, he knew he would be sick. He wished he were home.

Home. Where was home? He was a stranger here—he knew no one this far north, and Miriam was nowhere to be seen. She had deserted him. He must go to Robert. The way he'd come... south. Yes: Robert was south. The horse whickered softly, summoning him back. He hadn't even strength enough to pick up her castaway things and climb up the bank again. He would have to go back to the path and up that way. It seemed to take an hour.

Looking around dazedly, he took the halter. He was no rider. But here was a horse wanting to escape this wretched place, and here was a man already flush with fever and needing to go home.

Now, how to get atop the thing? Could he even keep his seat? Well, he would have to try, that's all. There was a smallish boulder—he could mount from that. How he would get down again was anybody's guess. Clutching his own mantle tight, he spread Miriam's cloak over the horse's back. Then, with a great heave, he threw his good leg over and grabbed its mane with both hands. There was no need for goad or whip; the mount took off down the path, spurred on by a holy madness, to take Michael homeward.

Twilight hung in the west when the journeyman rode through a rustic gate. The innkeeper whistled.

"Whoa, now. Been riding too long and hard, I sh'd think. Your horse is spent, Sonny." But Michael stared with glassy eyes and tumbled off on top of the fellow, who cursed and laughed, and hollered to his ample wife to stable the beast while he led his mindless and bedraggled guest into the house.

"Poor devil. Been chased, eh? No soldiers, I hope." Michael shook his head violently; the movement made him feel even sicker. Slumped on a bench, he didn't open his eyes until his host had splashed some water in his face. It mixed with the sweat on his forehead and trickled down his back. He shuddered and began to wretch. "You're sick, all right. God, I hope it's not plague. That's been through here once already."

"Holy Virgin, he looks just like 'is horse," came the comment from the doorway. "'At's not plague, man; it's some shock 'e's had." She went to brew some mint tea, practical woman that she was. The beast would be well-bedded and have hot mash and oats, the man a warm bed. He was about as old as her son, she thought, who had left years ago to fight in some war and never came back.

Michael wiped his mouth on his tattered sleeve and groped for his tinder box. His shaking hands took out a gold coin.

"No, Sonny, I ha'n't got change for that. Put it back."

"There's a cloak on the... the horse," he stuttered.

"I'll bring it to ye. That poor creature needs a rest, just like yerself. Where're ye off to, so fast?"

"South. My master's there." Michael's eyes bore into the innkeeper's without apology. "I have to get home," he said in a choking voice.

So, the innkeeper surmised. A craftsman, probably stripped of his goods by thieves and somehow managed to escape with his life. He looked like a working man.

"So you shall, m'boy. But now's the time for sleeping. You can't ride in the dark." He couldn't ride at all, not in this condition.

The innkeeper's wife rose to feed her chickens early and found the stable door ajar. Her husband came at her call to find the horse gone and their wooden saddle missing. A gold coin shone from the empty trough. Their guest had gone.

"Yer saddle's missing."

"Aye," said he, picking up the money. "But it weren't worth half a silver piece, even. Pray God gets that fellow to his journey's end, my dear, 'afore he kills hisself on the way."

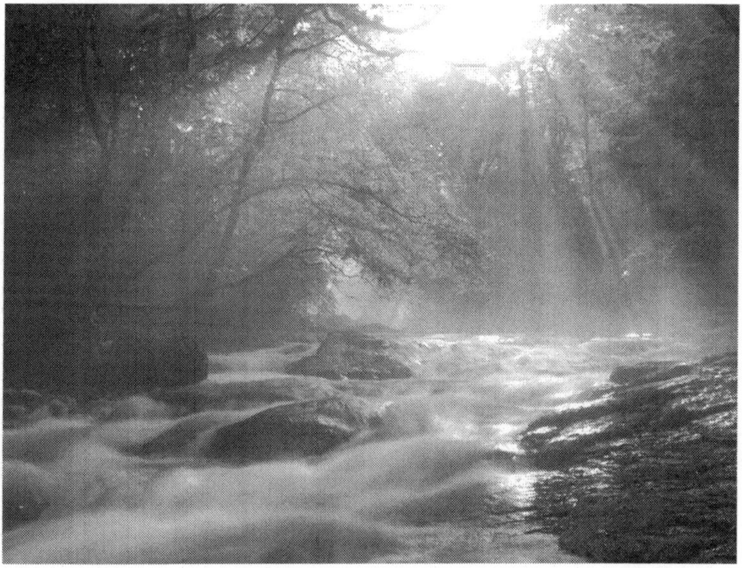

In a dark night, forth unobserved I went,
In secret, seen of none, seeing nought myself,
Without other light or guide
Save that which in my heart was burning.

If, then, on the common land I am no longer found
You will say that I am lost;
That, being enamored, I lost myself;
And yet was found.

– Saint John of the Cross

XXV

Sunlight

A passing zephyr rippled the surface of the murmuring brook, wooing the still form at its bank to wakefulness. Miriam heard its whispered call and smelled the sweet damp earth, greening beneath and around her long before she opened her eyes.

She found herself lying almost face down, growing aware of the brook-song and the new-waked thought sprouting from the loamy, dark soil of her steady heartbeat. Her eyelids lifted to unveil the sparkle of sun dancing brightly upon underwater stones; she felt its warmth clothing her back, the breath of wind caressing her face. She sat up. Gone was the hollow, the biting wind, the snow—gone even from her distant memory. The air shone clearer than even the crystalline stream, with the warm, vanilla-like scent of mountain pines floating upon it. She reached up to smooth her hair, blown loose as drifting dandelion seeds about her, and noticed her bare feet, fair against the moss of the bank. Instinctively she reached for her cloak, but it was nowhere near.

It was mid-afternoon, and Miriam sat in an unknown forest glade drinking in bird songs and small flower-bursts of color that sprang fountain-like from the short grass. She stood, bewildered: a tight-woven linen garment, pale as cream, fell almost to her feet—she could not remember where she had gotten it or having worn it before. She wandered upstream, toward a craggy ridge, but an inner compass needle swung her round to the west. Meandering along the stream, she grew thirsty, and stopped to drink its glass-clear water.

As her hand sank beneath the surface, she withdrew it in quick surprise—the coldness of the water stung her. Some nearby spruces seemed to bend to watch her lift her fingers to her face, curling and uncurling them in wonder. She gasped when they touched her cheek. They were warm. And the long scar on her arm—it was still there, but now a fine white line instead of a jagged red one. She fingered the moss at the stream's edge, tracing its contour against the smooth worn rock, marveling at its soft resilience. Lifting up her head, she saw an eagle circle, coasting along on an unseen current of air. Big trees and rushing water...

Only then did she think of Michael.

The unfamiliar ridge behind her loomed up as an impenetrable wall; she supposed he must lie somewhere on the other side. Her eyes wandered, searching the strange country, longing for a landmark, a signpost, a path. Her hands, though warm, were empty; she thought her heart was too. Sorrow overshadowed the sunlight, grief welled up afresh, and the cry of her voice erupted like a geyser from a black crevasse.

Seconds later, she felt the warmth of tears coursing down her face to dampen the strands of hair at her neck. She had lost all, but what was this she had found? She must know. Resolve prodded her to follow the calling of the stream. Wiping her cheeks with the fresh sleeves, she set her feet alongside the curving pathway the water made as it wound through thick forest and rock outcropping, to meld with a river below.

The plash of the stream measured her steps, slowly crossing a meadow, then with a quickening tempo as the hill steepened downward. Her unshod feet glided sure and unstumbling over glacial rock, springy turf, and warm shallow puddles. How long had it been since she had left that frozen, ice-bound world, that howling blizzard, that blinding cloud of whiteness? Was this new season Death? She was alone but not afraid. And with the lengthening shadows of the spring-like day came another realization: she felt cold.

Even with the thick forest about her, she knew by her footfalls that the hill had leveled. The stream, deeper and quieter now, swung away to her left, but she continued arrow-straight. Silhouetted tree shadows fell across the duff, mixing with sunlit shafts of light slicing through from just ahead. Every now and again, the edge of a fir cone or a pine needle would prick her feet. What little part of the horizon she could make out seemed to be peppered with the rooftops of an ancient town. Suddenly the forest ended—she stood in the thick shade of a towering stone castle set on a hill directly in front of her.

Miriam whirled around, fully expecting to see the yawning blackness of her dream-tunnel behind her, but there were only the silent trees standing guard, barring her way back. She must go on.

No—she was free to go on. A new strength filled and steadied her. She knew that the dry sands had at last run through the old hourglass. The curse was broken. Somehow. Even the thought of Michael seemed far away as she approached what lay before her. She was not conscious of the remaining distance, nor of the fact that she was coming to the back gate.

The shadow deepened as she ascended the smooth-grassed pitch of the hill and stood upon a drawbridge, catching her breath. Dressed stone walls rose vertically, the evening sun striking the edges of the ornate battlements on top in a pattern that reminded her of some of Chantal's embroidery. It was a fine, sturdy castle, but a cold and unwelcoming one. She prayed there would be warmth on the inside. The portcullis was up; she drew a deep breath and knocked on the heavy door. Beginning by now to shiver, she wrapped her arms about her while she stood waiting.

A small view-door opened, and a suspicion-laden face peered out, back-lit by a dusty light from the inner courtyard.

"Who are you and what do you want?" He seemed to take her for a beggar, and his gruff manner surprised her. She was craving a touch of kindness, about now.

"Good even, sir. Would you be so kind as to give me shelter for the night?"

"Why didn't you seek lodging in the town when you came through?"

"I didn't come through the town, sir."

"No? Then how did you come?"

"I followed the stream down from the forest ridge."

"Oh you did, did you?" His eyes narrowed. That was a dead end.

"Yes, sir. And I am beginning to be cold." He eyed her meager dress, puzzled that she carried neither bag nor cloak. "I do have some business within, sir," she explained, hoping to speed things up a bit.

"Oh? And what is that?"

"I wish an audience with the king." She struggled to maintain her courtesy, feeling so chilled, but with the force of will kept her tone polite.

"Now? For what reason?"

"I'm his daughter." There, it was said. She heard a deep grunt and with it the sound of a bolt being drawn back.

Another one, thought the gatekeeper. A number of young women had turned up at the castle lately. He'd heard about them from the porter. But they had all come to the front gate. Well, he had his orders. The door swung heavily open, groaning with age and a lack of grease, and the very odd visitor stepped gratefully inside.

The gatekeeper slammed shut the iron-shod door and fumbled with the bolt. She doubted seriously if she were really there, or if she was imagining the whole thing. No, she was too cold to be dreaming. She stood on the flagged stones, feeling the dust beneath her feet. The afternoon light gave way to a mud-colored dusk. Smoke crept out of a gaping casement nearby; all the doorways she could see were either shut or dark. She set her jaw to keep her teeth from chattering.

"Wait here." The disgruntled guard walked unhurriedly to a tall man in a hauberk, bearded and sullen, with keen eagle eyes and as great an air of authority as she'd ever seen. He listened to the little gatekeeper with bent head, nodded fiercely, and flicked his gaze toward the uninvited guest. He then strode over, towering above her with his hand resting nonchalantly on his sword hilt. An unfamiliar golden sunburst medallion shone dully at his shoulder. His first impression of her made a greeting apparently unnecessary.

"What is your name?"

"I am called Miriam, sir," The calmness of her voice steadied her. He scanned her intently.

"Let me guess. You're from somewhere south, and you're here with a claim to be the king's long-lost daughter. Isn't that so?" Amazed at his insight, she was about to answer when he cut in, "Well, my lady, you're not the first. Why didn't you come to the front gate?"

"I found myself at the back. Should I have walked 'round, with evening coming on?"

"Saucy little thing, aren't you? No, you shouldn't. But it's a strange time of day to seek an audience with his Majesty. I shall, however, tell him you're here; please wait until I return."

"Certainly, sir."

He made a brisk token of a salute and set off at a soldier's pace, entering a door near a thickly-leaded glass window. The gatekeeper kept his eyes on her and resumed his perch, but there seemed to be no other place to sit, so Miriam remained standing. Another man-at-arms, stationed near turrets flanking a low archway, stared with a hungry smile lurking at his mouth. There were few others about, mostly poor squatters who supplied the wants of the great house in a thousand menial ways. Only children smiled at her. A rough leather patchwork ball tumbled down the dusty stones. She bent to pick it up and toss it to a dimple-kneed boy of three, who ran off, pretending to be chased.

"There's not a speck of decency around here anymore! Fie on you all, to give such a welcome to a weary traveler!" a dowdy woman clucked, approaching and scattering most onlookers with her scolding looks. The turret guard sniggered and resumed his visual feast at Miriam's expense. "Now then, lassie," the older woman said, "won't you step over this way, please, where there's a wee fire burning and a bit of blanket for your back." Miriam glanced about. "Never you mind them, dearie. They're a shameless lot." She smiled and took the woman's proffered hand, to be led across the courtyard to a coarse hut built leaning against the smooth, cold stone of the castle's interior wall. Before they reached the low entrance, the armed knight had returned.

"Lady Miriam," he summoned, his voice full of official—and feigned—respect.

She stopped. "The king is indisposed at present but will see you after breakfast on the morrow. You can present your claim then, if you still have one."

"Thank you. And where, sir, am I to pass the night?"

"It seems you have already made arrangements." He raised his eyebrows at the matron, who smiled and curtseyed proudly.

"Yes, I have," answered Miriam, pleased.

"I bid you a good night then." He made an automatic bow of his head, turned on his heels with a flourish, and left.

Silver-haired Basil, the king's counselor, stood concealed in the shadowed frame of a nearby archway. He retired with the knight to report that satisfactory arrangements had been made for tomorrow's audience.

"Most fitting lodging, Sir Gustav," he remarked.

"Thank you, my lord," returned the knight. "I thought it appropriate."

Their sharp footsteps struck the flagstones in quick-tempo'd unison.

"How many does that make now?" the knight ventured.

"Five."

"Upon my word!" exclaimed Gustav. "However did they all hear about that ridiculous tragedy that happened, if it happened at all? No one around here ever mentions it now." He paused to kick some dust into a chink in the pavement. "How long will this go on?"

"I wish I knew. He's wasting his royal energy on all these interviews." *Lost princesses, indeed,* thought Basil. They paused in a dim passageway, not far from the king's chambers. "Good night, Gustav."

"Good night, my lord."

A heavy burlap curtain hung across the low doorway, shutting out the gray murkiness of the courtyard and its ogling stares. A lone candle set the timbered niche aglow with warmth and the welcome only a poor person can give. Something steamed from a bowl in the corner. Miriam was handed a patchwork blanket, the faded cotton threads worn soft. Eagerly she wrapped herself in it, and a new sensation of warmth welled up afresh. She smiled and relaxed, watching her hostess bustle about as if she had the queen herself to entertain. Outside the dingy door-curtain a dog barked, but it seemed miles away.

"Bet you're tired," remarked her hostess, ladling some soup into a wooden cup.

"A little."

"Come a long way." It was a statement, not a question.

"It seems so. I don't know how far." Her eyes had by now grown used to the light; there was a stool, a small fleece which served as a mat, a coarse table, a single shelf, and a pile of clean straw. The older woman seemed to find it comfortable enough, though it was a lonely corner of the world.

"I'd like to thank you, but I don't know your name." How those words reminded her of Michael!

"It's Brigid, and you don't have to. I know yours, though."

Miriam looked up while reaching for an offered oaten cake, a longing overshadowing her appetite. "From the man in the courtyard," she guessed.

"No, lassie. The one your mother gave you. Ah, faith, it's been a long time! But you've come at last. I always said that the prayers of them that love God get answered."

"I know nothing about my mother," Miriam confessed in a trembling voice. They sat in the straw together like old friends to share the simple meal.

"You should, though. She was dark-eyed—but fair, like you—an' slight, but she was a strong woman an' the truest lady ever I knew. Treated us like treasures, she did, all of us. Always looked us in the face, like we were real people an' not servants." She took a meditative sip from a chipped cup. "There was something deep and faraway about her, too. I don't think even your father knew her too well."

The candle flame flickered in an unfelt draft.

"When did she die?"

"Years ago—just a few months after you were born. Before you were sent off."

"Was I sent? Because of the curse?"

"You know about that, do you?" Brigid took hold of Miriam's warm hands, looking at and stroking them. There were tears in her knowing eyes. "But all that's done now. You're home."

"What about my... the king?" She dreaded to hear more, knowing that he had sent her away once, but still she ached to know.

"He remarried, but that did him little good. That one died in the plague. Gave him a son, she did, an' it almost made him happy. 'Cept he missed you and your mother too much.

Never said anything about either of you, not to me anyway, but I could see it in his eyes."

"What was her name?"

"Isolde." The woman sniffed; the cup was wiped dry and covered with cheesecloth to be washed in the morning.

"Isolde."

"Don't you want to know yours?"

"I think I'll find out soon enough," she answered hopefully. "Will he believe me?"

"He'd be a fool not to. You look like your mother, so much. You even talk like her."

"Is that how you knew me?"

"I was her lady-in-waiting."

* * *

"She's probably dead, Sire," said the counselor in exasperated tones. This conversation had happened too many times before. The flickering fire made his face dance with distorted light.

"It may be," came the usual answer, with the usual sigh. "Good God, they can't all be dead."

"Your son's very much alive. Look, my lord king, you've spent enough of yourself on these girls. They've all heard the same silly tale and thought they'd take a risk to make it come true. It's been nineteen years, Sire."

"Twenty."

"Twenty, then. Leave this curse of yours buried in the past, where it belongs." Basil urged, with an edge of impatience. "No one thinks about enchantments anymore."

"No one?" the king nearly shouted. His knuckles grew white with suppressed rage. What about that mad woman who turned up just last month, demanding payment for a purchase made long years ago? Nineteen gold pieces she wanted. It was a debt he owed her, she said. *She* thought of enchantments. She *made* them, binding and chilling. No—he would not be indebted to her, or intimidated by her, even if she did claim to know where the princess was now. He had turned her away and she had gone off, laughing at him this time. There must be a power stronger than hers, but he had failed to find it. He unraveled his thoughts and let them rise with the sparks in the fireplace, to be set free upon the night air.

Basil was right. His daughter was probably dead. He smiled a sad, defeated smile. Then he sighed and turned toward his counselor.

"Very well. This will be the last claim I consider. You say that she has no proof, so the audience will be a short one. But I have given her my word, which is still worth something." It was all he had, anymore. "You may go."

"Good night, Sire."

The king kept his back to the door as it opened and shut again. He was alone. He reached for the pewter figure on the mantel, to hurl it into the fire. But there was only a small, dustless pool of glistening marble where it had stood only the day before.

It was gone.

* * *

The candlelight brightened as dusk became night.

"I'm so glad you're here, Brigid."

"I've prayed for you every day... your highness." Miriam fell silent; even thoughts deserted her. Tomorrow was a mystery, like yesterday. But tonight she would sleep in the warm welcome of her dead mother's maid. The feeling became an incoherent torrent of gratitude, while Brigid tucked the cloth around her feet and kissed her forehead. She drifted like a dying ember into a soft, dreamless sleep.

The old woman's face crinkled in a tender smile. She blew out the candle flame and whispered the name of her goddaughter into the hovering darkness.

"Kristina." It was prayer enough, thanksgiving and supplication woven into one.

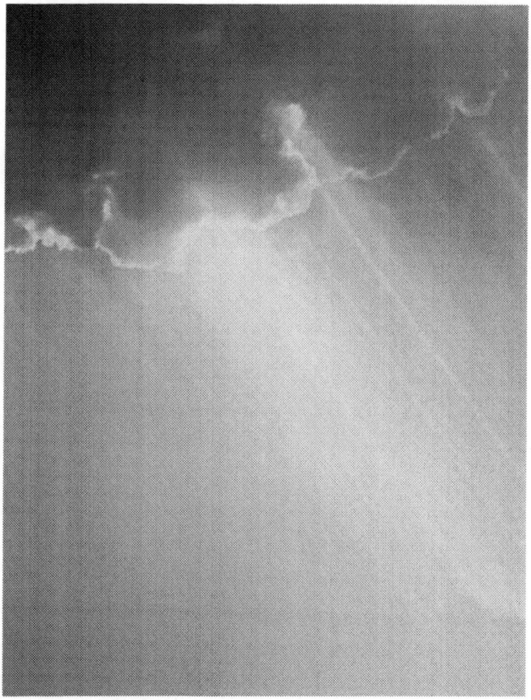

Revelation is not in Reason's realm.

– Carlo Carretto

XXVI

Stranger at Home

The great hall stretched before her—like the tunnel in her dream, almost. The king sat at a heavy table at the far end. The table was covered with books and parchments and stood not on the dais but on the stone floor in front of it. A richly dressed man, decorated with a gold chain of office, stood to the king's right, bending over him and speaking in the hushed tones of a polished consultant. The emblem on the wall had just caught the morning sun, which filtered through the mosaic of amber to mist the room in golden light.

When the great doors opened, the monarch in his nervousness did not look up; he wanted to complete the business at hand before being interrupted by the last of those young-woman glory seekers. What he did notice was sudden silence, as one by one the courtiers caught sight of the visitor in her simple dress and naked feet. So he lifted his head to greet his guest with kingly eyes.

But the whirl of years fell away—he was thrown backward in time. The face before him held the image of the wife he had tried so hard to forget. He saw no resemblance to himself; he did not even think to look for one. His hand searched for the edge of the table... for something to hold on to.

Without a nod or any welcoming gesture on his part, the maiden walked escorted by Gustav to the front, dropped down on one knee, and said softly, "My lord king."

He recoiled in wonder. Here was a girl, with his dead queen's look and voice, kneeling as a knight would—and hardly dressed for the occasion. It was a cosmic joke, a divine hoax. Not what he expected at all. Somehow, the color returning to his face, he spoke. Regally enough, to his great relief.

"Rise." He sat back in his chair, trying to force back the notion that the discarded dragon seal was clawing its way through the wood of the carved sunburst now mounted in its place on the front of the table. She obeyed and stood quietly before him. "I understand you have come to present a claim to be a lost princess of this realm." He would not mince words, nor would he use the term "daughter" if he could at all help it.

"Not a claim, Your Majesty. Only myself. I have no claim; I'm here."

"If you are so very sure of yourself, then, why do you not address your sovereign with a more familiar title?" The others had, with audacity.

"Forgive me, my lord," said she, unshaken. "To use a more familiar title would not be right at all—until Your Majesty acknowledges the relation." Where did such words come from? She had never studied rhetoric; she had practiced nothing.

The king glanced around the room; the few there were attending to the conversation with interest. Everyone was a potential witness—he would have to be careful. He had to break this grip of silence before they grew suspicious at his hesitation.

"From where do you come?"

"Well below the mountains, to the south... across a river. I couldn't show you on a map, though."

He leaned forward, perplexed.

"Then how exactly did you come to be here, if you are not altogether sure where you came from?" His tone had regained control of the company, and there were amused smiles on several faces.

"I found myself in a meadow, just beyond the forested ridge to the south. I followed the stream to your castle, Sire."

He was intrigued, now. *She had found herself?*

"And how exactly did you come to be there?"

"I don't know. It happened when... when the curse was broken." The court froze, waiting to hear more of the story, but it did not come. The king had changed the subject.

"My guard tells me your name is Miriam." A Jewish name. Unusual.

"That is what the shepherd couple called me. But I don't know, and neither did they, how I was christened. Perhaps you could tell me, Your Majesty..."

"Where are these—parents—of yours now?"

"The plague took them."

"I see." He didn't. He had dismissed the others so easily. Whispers drifted from the fringes of the court, echoing the one in his head: "She could be the prince's sister." The king cleared his throat, but Basil intervened.

"She cannot make good her claim on such evidence, Sire." *Of course she couldn't*, the king told himself. He needed time, to think, to strategize, to consult.

"We shall discuss this matter further, in our private chambers," he announced. "Tomorrow." The court nodded its approval; they were beginning to be embarrassed for the poor girl. "Mistress Friede will prepare a modest guest chamber in the eastern tower for the Lady, ah, Miriam…" It was a good distance from the royal apartments. "Sir Gustav, kindly escort this damsel to her quarters."

"By Your Majesty's leave," she spoke, unbidden, "I would like a companion during my stay—seeing as I am a stranger here." Quite right; it would be civil.

"You may have one."

"I request the lady Brigid, my lord king." A wave of smothered laughter rippled through the courtiers when they paired the underdressed girl with the old woman of the dust heap—a remnant of bygone days the king still sheltered for some unknown reason.

"So be it." Brigid would fuss over her, keep her occupied. He significantly lowered his eyes to an open ledger on the table, but the figures were all blurred. No one could hear the pounding of his heart; they were all too busy murmuring about how different castle life had become since these "lost princesses" began turning up.

Miriam's designated escort approached. They turned and were halfway across the room when an older knight entered. He saw her as one sees a specter and paled, taking a slow step nearer to where she had stopped. She lowered her head in a gracious nod and waited. The man was at the point of kneeling…

"Ah, Sir Pieter, there you are!" called the king, averting a catastrophe. He was not ready to be upstaged. "Come here, my good man. I should like your opinion on a most pressing matter." He rose and left the table to accompany Pieter to his royal chambers, motioning Gustav to continue his assigned duty. Basil hastily eyed the sovereign, calculating an appropriate moment to offer his own opinion on the matter. He bowed deeply as the king passed, and the crowd, small as it was, parted before the two, the king and his knight.

Pieter shut the iron-studded door behind them. The king silently walked to the window, where he could see the river wind through the town below—a silver snake hunting its prey. It had been a shock to both of them. All the careful words he'd rehearsed, all the questions he'd meant to ask had failed him. How could he be so held at bay by a strange girl? *Unless,* he thought, *unless...*

"It is she, my lord," came Pieter's voice. "How can you doubt it?" He turned again toward the carved stone mantel which rose like an altar at the end of the room. Gone.

Brigid had disappeared with the housekeeper to "gather some things." The king's daughter looked out of the high turret window, surveying the island world of the castle, taking in its courtyards, towers, people; the stables, the smithy; and then letting her gaze drift over the walls to the river valley and the protecting mountains beyond. Michael was out there somewhere, alive and lost, or frozen and dead. But he had a Friend in either case, she remembered, and besides, he was not hers to worry over.

The door opened clumsily, and Brigid bustled in with her arms full of linens. The princess rose to help her.

"Well, my lady, we'll do well enough in here. Coo, but the wind blows! You aren't getting cold again?" She shook her head no. The fur-lined mantle provided by the pitying housekeeper kept off the chill. "I'll light the fire anyway. It's not the best room in the house, but there is a small hearth." Brigid piled fir cones on the grate while her new mistress returned to the open casement. "You'll find some clothes there, I hope they fit. Found them in an old chest."

"Thank you."

"You're no prisoner, you know. Mistress Friede made that clear to me. We've our own key, an' you're free to move about. 'Cept his Majesty would rather you not leave the castle grounds. Here, come take a look."

"I'd rather take a walk." She felt cooped up already.

"Yes, my lady." She wasn't a child, after all. Brigid had memories to outgrow, but she did know who was mistress and who the servant. "Do you care for company?"

"Only to the chapel."

"At least wear these slippers."

With a grateful smile, the princess obediently put them on.

They passed a hidden courtyard on the way, where a well stood amidst a small herb garden. The chapel awaited them, cool, bare, and empty. Miriam sat, as was her custom, in the back.

"Shall I come back for you, then?"

"Yes. Meet me at the well, just below." The swish of the waiting-woman's garments faded, leaving behind a lonely silence. Someone had placed a small vase of flowers on the altar table, but otherwise the room was undressed stone and polished wood. Her eyes wandered about the lines of vault and niche before resting on the empty cross. She had grown used to seeing a dagger unsheathed in its holy shape, but the image was no longer there. Instead, the arms of her Beloved stretched out, reaching for her, drawing her. She knelt down on the terrazzo floor, sheltered in his acceptance, weeping at the hem of his invisible garment, and strangely assured that—whatever the king might say to her tomorrow—she was a princess indeed.

The sun had not risen before she woke to a lavender-gray dawn. Her eyes opened upon the carved wooden beams of the ceiling, expertly joined in intersecting patterns—with empty places where the dragon emblem must have been once. Another bare spot interrupted the design in the stone mantel. They had all been removed.

She realized that she had slept two nights now without dreaming. Since she'd entered the castle, the dream-book had closed, leaving her to go on into the unknown without a vision—dark as it was—to light her way.

She left the too-soft bed but saw no sign of Brigid, though the fire burned cheerily. The thick nightdress fell in folds to the floor—how much cloth there was! A linen gown lay draped across the back of a chair, inviting her to don it. She did, and was just smoothing it into shape when the latch lifted and the door swung open.

"Oh, my lady! How beautiful you are!"

"Brigid, where have you been?" A steady rain began to tap against the stone slates above them.

"I've brought you a bit of breakfast, my lady; then I thought I could help you prepare for your audience."

"Haven't you done enough already?" she asked, putting her hands to her waist to show Brigid the dress. Full, flowing, and seemly it was. It looked beautiful, it smelled pleasant, and it fit perfectly. "How ever did you manage it?"

"It was your mother's. But her hair was darker than yours, and longer. I used to comb her hair..." The years had melted away; Brigid's tears stole whatever words that followed.

"Won't you do mine, then, Brigid?" came the tender voice of her new mistress. "For love of Isolde."

"No, my lady. For love of you."

Soon there were two sets of eyes to dry, before the man-at-arms came to announce the king's readiness to see her.

The king sat in a great chair facing the hearth, letting daylight illumine the young woman who stood once again before him. Pieter, statue-still, stood in attendance, framed against the warm panels of the oaken door, the muscles of his jaw working from clenching his teeth. All of this interrogating reminded him of a cursed inquisition.

"Tell us again how you came here," Basil asked her, crossing his arms over his gold chain of office.

"I told you, sir. I just found myself up on the forest ridge. I followed the stream..."

"Right up to the postern gate. Where were you before the ridge? Eh?"

"Somewhere else. In a snowstorm, near a high mountain pass." Her voice was calm.

Ah, so that was it, thought Basil. *A memory lapse, coupled with romantic notions after hearing that damned faery tale.* He'd seen this kind of thing before..."Are you not subject to fits and mental wanderings?" She did not answer. "And what token have you to offer us in proof of your claims?" He had her now.

"I had a brooch, sir—a beautifully wrought dragon in silver, with a red stone."

The king leaned forward. *That hadn't been part of the troubadour's story*, he thought.

"And where is it now?" probed Basil.

"I did not wake with it in my possession, sir."

The king had had enough.

"Faith is worthless, Basil, when you require so much in the way of proof. There is the witness of my own eyes…"

"She's wearing your first wife's dress!" exclaimed the counselor. "Surely, Sire…"

"…And Pieter's eyes too. There is her age." *And there is more to her than her dead mother's looks*, he thought. A fiery spark of soul. It warmed him.

"And I knew my home was in the north, sir," she addressed Basil, "even before I heard the minstrel tell his story. My heart led me here, not my imagination."

Basil stood unmoved. "And what exactly did you come here *for?*"

She looked shocked, that such a question should be asked or even entertained. "To submit to my lord king," she quietly answered.

"You're too much like Isolde, God rest her soul," admitted the king jovially. "Well, she named you, not I—Kristina."

She breathed in of a sudden, as if the sun rose on her face.

"You—you own I am your daughter?"

"Yes. I have no doubts." He was glowering at Basil.

"And what am I to call Your Majesty?"

"Sigismund calls me 'Father'," he said glumly. "What did you call your guardian—the shepherd?"

"Papa."

"Papa." The corners of his mouth turned up; his eyes danced, as if his infant daughter had just spoken her first word. Pieter's face softened. The king leaned forward again, asking in gentle earnest, "What is it you want, Kristina? An inheritance? I have none left to give you. A title? Riches?" She shook her head. "Come, come—there must be something."

"There is. But I don't know if it will happen."

"Why ever not? Confound it, girl, you speak in riddles."

She looked him full in the eyes. "I want to be married."

He laughed outright. What a relief, to be married—that was all!! The ideal solution to his dilemma: let someone else give her an inheritance! He should have thought of it before.

"Have you a suitor of your own, then, or shall I scare up a few knights for you to choose from?"

"There's no need—Papa." There was that music-word again. "He'll be here soon." Her childlike faith was beyond speculation; it was so refreshing! But he wasn't looking at a child now. Fatherhood stung after so many lost years. He was beginning to like her.

Word spread like wildfire. The princess who had vanished twenty years ago was back in the castle, and staying secluded in the queen's chambers until her future should be decided. But before Kristina could arrange her first outing to visit her mother's grave, Basil had contrived to slip in further details: that she lacked adequate training for the rigors of government (unlike her royal half-brother); that she suffered from an unknown malady and therefore was not fit to reign...

The princess would readily have admitted to this. She was lovesick.

"Your Highness?"

"Brigid, will you stop that? We're alone." They sat before the huge hearth in the hall. It was still early; most of the great house had yet to breakfast.

"Kristina, I want you to meet someone." The princess looked up. Of all the introductions made to her so far, Brigid had not made any. She smiled a half-smile and nodded. The older lady went quietly to the courtyard door and opened it. "Come in, dear Nigel." A young man entered, rather bashfully, and the king's daughter rose to greet him. When she saw his face, she took in a sharp breath and stood motionless. "Your Highness, this is my nephew, Nigel."

The minstrel in the harvest fair, another world ago.

"My lady," he said, reaching for the hand that hung limp at her side. He kissed it with reverence rather than the drama she expected. Somehow she found her voice; to him, it sounded calm and gracious.

"You are welcome, sir. Please sit with us."

"With a good will, Princess." He took his seat, relaxed and at home here as anywhere.

Kristina, for all her serenity, could not hide her wonder. Resuming her place, she turned to him. "The story you told, south of the mountains. Where did you get it?"

He answered, nearly grinning, "From Auntie. But I had to change it some."

"Brigid, you didn't tell me…"

"That I sent him? No, my lady, why should I? I didn't know if he would find you. But now you're here, and so is he." She was obviously pleased, and she left to get them a hot drink. She knew they would talk awhile.

"Did you know me, then, for who I was?"

"No, my lady. I kept on. When you arrived here, Auntie sent someone to fetch me back."

"But that wasn't much more than a week ago."

"Well, I made extra haste," he confessed. "I was eager to hear the rest of the tale. How it ends, I mean."

The princess demurred. "It hasn't an ending, yet."

"No? Then I'll stay around long enough to see that it does." He was young and boisterous, cock-sure of himself and loveable. He raised his cup in a confident salute while she blushed, unashamed.

"And will you have to 'change it some' again?"

"Only if your ladyship desires me to. Any story is only a shadow of the true tale, after all. That's what Auntie tells me. But I do have a promise to keep."

Of course, thought Kristina. *All those people waiting to hear the end.*

"Yes. Well, I shall tell you what I know, and if you are here to see an ending, you may amend it to suit your voice and art, with all my blessing."

He smiled radiantly upon her and waited expectantly as the sun struck the coat of arms and the room was changed from gray to gold.

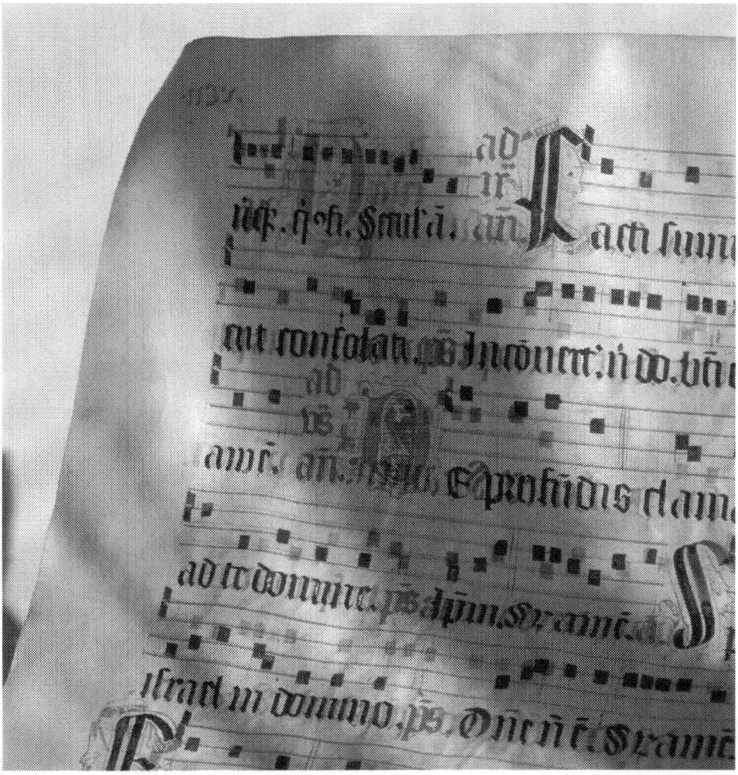

Love, I believe, can never be content to stay for long where it is.

– Saint Teresa of Avila

XXVII

Locksmith

People stayed well clear of Michael; he didn't appear at all safe. In unwashed, disheveled clothes, his beard untrimmed and his eyes glazed, he spoke in the quavering voice of a madman. Besides, everyday folk had other matters to attend to: fields to cultivate, sick to tend, gossip to share, prayers to recite, dead to bury, winter food to store. And he rarely stopped long enough to buy a loaf or some cheese. The nameless horse fled on, content with a wayside drink and a mouthful of grass now and then. They were a well-suited pair. Michael reached the thatched cottage of Master Crafter in less than a week.

The seasoned carpenter sat outside on a wooden stool, vacantly chewing on a dry bit of straw. The flowers had gone in for the winter; a few flies buzzed aimlessly in the dry afternoon air.

"Michael, is that you?" His poor horsemanship and haggard appearance couldn't deceive the old man. The journeyman dismounted and hobbled to the door, but he could not answer for the tears choking him. He fell into Robert's arms, sobbing pitifully.

Robert had no one nearby to call for help, so he held Michael there while the shadow of the eaves crept over them. Gradually the cries gave way to short, sucking breaths and long sighs.

"Where'd ye get the horse?"

"It came to me." So typical of his nephew, his need always met so close at hand, somehow.

"Well, now, it wants a drink and some vittles—and so do you, I daresay." Michael looked around, his head clearing a little at the mention of food.

"Where's Aunt?"

"Gone."

"Plague?"

"Aye. Mowed down a third of the town."

"Jon?"

"He survived it. So'd I... sometimes I wish I hadn't. Did it catch up with you?"

Michael nodded. "Few months after I left." The light ale his uncle offered jostled his memory, though his hand shook as he raised the cup to his mouth. He was very tired. "Found a new line of work, making coffins, and then digging graves." The musty feel of death made them both quiet. Robert at length sniffed and went without a word to tend to the spent horse.

He unrolled what he thought was Michael's bedroll, wondering what had become of his tools, only to find an extra cloak, well-made but worn. A nobleman's, something prickling in its deep pocket... He went to ask his nephew, but when he returned, Michael lay across the sturdy oak tabletop, fast asleep.

Locksmith

He woke to see Robert sitting pensively, swathed in candlelight. Black bread and hot mulled cider greeted his new-found appetite.

"Go on, I've had mine," said his uncle in a distant voice. "Ye'll have to tell me what's brought you home." He went on as Michael fell to. "And what it's got to do with this." He held up the brooch, new-polished. It shone like fire in the candle's tiny beacon. Then, to himself many years ago, he said, "I thought he destroyed them all."

"Who?"

"The king I used to work for, way up north."

"Above the mountains."

"'At's right."

"You mean you know him?" Michael looked terrified.

"Not too well. Do you? Where did you meet him?"

"I didn't. But I want to, more than anything."

"Then where in blazes did you get this?"

"From his daughter."

"His daugh—"

"My lady." How would he ever explain it all? He looked down. "Our paths crossed, we were both heading north... She looked like a common peasant."

"But she wasn't." Robert scratched the white stubble on his chin. "The princess, Michael—you found her! So where is she?"

"I... I don't know." The younger man's voice caught again. Robert poured more cider and laid his work-weathered hands on Michael's shoulders. "We were heading there... I lost her somehow, up near the mountain pass. It was snowing... there was a fire." He began to shiver, his face working in anguish. Robert wisely saw that words wouldn't do, not for this. "We were supposed to go together, but..."

"We'll just have to go and find her, lad."

"How?" She had vanished; to him it was impossible.

"We'll start with her father."

"It's a hard road, Uncle."

"Not if you go west; it's shorter that way, and there's a lower pass. Looks like your road might be different than hers, but I think your paths are meant to cross again. Must be. I'll talk to Malcolm about lending me a horse."

"You're coming?"

"Well, I'll have to. You've never been there before."

"What about Jon? Won't he miss you?"

"Nah—he hardly talks to me anymore. Busy in the merchant guild, nowadays. Besides, this lady's father needs to know this has been found; it may help him find her as well. Who knows? Shouldn't keep secrets from people like that."

"Will he recognize you?"

"Don't know. But we've this old seal of his to gain our entrance."

"What if she's not there and no one's heard from her?"

Robert tugged at his moustache, thinking. He rarely spoke before he thought. Michael ever admired him for that. He answered after some consideration.

"She may not be. But it's the next step. Not many folks know much, Michael, beyond the next step. And I think you're far too taken with her to not find her."

"So when do we start?" He feared the preparations of an old man would take days.

"Tomorrow, early—if you're rested up."

"Is it a good time to travel there, Uncle? I mean, can we beat the winter storms?"

"I think so. Michael, m'boy, the best time to go on a pilgrimage is when everyone else is staying home."

"A pilgrimage?"

"You love her, don't you? Then it's a pilgrimage. Sure you're strong enough for another journey?" he added as an afterthought.

"I will be, if love is really stronger than death, like they say." He was blushing. Robert took it as a good sign.

"Good lad." He leaned back to celebrate silently, lighting his clay pipe. "I've always wanted to meet a princess."

That night Michael lay in his old berth, his only lamp starlight slipping through cracks in the roof. The pang of loneliness was over for the present, soothed by Robert's company and the slowly-returning memory of Miriam crouching over him in a high mountain cleft. Could someone love him, after all? He wished his mother were there to talk to, before sleep overcame him like an incoming tide.

* * *

Kristina had retreated to her chambers, weary of learning names and faces, wanting stillness. She sometimes wished she and Brigid were still lodged in the turret room; all the rich ornaments of the queen's apartment fatigued her. She sat in the alcove and searched for patterns in the grains of the paneling, wondering where Michael was. What was most strange was accepting that this was her birthplace. "When love grows, so does sorrow," Brigid had told her, but sorrow came now without suffering, and without shame. She caught her mind wandering the foothills again, watching sheep. The embroidery sat long and idle in her lap.

A noise drifted through the open window from the front courtyard; she went to look. There was some sort of skirmish at the gate. Well, a minor tussle, really. Two men were in earnest confrontation with the porter. Her hand went to her mouth.

"Michael," she whispered, and she headed for the door. Brigid smiled serenely and rose to follow her down the stairs; she wasn't going to miss this for anything.

Kristina stole through the now-known passages, her slippered feet making no sound. The well was just below the king's parlor—she would wait there.

Agitated voices drifted down the hall.

"Sire, there are a couple of plebian guildsmen outside, demanding an audience."

"Complaint?"

"No, Sire. One says he has something that belongs to you. A piece of jewelry you lost once."

"God."

"Sire?"

"Let them in."

The king received the brooch from Michael's hand while looking straight into the young man's eyes. Walking to the casement window, he lifted it to the light and inspected it slowly.

"My deepest thanks, Master…"

"Carver. Michael Carver, sir."

"You needn't tell me how it came into your possession. I already…" He caught sight of the older man, and his eyebrows rose in surprise. "I know you. The woodcarver. Master, uh, Crafter, is it? You left when…" They shook hands, almost apologetically. "Well, gentlemen, I'm so glad you've come."

"You seem to've been expecting us," remarked Robert. Michael shifted his feet nervously back and forth.

"Well, one of you at least." The king turned to face the journeyman. "And not me, Master Carver. The princess told me you'd be here soon."

"She's here?" He was horrified now. And she was beyond his reach, surely. No king would allow a working man to… It was a victory that felt like defeat.

"She arrived—rather mysteriously—less than a fortnight ago. She knew you'd get here, eventually. I assumed, since you had the brooch… You *are* her suitor, are you not?" What had she told her father? Michael's head swam in bewilderment as the king went on. "You must be. I've never seen anyone so tongue-tied at the mention of a woman." He had been too, once—but that was long ago.

"Indeed, Your Majesty." Robert was backing him up.

Basil had slipped in, uninvited, early in the interview, and now spoke up.

"What are your assets then, young man?" he asked pointedly. Assets. What had this suitor to offer a king's daughter? "Your assets, sir: lands, titles, endowments…"

"Just these, my lord." Michael held up his hands in display. Basil frowned, but the king leaned back to stroke his chin.

"Are you as able a craftsman as Sir Robert here?"

"Not quite."

"More able," piped in the old master.

"And you are fully capable of supporting her—on your own?"

"Well..."

"Absolutely, my lord," said Robert.

"Because I have only a small dowry to offer..." He glanced at Basil, who stood listening with restrained approval. "It would be enough for a house, perhaps, and tools—or did you bring your own along?"

"No, Sire. I... I didn't come prepared to stay," answered Michael. Robert rolled his eyes—the boy had a few things to learn.

"Why? Have you other plans?"

"No, sir."

"Then you must stay. Let's see..." The king was having a glorious time, watching the loose strands come together. "Timber." He pursed his lips and pressed his fingertips together. He turned toward Basil. "Lord Counselor," he said, "Prince Sigismund is fond of hunting. Who manages the forest behind the castle?"

"Some hired men, my lord."

"Then put them in this fellow's service. That is, if Master Carver will consider taking the position of the king's forester. It's not much in the way of salary, you understand, but the trees would be your responsibility." He noticed that Michael looked puzzled. "Would you rather live in town?"

"No, Sire."

"Good. It would be better if you could build a modest cottage—to suit your taste—about halfway up the mountain."

Michael heard very little after that; he was trying hard to keep from fainting.

"Ye'll be needing some clothes, I think," said Robert, prodding him down the hall.

"Clothes? For what?"

"For your wedding, ten days hence."

Holy Saint Joseph, he hadn't even asked for her hand.

The monarch tossed the brooch on the cherry wood tabletop.

"Here's your proof of kinship, Basil. What do you have to say now?"

"He seems a bit giddy, Sire."

"They're all like that at first. He's a fine, sturdy fellow. We could do with more of his sort around here... Don't worry, Basil. She'll calm him down."

"Your consideration of your son's interests is worthy of merit, my lord." His diplomacy never lagged.

"Sigismund? I'm so glad you approve, Basil. Things do seem to be working out nicely for him, don't they?"

Basil nodded gravely. With the marriage of the king's daughter to a simple craftsman, the prince's future was guaranteed.

A few snowflakes drifted in the graying sky. The whole atmosphere of the castle seemed changed to Robert. It wasn't the new emblem so much as all the different faces.

"Is there a chapel around?" Michael asked. "I'll... I need to say thank you."

"Of course, m'boy. Right this way."

They almost passed her by. As they came around a corner, she froze, trembling, her hands in her lap and warm color rising to her waiting face.

"I'll come anon, Uncle. I just want to wash the dust off first..." When he touched the windlass on the well, she almost cried out, but instead she raised her eyes, slowly lifting her head toward him. He dropped the bucket down the shaft; it echoed with a splash. She rose to meet him. He sank down at her slippered feet, embarrassed, afraid—and so glad from relief that his insides ached. He didn't have the nerve to even take her hand. She reached to touch his head; he began to cry.

"Don't, Michael." She bent lower, offering to raise him up.

"I can't help it, my lady. I—I owe you so much."

"You owe me nothing." She guided him to sit on the edge of the well and stood silently beside him, letting him press her hand against his wet face. It was warm, warm as the wheat fields in early autumn and soft as the moss on the riverbanks.

"Michael?" Robert peered out of the chapel door. "Oh my God."

She saw him and, with a gesture, bade Michael rise to his feet.

"Ah, Uncle," he said, sniffling. "This is, uh, my lady…"

"Kristina," she smiled, extending her hand.

"You look just like your mother." Robert had forgotten all his court manners, but she didn't seem to mind at all.

Autumn lingered in the valley. Set against the rugged mountains already dusted with snow, the pavilion of dying leaves spread out over the town in a mosaic of color.

Michael Carver stood shaven and dressed at the church door, chatting amicably with knights who dwarfed him. The fall breeze drifted through the fine cambric of his shirt, keeping him from perspiring. Pieter stayed close by, listening attentively to his efforts at small talk and asking questions that put him at ease. Not six paces away, the king had cornered Robert.

"Won't you stay on as well, Master Crafter? I could use some new tables."

"My home's in the south now, Your Majesty."

"Well, at least winter here. That new son-in-law of mine would like some help building furniture for his cottage—don't you think? And I could do with some, ah, manly company."

Robert thought. Jon would not be needing him anytime soon... He and Michael could work together again, catch up on old times.

"Very well, Sire. But I'll be leaving come spring."

"Fine, man. Now, if you'll excuse me..." He had seen Sigismund out of the corner of his eye. It was fitting they should stand together.

The prince had been at his grandfather's court when Kristina came to the castle; he had met her a few days after. Her breeding being inferior to his own, however, he spent little time with her. They had little in common.

She appeared from the sacristy door, shrived and ready—though she wasn't used to wearing silk. The flowers had all frosted away, but Brigid had plaited some bright ribbons together for a garland. The priest held up his hand, and Michael stepped forward. He looked smaller to her, without his beard. *He has a nice face,* she thought.

He heard himself plighting his troth to her at the church door. Somehow his bumbling fingers had produced the silver ring. Her hands were so much softer than he remembered... there. It was done. He was married.

When the nuptial Mass was over, the procession moved in a bright stream to the castle. There would be feasting tonight, and dancing. Nigel might even tell a story. Only the king,

Pieter, the Lord Counselor, and Sigismund rode. The princess walked with Michael, her arm on his, beneath a silken canopy while fiery leaves rained down upon them from the baring trees.

At a lull in the glorious meal, Sigismund strode gallantly up to the head table to bid his half-sister good night. The wine didn't agree with him, he said. It was—as he intended it to be—a statement. He clasped Michael's hand in a competitive grip, smiling with satisfaction. A simple forester, not even a knight. Probably illiterate. Here was a fitting match indeed for her, his father's bastard daughter.

Secure in his inheritance and courtly education, he nodded politely, bowed to coldly kiss the princess' hand, and left.

* * *

Above the castle on a little knoll early the next day, beneath the reaching arms of a half-bare maple tree, Nigel sat crosslegged, bending over his lute. He looked over the sleepy town and cleared his throat, sketching the bare outlines of his tale and practicing its telling to the wind:

"Stripped of all comfort, bereft of all she had known, she fled the hilly meadows and made her way down to the lowland plain, seeking shelter and warmth in the holy houses. Tending the sick and carrying water from spring to cloister, the forgotten princess passed the winter in solace. And yet, an ember of longing began to burn within her, in the very center of her heart. It drove her to take up her wanderings again when spring came, to answer an inner pull drawing her northward. She slept in the open, unfearing, unfeeling—or so she thought.

"Along came a simple forester, his leg sore wounded in battle. One morning in May, he stumbled over the sleeping form of the enchanted princess, mistook her for a beggar, and fell headlong into the glen. Moved with pity, her cold hands soon tended to his hurt…"

He broke off, mumbling. "Hmm. It needs work."

By the end of the morning, he was putting the finishing touches to the song he would end with:

Beneath lichen blankets, cold gray stone
  Drops forth a river—not its own—
    that flows down from a higher place
      Where a princess melts.

Through caverns cracked and deep beneath
  Earth's cloak of fragrant, purple heath,
    rain showers salty, warm, and dark
      From where the princess melts.

From out her heart, her tears stream down
  And pain, her passion—now her crown—
    wears Self away to bring new sense
      As the princess melts.

The stream runs on to overcome
  A man, who, freezing cold and numb,
    lies covered by her cloak, not far
      From where the princess melts.

He wakes to Spring, and searches wide
  To find the one who knelt and cried
    for him alone, while winter fled
      At the princess's melting.

Flowers fresh stretch up to meet him
  On the path whereon his feet fly,
    knowing, to the warm embrace
        Of a melted princess.

Spring water clear—not bitter brine—
  Flows on to quench their thirst. They dine
    on raisin cakes, and apples cool
        And still the princess melts.

She melts to him in caverns deep
  Where mosses grow, and soft ferns sleep.
    Their very souls entwine in joy
        Whene'er the princess melts.

The minstrel bagged his instrument and rose, dusting himself off and taking a drink from his skin bottle before climbing the ridge to the south. He had a promise to keep, the ending of a story to tell.

"I hope they like it," he told himself. "Because it's true."

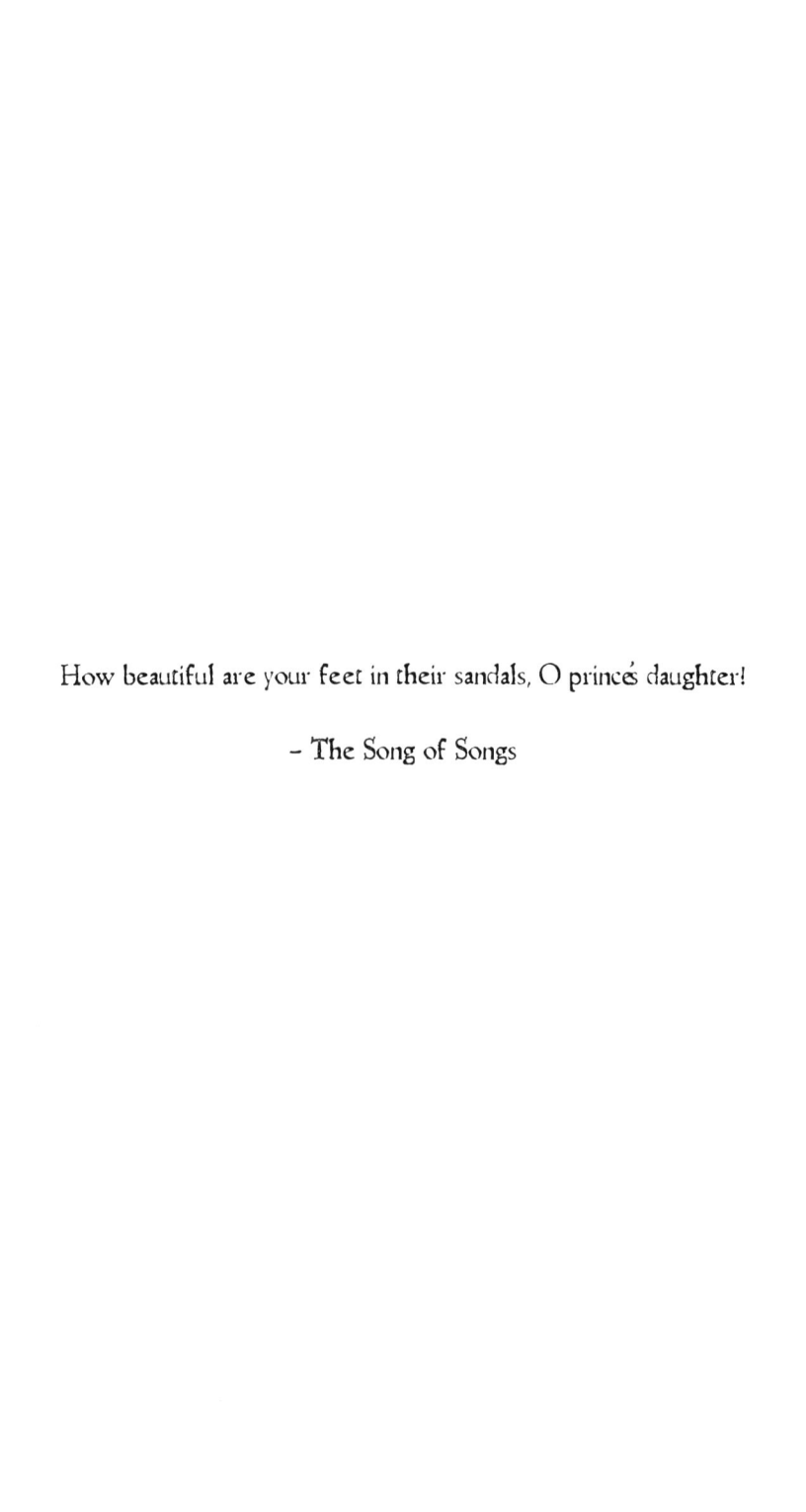

How beautiful are your feet in their sandals, O prince's daughter!

– The Song of Songs

XXVIII

Summer

The heavy beams of the waterwheel turned sluggishly in the warm air. Michael had gone up into the forest to fell timber, and Brigid had taken the children to the fair in town.

It was glorious to be alone, solitude falling about her with the sunlight. She knelt over the little mound of earth at the edge of the garden, planting an apple tree next to the tiny grave of her seedling child, stillborn and too small for even the church to trifle with. Brigid insisted she stay at home until the bleeding stopped, so she moved slowly, freely drinking in the bittersweet smell of the cedars. The music of water falling over the wheel measured her day. When the sun was high she slept, to wake refreshed and bathe before she set her hands to the evening meal.

The slope of the hill carried voices to the house long before swarthy little Robert came bouncing into view; how he could climb so quickly up such a steep path on his short legs amazed her. Kristina smiled to see Brigid, basket on arm, and Johanna, who bent to pick wildflowers, talking and laughing their way homeward. How old were Gerda's children, now? She had lost track of time.

She wiped a wisp of hair away from her face and shook the water from her hands before drying them on the coarse, clean cloth of her apron. Then she spread her arms wide to catch the boy, who hurled himself at his mother.

"Why, how now, my lady!" said Brigid loftily. "Working, when you were to rest! Fie on you!"

"And how was the fair?" the princess asked her daughter.

"Oh, Mama, it was wonderful! There were sheep—like you used to tend—and jugglers, and sweetmeat sellers… and a man who ate fire! And Robert got into a fight with another boy…"

"A fight?" He wasn't yet four.

"It was so funny, Mama. The boy was oh-so-much bigger than him, but Robert pushed him down. Then the big boy got up and jumped on Robert and they rolled around and around. They were both laughing in the end, so it couldn't be a real fight, could it?" Kristina smiled; how Johanna liked to talk. "And Mama, there was the bestest story time. It went on and on—I didn't want it to stop."

"Do you remember what it was about, child?" asked the mother, casting a sidelong glance at the very amused Brigid.

"Oh yes! I could never forget it. It was the story of the Ice Princess. Nurse has heard it before, but she always likes to hear it again."

"Couldn't tear the girl away," confessed Brigid, winking. "Come, Johanna, let's take Robert down for a wash. I daresay he needs one. Master'll be home soon, no doubt." They bustled out of the open kitchen, leaving Kristina alone with a flood of memories. It was someone else's story now, no longer hers—embellished, embroidered, and made magical by mystery.

A horse's nicker brought her to the oak frame of the doorway. Across the glade walked her husband, shouldering an axe and leading his sagging (but faithful) piebald nag. In the sylvan light and in dashing contrast, the king rode lazily beside him on a bay mare.

"Hello, Papa!" She knew how much he liked to be called that. He came more and more often to visit and dine with them.

"God save you, Kristina!" he greeted, dismounting. He grasped her at arm's length and looked proudly into her face. After all these years, he was still afraid to touch her. "Michael tells me you had a loss... I'm sorry." She nodded, misty-eyed, and led them into the house. Dusk was falling; the lamps were lit.

"Sigismund at the castle?" she asked.

"No—he's still at court, being groomed for the throne. At least the prince is learning some manners and treats his old father with courtesy. It's sheer diplomacy—he didn't used to. But I hardly feel like a king, anymore. More like an earl."

"It suits you better, Your Majesty," said Brigid, boldly and lovingly frank, as she reentered with the children.

"Yes, you're right. Sigismund is in the hands of a better king anyway, one that deserves to rule an empire."

"Does anyone deserve an empire?" laughed Michael. "I wouldn't want one."

"That's because you have enough right here," answered his father-in-law, gesturing with a sweep of his hand over the glade and homestead now bathed in the cool evening light.

They sat together at table beneath the open joists of the ceiling, a wax taper spreading its halo against the smooth red wood and over the simple meal. Robert drank his porridge with noisy relish, but Johanna was subdued, staring distantly into the candle's flame.

"Nurse," she said quietly.

"Yes, child?"

"Who is the Ice Princess?" Kristina's eyes widened in alarm. She shook her head imperceptibly at the woman across the table. Brigid didn't bat an eye.

"Why, don't you know? Bless me! She's the Lady Poverty, sweetheart."

"Oh. I thought she might be somebody real."

"She is real, child," breathed the relieved mother.

"And beautiful, too, if you look long enough," said Michael Carver, his eyes twinkling as he reached to slice more bread. "Like the flowers of the field. Or the woodcutter's daughter." The little girl blushed and giggled, while the candlelight revealed Robert nodding over his bowl and the graying king nodding in forgiveness.

He returned to the castle early next morning, but he stayed long enough only to fill his purse. Then he went, on foot, to the town. How long he walked and wandered! Through the fields, greeting the harvesters, through the small streets, saluting the townspeople, he went; slowly quiet he went, as if listening to wind-borne words no one else could hear.

He was about to enter the churchyard when a crumpled figure sitting near the rusty gate caught his attention. Her begging bowl lay beside her. Thin feet and hands stuck out of her threadbare garment, and flies buzzed about her covered head. He stood beside her, wondering what to do, when she looked up into his eyes.

In spite of a visage marred by scars—scars that had melted her features, borne in some tragic inferno—he knew her.

She looked down suddenly, shamefully, as he knelt beside her in pity. Then from his belt he took his soft leather pouch and counted out, one by one, nineteen gold coins into her bowl. He paused, wanting to bless her, but no words would come. Her twisted hand reached for his and seized it, drawing it closer to her disfigured face. Tears overflowed her eyes, wetting the king's hand along with the beggar woman's kiss.

He walked softly away, feeling deliciously empty and, for the first time in twenty years, free. Some townspeople had noticed his actions; their talk spread quickly. From that day onward, his people began to love and not merely fear him, their King.

The bitter goes before the sweet, and because it does,
it makes the sweet sweeter.

– John Bunyan

XXIX

Candlelight

Kristina had gone to bed with a fever; it followed her into her dream. The same dream, left unfinished so long ago, made dim by time's passage and no longer a prophecy to be fulfilled.

The devouring pain in her shoulder had given place to a distant throbbing. The race, the dark tunnel-flight, even the rough cobblestones were gone now; she lay in a dark and scented chamber, too weak to even groan. There was a fleeting memory of being carried here, of the sharp pull as the quilled bolt was withdrawn. She thought at that moment she would split in two, but she fell into blackness instead. And now, voices. Low, worried tones of the men—a physician and a man-at-arms—who attended her.

"How she could stay conscious for so long... A clean bowl of water, please, Captain."

"Yes, sir." It was Michael's voice she heard, distant and low. The other's continued, but not to her—it was to himself he spoke.

"Bloody mess of a wound. Looks worse on a woman." She shivered as he removed the blood-soaked tunic.

"Here, sir—the water. May I go?"

"Certainly, Captain. Though most men would rather stay about now."

"Not me, sir. A woman's a woman. And I'm no doctor." His voice trailed off again as he turned toward the door. Water dripped from clean cloth.

Once again the dreamer's viewpoint changed; she was seeing the scene from above.

"You should be, though" said the physician. "I couldn't have removed that bolt without your help. You might consider…" His washing stopped abruptly. Time stood still; he saw something, there on her skin, once the blood was wiped away, just below the closed wound. "My God." He was hastily pulling fresh linens over her, draping her for modesty's sake. "Captain."

The man-at-arms halted and turned back. "Sir."

"I need you to see something—as a witness. Here." The physician pointed to a brown crescent shape there, just beneath her fair arm.

"Is it a birthmark, sir?"

"Yes. And I know it."

"You do? From where?"

"I delivered this child. She is the queen's daughter."

"I didn't know Her Majesty had a daugh—"

"Not many people do. The baby disappeared years ago." There was a pause. Crashing sounds and shouting drifted in the distance—the siege had begun. "The queen must be told that she's come back. You stay with her, Captain. I must inform Her Majesty at once."

Candlelight

Their voices faded and the dream muddled; she was once again inside her dream-self. She imagined shock in the calm eyes of the queen when the physician told her who his patient was. Then, a spark of knowledge that the sovereign lady knew already, somehow.

Kristina tossed in her fever upon the bed, her still-sleeping mind in limbo, filling in the blanks. How the dream-princess had been stolen away and raised as a foundling child, always bearing that hidden mark until the threat of siege forced her back, until the dark journey exposed her. Her own voice, crying out, seemed to come across a great distance as images tumbled one after another over her: Jacob's face, Chantal's hearth, the screech and squeak of cage and wheel in the deep blackness of the mountain.

And now a woman sat next to her upon the dampening bedclothes, a woman whose voice the princess knew, but didn't know. It was the queen's, and her mother's, voice.

"Hush, child; I'm here. Kristina." A cool, strong hand held her burning cheek. She pressed her head into it so that the lines of her jaw fell against the strength of the palm.

The dream-daughter reached up with a trembling hand to touch her mother's arm—and woke.

Michael's hand held her face. Bathed in candlelight, he sat beside her, looking down upon her with concern. Her eyes met his, and she smiled. The fever had broken. She stretched her arms up to him in thanksgiving, as if his touch had driven it away. Then she pulled him toward her, to melt again in his wordless embrace before night covered them both in a comfort without dreams.

She was home.

Let my tears drop like amber, while I go
In reach of Thy divinest voice complete
In humanest affection—thus, in sooth,
To lose the sense of losing! As a child,
Whose song-bird seeks the wood forevermore,
Is sung to in its stead by mother's mouth;
Till, sinking on her breast, love-reconciled,
He sleeps the faster that he wept before.

- Elizabeth Barrett Browning

XXX

Harvest

"Mama! Hurry! Robert's swinging the hen by her tail again!"

Kristina sighed and rose from the table a bit heavily. She glanced at Michael, who was engrossed in designing a better chair. He stifled a guffaw.

"There's seeds of the weeds in every garden," he announced, daring to look up. "Shall I give him what for?"

"Somebody's got to prune him, before we have a dead chicken on our hands."

"Hmm. Been a long time since we ate roast..."

"Michael!" she rebuked, smiling. They went out together, but the crisis had passed. Robert was squatting at the edge of the garden, where the tall trees began, peering into the undergrowth. Johanna tiptoed up on their left, whispering.

"He says there's a little man in there, dressed in leaves. I think it's an elf."

"No, Johanna," hissed the little boy in a husky voice. "A faery."

"What's the difference?" asked their father.

"Don't you know, Papa? Elves have pointy ears. Faeries have wings."

"Oh," Michael replied. Brigid had been telling stories again. "Well, he's probably gone, now the grown-ups are here."

"He'll come back later," said his son, convinced beyond all doubt.

"What makes you think so?"

"He likes Mama."

Michael grinned, shaking his head, and went back to his plans. Kristina gently led the boy back toward the chicken coop to make his apologies and learn some kindness. With Johanna still searching the wooded shadows, however, Robert chose to talk—while he had the chance.

"Mama, that funny man likes you so much."

"Really, Robert? Why?"

"Because once a witch locked him up tight, and you let him go."

"I don't remember that."

"No? But he does." He was so earnest, she laughed in sweet delight. Children knew things, even if they couldn't explain them. Before she could ask him more, her daughter had joined them.

"Can we go with Papa into the forest today, Mama? You should get some exercise"—she was parroting Brigid—"and I want to see Uncle Sigismund train his hawk. Can we?" Kristina considered; preparations for winter were well under way. It would be a lovely afternoon.

"Yes, sweetheart." She would ask Brigid to stay with Robert; he was too heavy to carry nowadays.

There were a few trees with glowing leaves still upon them; most had already fallen asleep, their summertime mantles carpeting the damp forest floor. Johanna looked high up to where the fir tops swayed above her, then reached for her mother's hand.

"Mama, if Grandpa's a king, doesn't that make you a princess?"

"Yes."

"They why don't we live in the castle?"

"Your papa wouldn't feel at home there. I don't think I would, either."

"You mean you'd rather be poor?"

Kristina stopped and bent down to look her daughter in the eye. "I'm not poor, sweetheart. I have you, and Papa, and Robert."

"Don't forget Brigid—and Baby," added Johanna, pointing to her mother's belly.

"Yes." And Chantal and Cyril, Gerda and Irina. Not poor. Rich.

"How long will it be now, 'til Baby's here?"

"A couple of months yet."

"Nurse says we must be nice to you. Why's that?"

"Because having babies is hard work, carrying them before they're born, and taking care of them after."

"A nice kind of work, though."

"Yes."

"Mama?"

"Yes, Johanna."

"Does it hurt, having babies?"

"Some. But it doesn't last long."

"Oh, good." Then off she flitted into the sunbeams that fell in pillared diagonals between the towering trees.

Kristina stopped again, to listen and remember: 'Who is like unto the Lord our God, that hath his dwelling so high, and yet humbleth himself to behold the things that are in heaven and earth? He taketh up the simple out of the dust, and lifteth the poor out of the mire, that he may set him with the princes, even with the princes of his people. He maketh the barren woman to keep house, and to be a joyful mother of children'.

God's ways are certainly past finding out, she thought. She was glad she'd somehow stumbled into them, and resumed her walk.

The wind whipped against the shutters, bringing the scent of coming storm. Michael had gone to see that the animals were secure in their stalls and roosts; Johanna and Brigid were sleeping already, the one worn out from a day in the wood, the other from chasing Robert.

Kristina bent to kiss the curly head of her son, when a sharp gust of wind slipped between casement and shutter to snuff out the candle. Night fell over them, dark as black velvet. Lightning flashed in the distance. Robert grabbed his mother's arm as thunder rolled.

"Stay with me—a little tiny while."

"A little tiny while." She climbed in next to him under the quilted coverlet. The boy snuggled close, putting his pudgy hands on her cheeks. She hummed a long-ago shepherd tune; he began to relax in the thickening darkness. The wind dropped, and quiet filled the house. The child in her womb stirred and stretched, and stilled again.

Robert spoke, fearless now. "I can't see you, Mama, but I know you're there."

"How, Robert?"

"Because of your cozy warmness."

A single hot tear rose and fell, splashing on the linen of their shared pillow. Let the winter come, she thought—the consuming fire within would burn through the night, right up until Dawn.

Afterword

In his book *The Living Reminder*, Henri Nouwen wrote, "We need to become storytellers again. We can dwell in a story, walk around, find our own place... As long as we have stories to tell each other there is hope."

In a short story written for my beloved years before I "met" the Christian mystics, Michael tripped over Miriam in a forested glade. Other elements of that little story recurred to me as I read the writings of Catherine of Siena (the *bridge*), Teresa of Avila (her *castle*), George MacDonald (the *king-papa*), Francis of Assisi (retreating to a mountain *cave*), the desert fathers (their *fire*), John of the Cross (the *journey*, the *wound*), and John Bunyan (*mountains* and *ice*). But the story is its own; I did not set out to 'weave a tale' around them.

The same threads, woven and rewoven into different tapestries. Thus, the words of Christian mystics, here uttered by Cyril and Giuliana, Jacob, Brigid, Robert, and even Michael, are not merely paraphrases of wise teachers. They have been spoken in every age, by every imaginable type of person.

Neither is this little romance set forth as an allegory (apart from the reference to the Lady Poverty) or historical novel. The nonspecific setting, a fragmented medieval Europe, is drawn impressionist-style as a backdrop, scenery on a stage. In light of the events of the period, though, with its heretic and witch hunts, the Black Death, famine, anti-Semitism, political instability, and threats of Marmeluke and Turkish invasion, Miriam's trials are far from being pure fantasy. I felt I had to present the medieval mystics' thought in the framework of their own time, out of fairness to them. I tried to enter their world. It was not difficult because the wide-spread poverty, the struggles for power, the continual threat of plague and epidemic which occurred in the Middle Ages continue as a present-day reality in such places as rural Uganda—where I finally mixed "my" short story with the mystics' ancient words. In the absence of electricity, the first manuscript was written in longhand, often by candlelight.

I have tried to let the reader's imagination have plenty of room. For further exploration, I happily refer the reader to Evelyn Underhill's book, *Practical Mysticism*, and the writings of Clare of Assisi, Julian of Norwich, Teresa of Avila, John of the Cross, Meister Eckhart, Catherine of Siena, and later works by Charles de Foucauld, Madame Guyon, and Thomas Merton. For a more spiritual storytelling style, I recommend George MacDonald, C.S. Lewis, Charles Williams, and Elizabeth Goudge.

Michael and the Ice Princess is a story meant for the old oral tradition, to be listened to, to be felt, to be imagined. There

Afterword

may be 'unreasonable' moments, but then, mystics are lovers, and lovers say unreasonable things. It is my hope that among these pages, the reader may find himself—and hear in his heart the call of the Beloved.

Acknowledgments

I can never adequately thank all those who have helped inspire this story: people who have lived it out, people I have listened to and learned from, people who opened their homes and hearts to me through the years. Jean Anne Conlon, high school poetry teacher; Ruby Shenk, Church of the Brethren mother and homemaker; Cully Anderson, Presbyterian pastor and his wife Julie, librarian and friend; Jill Herringshaw, songstress; Kim Robertson, Celtic harpist; several Franciscan nuns in California, England, and Uganda; and a handful of patient, listening priests. My young sons provided a willing audience as I practiced telling the dream sequences as a bedtime story. I am also grateful for the unself-conscious modeling done for me by a young Mufumbira woman named Jacqueline Kabanyana, who let me watch her and sketch the figure of Miriam. For confidence-building and technical support I am indebted to Pastor Hartmut and Karin Krause, my retired agent Arthur Fleming, and I. Kimmich, who painstakingly assisted in editing the Second Edition of this book. I realize that I have 'compressed' both literature and dates to suit the storyline, and I thank my readers for granting me some license in this regard. I also received tremendous encouragement and assistance from Michele Green, Elizabeth Sherrill, and, while he lived, Henri Nouwen (may light perpetual shine upon him).

Quotations from Scripture

Author's note: Although medieval churchgoers did not have access to the entire scriptural canon, they were allowed to read or possess a copy of the Psalter. Of course, books were still written by hand and hard to come by. Hence the use of verses recited from the Psalms, the preciousness of the hand-copied breviary (short service book), and the reliance on memory and oral tradition in *Michael and the Ice Princess*.

Quotations from the Psalms (as recalled by the characters in this story) are from the Miles Coverdale translation of the Bible, 1535. His work, translated from the Latin and Dutch (German), preceded both the Douai-Rheims and Authorized (King James) versions of the Bible and was used in the earliest Book of Common Prayer. More accessible English spelling is found in *Psalms: The Coverdale Translation*, edited by W.S. Peterson and Valerie Macys (2000) and is used with permission.

When used as chapter epigraphs and elsewhere in the book, scriptural references are derived from the *New Jerusalem Bible* unless otherwise noted.

Quotations from Scripture

Page no.	reference:	
90	Psalm 27:10	spoken by: Miriam
145	Psalm 31:20	Bernard
160	Psalm 62:1	Giuliana
168	Psalm 121:5-8	Miriam
259	Song of Songs 8:6	Michael
284	Psalm 113:5-9	Kristina

Chapter Epigraph Sources

Page	Source
–	"The Lady Poverty", from Evelyn Underhill's book *Immanence, A Book of Verses,* First Edition, 1912.
vi	4th century theologian; adapted from *Gregory of Nyssa*
6	Ecclesiasticus (Wisdom of Ben Sira, or Sirach) 20:12
14	II Samuel 1:19, *New Revised Standard Version*
22	From *The Pilgrim's Progress,* Part II
28	In his sermon, "Jesus and His Fellow Townsmen"
36	*The Proverbs of Ankole/Kigezi* by M. Cisternino
42	Antonio Stradivarius, in the poem "God Needs Antonio" by George Eliot
46	also attributed to William James, philosopher and psychologist
58	From *The Way of the Pilgrim*, translated by R. M. French
70	*The Dialogue*, chapter 73
74	Ephesians 2.10
82	Hosea 2.16, adapted
94	Matthew 5.4, from Christ's Sermon on the Mount
102	From *Till He Come*
106	From *Meditations of a Hermit*
118	From "East Coker", IV, *Four Quartets*

Chapter Epigraph Sources

- 132 From the 15th century hymn, "Come Down, O Love Divine"
- 154 "To be silent keeps us pilgrims", translation by Henri Nouwen
- 166 From *The Problem of Pain*, chapter 10
- 178 From "Piers the Ploughman", a medieval meditation
- 188 From *The Living Flame of Love*
- 194 *Revelations of Divine Love,* chapter 10
- 208 *Interior Castle,* First Mansions, chapter 1
- 216 Recalled by her sister Corrie Ten Boom in *The Hiding Place,* chapter 14
- 226 Verses from *The Ascent of Mount Carmel* and *The Spiritual Canticle*
- 240 Adapted from *The God Who Comes*
- 254 *Interior Castle,* Seventh Mansions, chapter 4
- 270 The Song of Songs 7.1
- 276 *The Pilgrim's Progress,* Part II, adapted
- 280 From her poem "Comfort" ("Speak to me low, my Savior…")

Photographs used with permission from Veer Images and The Microsoft Corporation

Minstrel Song

Mary Mendenhall

Be-neath li-chen blan-kets, cold gray stone drops forth a ri-ver not its own, that
Through ca-ver-ns cracked and deep be-neath earth's cloak of fra-grant pur-ple heath rain

flows down from a high-er place where a prin-cess melts. warm and dark from
sho-wers sal-ty

where the prin-cess melts. From out her heart, her tears stream-down, and pain, her pas-sion

now her crown wears self a-way to bring new sense as the prin-cess melts. The

stream runs on to o-ver-come a man, who, free-zing cold and numb, lies co-ver-d by her

cloak, not far from where the prin cess melts. He wakes to-spring, and sear-ches wide, to

find the one who knelt and cried for him a-lone while win-ter fled at the prin-cess's

mel-ting. Flo-wer-s fresh stretch up to meet him on the path where-on his feet fly knowing to the warm embrace of a melted princess. Spring water clear, not bitter brine flows on to quench their thirst; they dine on raisin cakes and apples cool, and still the princess melts. She melts to him in caverns deep, where mosses grow, and soft ferns sleep. Their very souls entwine in joy whene'er the princess melts.

Further Reading

Catherine of Siena, *The Dialogue.* Translated and introduced by Suzanne Noffke, O.P. New York: Paulist Press 1980.

Deansley, Margaret, *A History of the Medieval Church 590-1500.* London: Routledge, Reprinted 1974 (Original copyright 1925, University Press).

Hutchinson, Paul and Winfred E. Garrison, *Twenty Centuries of Christianity: A Concise History.* New York: Harcourt, Brace & Co., Inc. 1959.

John of the Cross, *The Mystical Doctrine of Saint John of the Cross.* Selected by R.H.J. Stewart, London: Sheed and Ward, Ltd. Rev. ed. 1974.

Julian of Norwich, *Revelations of Divine Love,* Translated and with and introduction by Clifton Wolters. London: Penguin Books, 1966.

Nouwen, Henri, *The Living Reminder.* New York: The Seabury Press, 1977.

Further Reading

Reade, Charles, *The Cloister and the Hearth: A Tale of the Middle Ages,* London: Bradbury, Evans, & Co., 1869

Teresa of Avila, *Interior Castle.* Translated and Edited by E. Allison Peers. New York: Image/Doubleday, 1989. Also, *The Complete Works of Saint Teresa of Jesus.* E. Allison Peers, New York and London: Sheed & Ward, 1946.

Underhill, Evelyn, *Mysticism: A Study in the Nature and Development of Man's Spiritual Consciousness.* 12th edition, 1930; Also, *Practical Mysticism,* 1914.

About the Author

Mary Mendenhall, a community health and hospice nurse, worked overseas for many years in church-related development projects. Passionate about all forms of communication, she's taught and performed music and drama, and assisted with health education in North America and with vocational education abroad. Her writing 'career' began in early childhood, right along with her attraction to mysticism. She's currently exploring ways to weave education, spirituality, health promotion, and writing together. Her first novel (the first edition of *Michael and the Ice Princess: A Mystical Romance*) was published in London in 1997; she's at work on another, set against the Rwandan genocide, and a meditation on the dream of St. Clare. She still engages in the performing arts, both as communication and as service. Mary lives in central Washington state and has three grown sons.

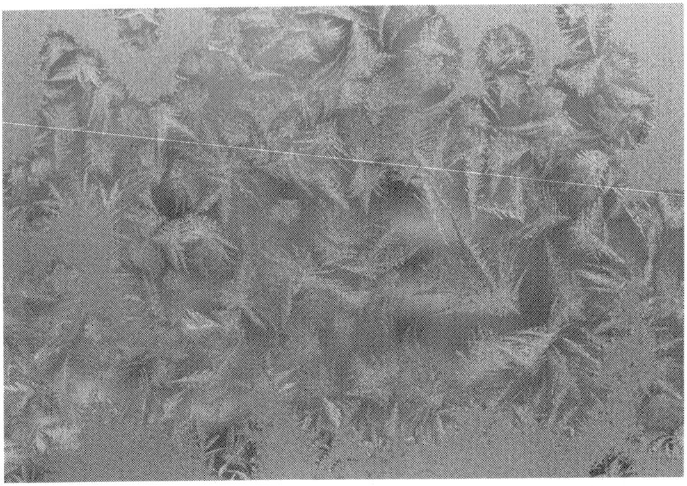

Made in the USA
Charleston, SC
26 October 2011